M000096545

1

ANIMUS

A Tale of Ardenia

By Scott McKay

To my parents, for a lifetime of love and support.

And to civilization, which must never be taken for granted.

Animus is a work of fiction. All names, characters, terms, places and events are either the product of the author's imagination or used fictitiously as devices of the story. Any resemblance to real persons either live or dead, events either current or historical, or locales is entirely by coincidence.

Copyright 2019 by Scott L. McKay.

All rights reserved.

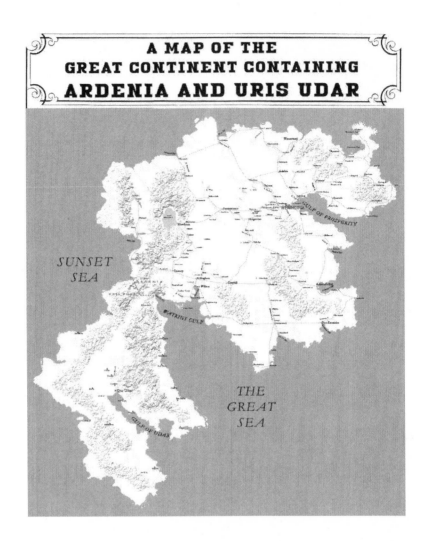

(see the Great Continent map in full detail at

http://talesofardenia.com)

Contents

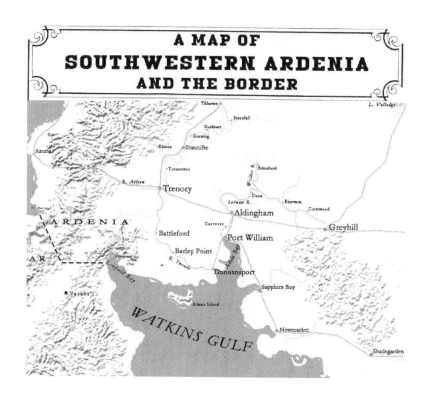

A MAP OF SOUTHWESTERN ARDENIA AND THE BORDER

(see the Great Continent map in full detail at

http://talesofardenia.com)

PROLOGUE

Gana'fali

The old man stood on a high plateau surrounded by mountain peaks, a place to which his aching bones had only just managed to bring him after a full day's climb. But to be here on this night, lit dimly as it was by a sliver of a moon, was crucial. It was from this place, after all, that the culmination of his life's work would originate.

For here his beauties gathered, and soon he would turn them loose to feed on the blood of the Profaners.

The old man had raised his beauties – his Vitau'hi – from hatchlings, and had tamed and trained them. It was under his tutelage that they had grown not into wild beasts wasting the land and the creatures on it, but rather into obedient and useful servants of the god Ur'akeen. It was that training which would soon deliver Ur'akeen and his followers a holy miracle.

Tonight the Udar would recapture the sacred shore of Gana'fali from the Profaners, who had seized it a generation hence, erecting a fortress with high stone walls and weapons of evil magic to protect their decadent hordes to the north. Tonight the Vitau'hi would be the tip of the spear through the hearts of the vile enemy.

After tonight, a Great Holy War would commence, which would finally end 1700 years of blood-struggle and deliver the manifest destiny for the Udar. Ur'akeen demanded it, and so it would be.

The old man looked over his pupils–three hundred in number. He walked among them, reaching up to gently scratch their breasts and necks, eliciting light cooing noises and the soft thump-thump-thump from their wiggling, excited tails. This activity went on for some time, as the old man insisted on giving loving attention to each before sending them on their mission.

Finally, he had completed his rounds. The hour had come, and it was time for the Vitau'hi to complete their destiny as servants of Ur'akeen.

The old man stood some distance from his beauties, who wobbled ahead to form a semi-circle around him, the rustling of feathers and the thump-thump-thump of expectation filling the air.

"Fefalo!" he called. The three hundred spread their wings. "Tonight you shall cleanse the land with the blood of the Profaner!"

The old man raised his arms, and the *Vitau'hi* leapt into the air, flapping their wings to rise into the night.

Turning to the east, the old man brought his arms forward in that direction. The three hundred began their short journey over the peaks to the sacred shore.

. . .

ONE

Hilltop Farm – Morning (first day)

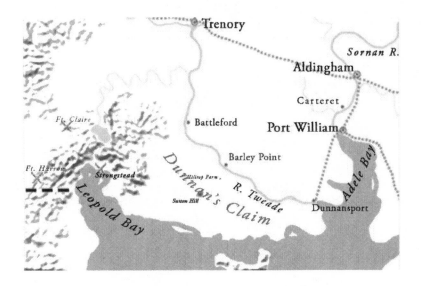

Sarah Stuart awoke before dawn on the morning of the sixth day of the tenth month as she had for most of her teenaged life. As the oldest child remaining in the Stuart household–that had been the case for the past four months–Sarah's morning chores kept her busy. First she had to light the fire in the kitchen stove and start the kettle for the morning's coffee, then feed the dogs from the scrap bucket and let them out for their morning haphazard patrol of the family farm. Then, with the help of her younger sisters Tabitha and Hannah, whom she'd awakened before tending to the three four-legged cattle herders, she'd begin milking the cows in the milking shed behind the farmhouse.

So much work barely before dawn wasn't unusual in Ardenia. As the third child of the most prominent family in

Dunnan's Claim Sarah had certain standards to uphold, and she took pride in displaying the work ethic and sense of duty that her people, and her family in particular, expected of their children. Her older brothers, Matthew and Robert, had set an example for Sarah before departing for the prestigious military academy at Aldingham, and in Matthew's case, thereafter for a deployment to the citadel at Strongstead, near the dangerous southern border. That made Sarah the oldest of the Stuart children still at home, and she wouldn't shirk the responsibility attendant in her status.

Soon, she knew, she would own a farm not dissimilar to this one with the man she would marry. When that happened, Sarah would become a full-fledged citizen of the Ardenian Republic, in which property ownership and the taxation it carried were prerequisites for citizenship and voting rights.

The Stuart farm was one of thousands springing up in the lush, newly-settled lands south of the river Tweade. In the 25 years since the Ardenian army had driven their longtime enemies the Udar far to the south, Ardenia had converted what was a frontier too dangerous for agriculture or any other civilized pursuits into the scene of a land rush of massive proportions. In short notice the influx of investors, homesteaders and military veterans created a thriving agricultural expansion surrounding three bustling new, if thus far small, cities – Battleford (population: 8,000) up the Tweade to the northwest, Barley Point (population: 3,000) just to the north of Sarah's home, and Dunnansport (population: 5,000) to the east at the river's mouth.

That burgeoning expansion included the Stuarts. Sarah's parents George and Judith were among the early transplants to the area, riding the sternwheeler steamship *Fredonia* down the Tweade from the bustling city of Trenory to the southern landing across from the river port of Barley Point, then embarking by horse-drawn wagon for the 200-acre parcel ten miles to the south. George had received the land in a grant by the Societam, which was Ardenia's parliament, in recognition of his military heroism. It was the most desirable land in the territory: lush, verdant savannah dotted with stands of Moss Oak and sweetgum trees. There was a breathtaking vantage from atop the hill where the manor sat, along the newly-cut road from the landing across from Barley Point to the north running south to the wilderness, with several small streams flowing through the land to provide natural irrigation.

George was just 25 then, a year beyond his five-year term in the Ardenian cavalry which had performed so brilliantly in the war against the Udar. He'd been discharged with the rank of Colonel, earning the Order of the Elk for valor in the Battle of Rogers Rock at the tender age of 20. He'd then served as an adjutant to the great general Henry Dunnan, before emerging as the hero of the great battle of Sutton Hill at only 21, which earned him the Parliamentary Star. In so doing, George earned a priority in the military emoluments which followed Dunnan's driving out the Udar.

George and his brother David went into business following the war; moreover, while George claimed double the allotted acreage (half in David's name) from the spoils of Dunnan's War, his older brother settled in the newly-founded city of Dunnansport at the mouth of the Tweade to manage a cotton and grain storehouse business the two had borrowed against the land to establish.

David, four years George's senior, had lost his left arm below the elbow in the first year of Dunnan's War courtesy of a well-placed strike from a Udar halberd in the battle at Strongstead. With that injury his talent and taste for agriculture was thus dissolved. So it was George who farmed the land, and those rich 200 acres made for suitable collateral to launch the commercial venture in Dunnansport. David, it turned out, had a brilliant head for business. Soon he wasn't just storing cotton, wheat, sugar and barley raised on the farms in the new land, but also brokering the commodities to the major exchanges at Port William to the north and Port Excelsior to the east along the seacoast. The profits rolled in.

Sarah knew the two had also collaborated in speculation in the share markets in the Ardenian capital Principia, with some significant degree of success. The true size of the Stuart holdings, after several stock trades amid what had been a boom market over the past 20 years had in recent years been the source of rumors and tall tales all through the territory. But George and Judith never discussed the stock transactions with the children, so Sarah couldn't say with any degree of specificity how rich the family was. She had her suspicions, though, that the family was wealthier than anyone knew.

David and George's success in business, stock speculation and agriculture quickly paid off the mortgage, and more, and by the time Sarah was born six years after its establishment, Hilltop Farm had expanded from a small log cabin built by George and six hired hands to a tidy stone manor at the center of a state-of-the-art, mechanized Ardenian farm with all the latest technological accoutrements.

Further, in the last year David had secured a franchise to sell steam tractors shipped down from the Somerset Company factory at Port William, and George was the sales agent for the Barley Point territory. The Somerset Company was the dominant player in the manufacture and sale of farm machinery, one of the fastest-growing sectors of the Ardenian economy. Agriculture, moreover, had become a major driver of prosperity as the nation became not just the world's breadbasket, but also its leading source of agricultural materials from cotton to rubber to hemp and beyond. Having a commercial hand in the mechanization of agriculture in this new territory, which was quickly proving to be the most fertile farmland in all of Ardenia, was a privilege and a blessing few could even dream of, but given George's reputation as a celebrity and potential figure of political leadership in Dunnan's Claim, the Stuarts looked upon his appointment as the company's representative as only natural.

Hilltop Farm was becoming the envy of the territory. George planned to make sure everyone knew it. That very day the family expected a visit from one H.V. Latham, an architect from Port William, who was to present plans for a total rebuild and major expansion of the manor house, to create the first Great Estate in the new Dunnan's Claim territory. Construction was to begin in the spring, and the Stuarts planned on spending much of the next year in Dunnansport as guests of Uncle David and his wife Rebecca.

Sarah was peeved at that, of course, because while all the exciting developments were taking place at Hilltop Farm she would be off at the Waldiver Finishing Academy in Trenory, where her mother had been a student and to which Sarah had recently been accepted. She was set to matriculate in just a few months to learn the finer points of becoming an urbane lady of means: the finer points of how to be a proper hostess at social affairs, the science of running a proper household, fashion and art, culture and philosophy and, of course, the deportment and etiquette of a well-bred Ardenian lady. On the latter two subjects Sarah had been adamant toward her mother that such instruction was anything but necessary. Judith's response was unfailingly dismissive. "You have the grace of a dyspeptic jackass," her mother had told her last year during a discussion of Sarah's refinement.

A few months later, though, Sarah sat with the admissions officer at Waldiver in the salon at the Hotel Danvers in Barley Point the day after her sixteenth birthday, and impressed the woman enough with her sophistication and erudition to earn her admission. When the letter came she had triumphantly waved it in Judith's face, earning knowing smiles from both of her parents. At the time Sarah thought nothing of that exchange, but since then, she'd entertained creeping doubts that perhaps her success had been driven more by the family's contributions to the school's endowment than her elegance and charisma.

She'd find out soon enough, she figured. What Sarah knew about herself was that she was pretty. She had her mother's looks, after all, and Judith had been the queen of the pageant at the Trenory Convivium, one of Ardenia's most prestigious beauty competitions, some 25 years hence. At sixteen Sarah had grown to 5-foot-9, two inches taller than her mother and the same height as Robert, her brother a year older, which was the source of no small irritation to him. Sarah's large brown eyes, high cheekbones, graceful neck and shapely legs were features she knew the men in her midst appreciated and the women envied.

She was also quite intelligent, having passed the standard Ardenian academic aptitude test for fifteen-year-olds with a ninety-two-percentile score at thirteen, and at seventeen having already passed the eighteen-year-old test with an eighty-eight-percentile score. Had Sarah wanted to pursue a position in the scientific or technological trades she had a sure opportunity to do so, but her interests lay elsewhere. Sarah wanted to follow in her mother's footsteps and raise a family, and on the side, she fancied herself pursuing a career as a writer of social commentary and fiction, though to date she'd yet to venture into that territory. Sarah had opinions and insights, and people would want to know about them. If at times she was a bit direct and those who weren't familiar with her style of expression couldn't handle it, well...they would get used to her, and when they did, they would understand the brilliance they had been missing.

Sarah considered that future as she donned a workday attire over her loose cotton shift which looked nothing like what one might associate with the life of the mind: a tie-waist gray cotton skirt falling to mid-calf, a low-cut buttoned-up light brown woolen bodice, a pair of thick wool stockings with ribbon garters tied above the knee, a pair of open-backed clogs, a wide blue cotton shawl draped over her shoulders and tucked into the vest, and a pinned-on cap covering her voluminous dark brown hair.

In Ardenia, though, or at least here in the new territories, the elite didn't associate high fashion with good breeding. Though in the throes of a technological revolution that over the past 100 years had transformed it in remarkable ways, this was very much a society built with agriculture at its foundation and forefront. Sarah's holding the aspirations, values, culture and vestments of a farm girl was still the sign of quality and status despite Ardenia's modernization.

Her future intellectual stardom wouldn't produce milk from those cows, though. Sarah led her younger sisters Tabitha and Hannah, who were similarly dressed, out to the shed in the humid pre-dawn air. Two dozen cows awaited their morning milking, and the three girls would have that chore finished and the milk poured into the bladder in the ice cellar by 7:30. That should be just in time for the girls to join George, Judith and the youngest brother Ethan, whose specialty was harvesting eggs in the hennery when he wasn't chasing the dogs around the manor house, his little legs only a bit longer than those of the hounds, for a hearty breakfast.

It was to be a rather light day on the farm, as the harvest labor team contracted from Trenory wasn't due in for another week, and Mr. and Mrs. Carson, the farm's foreman and his wife, were away in Port William to visit her family for the next four days. It was just the Stuarts this week at Hilltop Farm, and while George was keeping the girls and Ethan busy with chores, there wasn't a whole lot of major activity going on. Sarah was looking forward to an afternoon walk with her father, as he imparted to her another of his famous stories; she'd heard most of them already, but the sound of his voice alone was still enough to hold her interest; that hadn't changed since she was a little girl. Later, she'd have a chance to curl up by the fireside with a novel after the family dinner.

"Sarah, will you dance with William at the ball in Barley Point on Saturday? He'll truly ask you," teased Tabitha.

"Shut up, you," came the good-natured response. "I'll bet he won't even be there."

Tabitha wasn't giving up. "Of course he will," she retorted. "He'll be home from Aldingham for the harvest by then, and he's going to be looking for you…"

Sarah cringed.

William Forling, who was, to the day, three years older than Sarah, was the youngest of seven boys. He hailed from Grayvern Farm, the 100-acre parcel bordering Hilltop Farm to the west, and he had fancied himself Sarah's sweetheart since the two were small children, with the not-so-silent blessing of both Will's and Sarah's parents.

Sarah long considered William a friend, but a match? The Forling boy was tall – too tall – and laughably clumsy. George had teased the neighbor boy as he grew up by likening him to an unmade bed, and that had stuck with both the Stuarts and his parents. Will had shocks of flowing blond hair which grew so quickly he was seemingly giving it a fresh cut once a week just to keep it out of his eyes. He was frequently tripping over a pair of snowshoe-sized feet and his confidence in front of the community's adults was somewhat absent, leading to a comical stutter.

Since his departure for the academy two and a half years earlier, the younger Forling was also a frequent correspondent via post. Those of his letters she did read were filled with awkward romantic overtures. As she became old enough to recognize boys approximating her age as potential husbands, Sarah crossed William off that list. Emphatically.

No, Sarah would not marry William. Sarah would do much better. She'd had that conversation with her father and made her stance clear, but it was the source of some consternation to her that George didn't seem to take her very seriously.

"Such obduracy in matters of the heart!" he'd said with a grin, upon Sarah informing him of her rejection of William, just before his departure for the academy. "Young Forling shall lament the day his parents settled in the vicinity of so demanding a belle."

After such a mocking response from her father, Sarah had turned to her mother for support. "He thinks I'm a silly girl!" she'd cried. "How can you let him be such a brute?"

Judith had merely cast her eyes up from the novel she was reading. "I always say that time solves these questions," she said, in her languid Trenory drawl. "But I do expect you, as the oldest of our girls, to be the first to marry. If the Forling boy isn't to be your betrothed, I trust you will surprise and delight us with a young man of means and culture to join us as our son-in-law."

Sarah knew then that it was time to shut up and let the matter drop for the time being, but she was right about William Forling and her opinion of that boy had been well set. No one was going to change it.

"Maybe he'll dance with you, Tabitha," Sarah said.

"Is it dancing when you trip and fall on the first step?" her sister, the comedienne of the family, wondered. "Besides, he's certainly not interested in me. You're what he wants."

"Ugh. Poor boy. He needs to find a nice girl who'll appreciate him and won't mind how floppy and ungainly he is."

Tabitha wasn't ready to give up. "It's funny you say that. Robert's letters make him the luminary of the student body at the Academy."

Sarah found that hard to believe, though perhaps not impossible. She hadn't laid eyes on the Forling boy in over two years, though his letters to her had come in a steady stream that had declined from weekly in his first year at the academy, to monthly in his second year, to a bit less regularly so far in his third until the last few weeks when they'd resumed their initial pace. She'd read them occasionally, and, less occasionally, sent polite responses.

"That's most wonderful for him," she replied to Tabitha sarcastically. "I'm sure he'll do very well, and make some other girl a capital husband."

It was then that Sarah noticed Hannah wasn't seated at the milking bench, her cow mooing in an irritated fashion.

"Hannah!" she snapped. "Get to work!"

"Something's wrong," the youngest sister said, as she stared out of the shed's door facing to the south. "It looks like Thistleton Farm is on fire."

Thistleton, due south of Hilltop, was visible from the Stuart family manor and its outbuildings because of the height of their vantage. It was about three miles away, and it was occupied by the Hawklines, a young family with four children: three boys and a girl all younger than Ethan. Judith had struck up a close friendship with the mother, Evelyn Hawkline, who, like Judith, had grown up in Trenory. Mrs. Evelyn was something of an aunt to the Stuart children. The father, whom they didn't know as well, had been a merchant sailor and was originally from somewhere in the Northeast.

Sarah raced to the shed door to share Hannah's view, and Tabitha followed just behind. The three gawked, as dawn broke, at a pillar of fire and smoke emanating not just from the Thistleton farmhouse but also from its outbuildings, and they could make out amid the pall several – more than a dozen – of what looked like horsemen with torches.

"Those look like Udars!" Tabitha whispered, paralyzed with fear.

"Go inside the house," Sarah barked. "Tell Father. Get the rifles from the hunting closet, and as much ammunition as you can carry. Now!"

No time to spare, she thought, as she threw open the cattle door and clapped the cows into the pasture – if this was a Udar raiding party, something she'd heard about but never experienced, perhaps if the cows scattered they could escape capture or slaughter. She needed to get Hannah and Ethan into the ice cellar, where there was a hiding space in which they could be safe, and then help her father defend the farm. On that score Sarah felt somewhat confident, if that was possible in circumstances like these, as she'd hunted often with her father and brothers and wasn't a bad shot. George had impressed on his children, particularly in the last couple of years, the urgent necessity of marksmanship amid what he saw was a flagging commitment by Ardenia's army to defend the settlers of the frontier.

Racing to the house with Hannah by the arm, Sarah found that the adults were already in the midst of preparation for what lay ahead. She bumped into her mother still in her shift just inside the side door as she entered the manor's kitchen.

"Take your sister to the cellar," Judith commanded, an unfamiliar urgency bordering on panic rising in her voice, which scared Sarah. "But before you do, get the strongbox from your father's office and bring it with you down there. You know how vital that is to us."

19

"Yes, mother," she said, as George, his nightshirt untucked over his britches and the buckles on his knee-high boots undone, blew past her with his arms stuffed with saddlebags, his carbine rifle and his scabbarded cavalry sword.

"Three rifles and a crate of magazines are on the living room table," he said over his shoulder. "Get those after you hide Hannah and Ethan, and bring them to the south balcony. You're going to need to take firing positions with your mother. Quickly!"

Sarah did as she was told, reassuring her terrified youngest siblings and admonishing them to "stay quiet until I come for you" as they tucked into the cellar hiding space, and she then rushed up the stairs as fast as her legs would carry her. The *clunk-clunk-clunk* of her clogs against the wooden stairs was, she thought, a good approximation of her heartbeat.

Atop the stairs, she turned left into the master bedroom where Judith was hurriedly donning a robe to go with her bedclothes. Tabitha was throwing open the double doors to the south balcony. Tabitha and Sarah turned a table on its side and dragged it out to serve as a shield against enemy arrows and throwing axes, and then Judith joined them in taking position near the southwest corner of the manor house's second floor balcony.

She could see her father outside. George was on his horse, thundering down the hill to the south to scout the trouble.

He didn't get far, though. Barely 200 yards down the road to Thistleton, Sarah could see him stop his horse, empty his rifle in a quick succession of trigger pulls and wheel around to his right. He sought to lead the enemy away from Hilltop Farm, at least as he reloaded a new magazine while riding in preparation for a new defense, but the Udar advanced on a full gallop straight for the manor house.

In strength.

Sarah had heard her father's stories of the fearsome Udar war party–thirty to forty riders, equipped with practically every implement of pre-modern warfare and deadly skill in their use. The short bow, the throwing axe, the *Ba'kalo* halberd, the curved *Gazol* sword and the barbed *Izwei* dagger weren't much of a match for a Thurman rifle or the chain gun, he'd said, but with superior numbers and in close combat the Udar could wreak utter destruction on cavalry or infantry alike. That came from a lifetime of military training for Udar men, for whom no other profession was considered acceptable. All occupations other than hunting, piracy or warfare were the province of women in that savage society, which meant the Udar could punch above their technological weight in the prosecution of violence.

And this was a full war party, thundering up the road to cut George off from his family. The lead Udar were approaching the low stone wall at the south end of the manor proper now. Sarah could see that these were powerfully-built men, shirtless under vests and britches to their knees made of some indeterminate animal skin, with boots of a similar material, and the unmistakable fearsome trademark headdresses fashioned from the skulls of various creatures, including those of the human species. They filed around the wall, emitting war whoops as they rode to surround the Stuart manor house.

Crack! Crack! Two Udar were unhorsed by George's rifle shots as he advanced on the enemy now from their rear. Sarah watched in horror as four more rounded on him, two unleashing arrows in his direction while two more rode at him brandishing *Ba'kalos*.

George dodged an arrow from one and shot the man square in the jaw from 25 yards with his Thurman rifle, but the other dismounted him with an arrow to his horse's neck. Sarah's father managed to jump clear of his mount, and rolled to a defensive position as he drew his pistol on the first halberd-bearing Udar. He fired, killing the raider with a bullet to the throat.

George wheeled to shoot the other man approaching him, but he was too late.

The mounted Udar gored George in the collarbone with the spear point of his *Ba'kalo*, driving him backward into the ground. The last of the four warriors, who had unhorsed him with the arrow, rode up and dismounted, drawing his *Gazol* and decapitating the head of the Stuart family with a cruel, unceremonious blow.

Now the Stuart women were all that was left of Hilltop Farm's defense. The last moments of her husband's time among the living had unduly engrossed Judith, and she and her daughters had missed opportunities to shoot the advancing Udar who were now inside the wall and busily setting fire to the outbuildings of the farm.

"Girls, shoot as many as you can!" Judith screamed. "We have to save ourselves now!"

Sarah ran to the west balcony, the one above the front door and facing the road. The manor house was festooned with columns and a second-story balcony bordering all four sides of the building. She took aim at one Udar who advanced on the front door. She shot him in the side, and he crumpled into the flower bed along the footpath. She sighted another leading two Stuart horses by the bridle from the barn, and hit him in the leg. The horses panicked at his fall, and he was trampled by one. She then took aim at a third Udar as he came for the front door – and missed.

Things then became considerably worse, as Sarah caught a glance of a pair of hands atop the balcony rail on the northwest side of the manor house. She pointed the rifle in time to see a head and shoulders rise above the rail, and let loose a shot.

It found purchase, as the Udar's face exploded from a bullet through his nose. He fell to the ground from the second story.

Back to the west, Sarah then shot an Udar rider as he raced around the house from north to south. She dodged a thrown axe, which landed barely a foot to the left of her head, bouncing with a spark off the stone wall, and she cast a glance toward the south in search of its thrower. Finding him, a dismounted Udar drawing his bow, Sarah drilled him in the stomach with another rifle shot.

Six shots, five hits. Four bullets left in the magazine, with another in the pocket of her skirt.

Sarah raced to the north, and saw another rider attempting to scale one of the columns to reach the north balcony. She killed him with a bullet to the side of the head. But her next shot at another Udar, wielding a torch as he rode back across to the west, missed, and she missed him again as he launched the torch onto the house's roof. Sarah began to smell smoke coming from inside the house, and looking into the second upstairs bedroom window, she could see the manor was ablaze.

One shot left. She hadn't seen her mother or sister since just after her father died. She stopped herself from thinking about what she'd witnessed and what might become of the family. *Concentrate on what you can control*, she thought. *There will be time for all of that later.*

Coming back to the south balcony, Sarah shot another Udar warrior as he ran with another torch toward the house. She stole a glance down the balcony as she reached for another magazine and reloaded, and that's when she saw with horror Judith's body, pierced through the heart with an arrow as she slumped against the wall. Her lifeless eyes seemed to look almost accusingly at Sarah.

By the Saints! she thought. *I've lost both Mother and Father in front of my very eyes. This is the worst day of my life.*

But the worst had only begun. When Sarah looked up from the remains of her murdered mother, she saw an Udar warrior holding a knife to Tabitha's throat as he turned the corner from the east balcony.

The man was the most frightening vision Sarah had ever seen. Though not quite as tall as her father, who'd stood a commanding six-foot-two, this warrior was at least twenty stone, powerfully built with an angry russet complexion set off by an impressive straight beard tied in a point a few inches below his chin. Iron rings covered his immense left arm from the elbow to the wrist, and a massive headdress topped with the skull of a Blood Raptor, a species of predatory bird Sarah thought was extinct on the Great Continent, adorned his head. He wore a black vest made of some sort of leather and britches to his knees of a similar material dyed blood red. On his feet were boots of a fleshy color. As he moved, she could see a long, dark braid of hair dangling near his waist from under his headgear, and as he glowered at her she noticed that his yellowed teeth were filed to sharp points.

"Rochat, mazeen!" the man spat. *"Avoy! Rochat!"* He made a move as if to slash Tabitha's throat.

"Let her go," Sarah said, in as calm a voice as she could manage while raising her rifle, "or I'll shoot you dead."

I have ten shots left, she thought. *But I don't know how many I can fire before he kills Tabitha. And maybe me as well.*

"ROCHAT!" he roared in a deep, intimidating voice. *"Avoy!"*

"I'm not dropping this rifle, you bastard," she said, recognizing it unlikely he would understand; the Udar were not known to bother themselves with knowledge of the Civil Tongue. "You can kill my sister and me, but I'll take you with me and we'll go in opposite directions in the afterlife."

She could hear guffaws of laughter from the ground below the balcony, which she assumed were in response to her defiance more than the specifics of her words. Some two dozen Udar warriors had gathered to watch the deadly drama as though it were a sporting event.

The Udar holding Tabitha looked down at his comrades, then back at Sarah.

And a smile crept across his face as he pressed the knife further to Tabitha's throat.

Her sister began to issue a scream, but was quickly silenced. Tabitha's final utterance was cut short as the *Izwei* ripped across her neck, nearly decapitating the girl in a rush of blood. Then the warrior advanced on Sarah.

Screaming with rage and terror, Sarah quickly fired, hitting him in the thigh with the first of three shots but missing high with the next two. The Udar was barely slowed by the bullet, and in seven steps of a dead run he tackled her, throwing her back against the doorframe. As she was catapulted backwards by his broad right shoulder, her head hit the limestone of the wall outside her parents' bedroom, and everything went black.

...

TWO

The Barley Point Road – Morning (first day)

H.V. Latham's real name was Henry Varlet Latham IV, which under different circumstances would have been a famous name worth carrying. For a time, his father Henry Varlet Latham III had been one of Ardenia's most famed stage actors, heading a dramatic troupe which performed all along the locomotive circuit from the capital at Principia to its far-flung destinations in every direction. It was on what turned out to be the last of those tours, however, when elder Latham found himself in an imbroglio involving a card game in the train's lounge car, that an incident ensued involving a pistol and a very angry man accusing the actor of dealing from the bottom of the deck. Henry Varlet Latham III was shot dead halfway between Belgarden and Valledge Lake.

The death of H.V.'s father hit the teletext wires within minutes and had made all the broadsheets by the end of that week, and what started as scandal soon became legend. The younger H.V.'s mother reacted by immediately putting her husband's property on the market, banking a half-share (H.V. and his sister were in for quarter shares each when the house and most of its contents were sold at a premium at the Brown's Auction House in Principia). She then promptly took up with a retired Navy admiral of her husband's acquaintance, and decamped for the mountain resort town of Guthram in the far northeast.

The antics and tragedy of the Latham family were a national obsession for weeks, and H.V., at the tender age of sixteen, was unprepared for the circus his life had become. Taking his inheritance in a dossier case of notes from the Mercantile Bank of Principia, he secured early admission to the new Engineering College at Seton Grove far to the south and left the capital without so much as a goodbye. His sister similarly made off, convincing her boyfriend to elope, and the two settled in the Far West city of Vinland to pursue horticultural endeavors in Ardenia's wine country.

Putting as much distance between himself and his troubles was the right tonic for the young Latham. He finished a three-year curriculum at Seton Grove in only two, and was recommended for an internship at Raines & Co. Engineers of Port William. While there, he became a favorite of the proprietor Laudun Raines, under whose tutelage Latham flourished.

He earned his keep. Just three years after joining the firm, Latham had become an assisting engineer in the construction of the rail bridge at Aldingham, which finished the locomotive line connecting Principia to Port William. He would then become the lead engineer building the state-of-the-art hydroelectric plant at Port William two years later. That plant supplied power to the entire city using water wheels to charge rows of dynamos along the bank of the Sornan River. It was a revolutionary design when Latham came up with it, and lots of newer hydroelectric plants were still copying his blueprint.

At 24 H.V. married Raines' young daughter Astrid, which very shortly turned into a problem.

The boss' daughter wasn't quite the spoiled brat the clichés would make her out to be, but Astrid was less than the companion H.V. needed for the quiet, un-outrageous life he sought following the fame and misfortune of his parents. Specifically, she was possessed with a thirst for whisky and a predilection for the frequent use of the cannabis pipe, and these habits manifested themselves in less-than-decorous behavior at the Port William Society Club, where the city's influential citizens shared membership.

Raines blamed H.V. for the frequency of Astrid's missteps, to which the young engineer reacted negatively, but he got nowhere in his demands that she curtail her self-destructive behavior. Latham went so far as to commit her to the alcoholics' asylum at Greyhill, only to see her return, stumblingly drunk, on the locomotive three days later with the explanation that she disapproved of the accommodations at the facility.

At last, there was a row involving an inebriated and combative Astrid and a flying plate at the Society Club, which was worse than any preceding event. This kerfuffle led to the firm losing a proposal to the Port William Transit Rail Co. for the construction of a trolley-car line servicing that city of 300,000. At that point Latham saw he had no option but divorce – a scandalous and extreme solution frowned upon by all in Ardenian society. The Chancery Court granted his suit and discharged him of his marital obligations, solely, the decree read, on the fact that no children were produced of the union.

Raines, however, fired his protégé on that very day.

Virtually penniless, with his good name in tatters and his personage the subject of cruel, twittering gossip, Latham strode into the Army recruitment office at Port William and signed up as a cavalryman at the questionable age of 30. Astrid, meanwhile, landed on her feet. She took up with a rather aged, thoroughly childless and rip-roaringly dipsomaniac shipping magnate and married him within weeks. Within months the old man had expired of liver failure, leaving Latham's ex-wife the richest woman in Port William. Her scandalous and embarrassing behavior had in no time become delightfully eccentric to the city's society; for Latham, climbing aboard a government-issued sorrel and riding off to the wild frontier to shoot Udar seemed like a far safer and more prudent proposition than sticking around town to endure Astrid's social revenge.

Latham's five-year tour of duty wasn't spent mostly on horseback, however. He and his regiment, commanded by, in Latham's view, an estimable major named Alfred Terhune, did patrol the new territory south of Port William won in Dunnan's War, from the south banks of the Tweade west all the way to the newly-built coastal citadel at Strongstead. Along the way the regiment encountered enemy raiders and the horrors of Udar depredations more than once in the first six months of his tour. Following that, Latham's regiment ventured into The Throat, the heavily-contested narrow valley cut into the massive Rogers Range to the west, for the next four months for even more dangerous contact with the Udar, including a major scrape at a place called Stone Lip, which Latham would never forget.

Suddenly, less than a year into his tour it was noticed that he was the Latham of engineering repute, something he hadn't advertised but didn't deny. At that moment he was plucked from his mount and put to work in the Engineering Corps at the army's base at Barley Point.

Latham didn't much complain over the rather radical change in his assignment. After seeing the enemy on several occasions, he felt as though he'd done enough duty and penance for screwing up his life with the boss' daughter, and he was grateful for an opportunity to camp behind a desk and do what he was trained to do. Latham resumed his former profession, designing ad hoc upgrades to the army's chain gun, supervising the construction of the military bridge over the Tweade at Battleford and performing other work.

Over time, though, Latham's interest in engineering faded along with his desire to work for anyone else. So when his time in the Army ended, he returned to Port William and opened an office as an architect. And of all the moves he'd made, career-wise, this was the one which served him best. Over the ten years that followed, Latham designed a few houses and apartment buildings in Port William, though nothing in the fashionable areas of the city. He would draw plans for much of the new construction at Dunnansport's wharves. He would designed several of the mansions in that new port city's fashionable Tweade Landing district. More recently he received commissions for designing new and improved construction of many of the manor houses on the plantations in Dunnan's Claim.

The planned addition at Hilltop Farm, where Latham was headed on the morning of the sixth day of the tenth month, was to be a spectacular undertaking and perhaps his architectural masterpiece. After spending the previous day riding the rails from Port William to Dunnansport and from there taking a steamboat up the Tweade to Barley Point, at dawn he led his horse onto the ferry across the river, with plans for the manor house and outbuildings, including a dormitory for the farm's caretakers and hired hands, in a leather case slung across his shoulder. At the south ferry landing Latham led off at a trot down the road into the barley and wheat fields for Hilltop Farm and a date with architectural destiny.

But while Latham had successfully reinvented himself from a professional standpoint, at least enough to earn a living if not emerge as rich, Port William certainly hadn't welcomed his return to city society. He'd turned into something of a loner of minor means, and a thorough workaholic with a quite limited and plebeian circle of friends: dock foremen, enlisted Marines and tavernkeepers. As to romance, Latham had gone fifteen years without prospects, and following the experience of Astrid and the social curse she had laid upon him in Port William, he'd more or less made his peace with the permanence of his condition.

But Latham wasn't in quite the rut it might have appeared to his few remaining upper-crust acquaintances. Dunnan's Claim being in the midst of rapid growth and accelerating wealth accumulation compared to the rest of the country, Latham figured, he stood to gain significantly from the expansion of Hilltop Farm. The Stuarts were the best-known family in the new territory, and the largest single landowners to date. Winning renown for having built an architecturally-significant structure on that site could lead to things H.V. had been planning since his Army days. He wanted to move his office from Port William, away from his former wife's continuing gossip about him, down to Dunnansport and ride the new city's growth to fortune and fame on his own terms. There wasn't yet enough population or business to fully support that move.

The rich expansion of Dunnan's Claim, he expected, would change all that. Over dinner at an inn at Barley Point the night before, Latham had reconnected with his former cavalry commander Terhune, now a colonel in charge of the base in that town. After a lengthy rant about the insufficiency of the troop strength of his command and the thoroughly disgraceful quality of their armaments and provisions, which Terhune said were inferior enough to their former materiel that he'd been scrounging relics to properly kit his regiment, the Colonel had told him of the plans to incorporate a new county south of the Tweade which would run the thirty miles to the seacoast along Watkins Gulf.

Those plans would mean founding a new county seat, which Terhune said was several years overdue, and it would mean the potential for years of lucrative and substantial architectural work for a renowned professional operating in the area. The rich lands being settled and the needs of those settlers could well make Latham wealthy beyond his dreams. Little wonder the plans for Hilltop Farm in his travel case would rival those of the grandiose estates in the Morgan River Valley west of the capital.

Latham was a veteran horseman, but his 45 years were beginning to take their toll. As he spurred his mount ahead down the well-lain gravel road to Hilltop Farm, he noted the discomfort in his back and knees. *You've grown fat from too much time in inns and ale-houses*, he thought. *You look like a tomato with legs atop this horse. No wonder you're already in pain.*

Latham considered Terhune's advice from last night's conversation. "Take a wife, and have her bear you sons and at least one daughter," the colonel, happily married with four grown children, had said. "You need sons to carry on your business, and until you're in the family way that trouble in Port William will never be behind you."

But who will want a fat old man with a balding pate like me? wondered Latham. *My economic prospects are improving, but my name is twice cursed. No one of quality would consider my hand.*

Latham knew the Colonel was right, though. Inns and ale-houses would be his death in shorter time than Latham wanted to consider, and he needed to press his marital options.

About two-thirds of the way to Hilltop Farm, an hour after starting his journey from the ferry landing, Latham's reverie was broken when he saw smoke rising on the hill. He

31

spurred his horse forward as his heart sank. *Just my luck*, he thought. *They're ruined from a faulty wire from the generator or a random spark from the fireplace, and my prized client is literally up in smoke.*

But maybe, if he couldn't help himself, he could help others if something had really gone wrong. Latham rode ahead, ascending the hill at a trot as the magnitude of the calamity befalling the Stuart estate began to manifest itself. He could see smoke columns from at least four – no, five – sources on the estate as he approached, and as he passed the stand of trees just north of the manor house near the top of the hill, he saw that the entire property lay ablaze.

That's no electrical fire, Latham thought. *This is something far worse. And I've seen it before.*

The manor house was more ruin and smoke than an active inferno. But as he approached Latham saw something more telling than just the charred timbers of the newly-exposed roof.

Blood. Trails of it dotting the grounds outside the house.

Latham knew what that meant. Udar raiders had come.

He'd seen the handiwork of the Udar before, including in the aftermath of similar pillaging – though never of a prize like this. But that had been as part of a regiment of 100 cavalrymen armed with rifles and pistols against a war party of 30 to 40 brigands; the odds of battle were typically stacked heavily on the Ardenian side in those engagements.

Here, he was alone. And unarmed. Against what could be a murderous enemy in strength.

It was damned foolish to remain long. But Latham couldn't come all this way without rendering what aid he could to any survivors he could find. *See what can be done, then get out on the triple-time*, he thought. *The alarm has to be raised at Barley Point.*

In designing the expansion, Latham had memorized the floor plan of the manor now ablaze in front of him. Seeing no one alive or dead on the premises, he felt safe enough for some rapid exploration and knew where survivors might be if there were any.

He knew there was a trap door leading to the hiding space in the cellar, hidden in the flower garden by the front porch. Latham moved a planter box from its spot over that door and there it was. He turned the latch and pulled it open. "Is anyone there?" he called down.

No answer, but he could hear whispering, as though from children.

"Don't be afraid. I'm coming down," he said, as he quickly descended the narrow ladder into the hiding space. At the bottom, he saw two terrified young ones – a boy and a girl – huddled together in one corner of the small space.

"You must be...Hannah and Ethan?" Latham said. "I've met both of you. Do you remember me? I was here some weeks ago to discuss expanding your house. Ethan, do you remember I showed you the plans for the dockyard in Dunnansport?"

The boy nodded.

"I know you're scared, but I've got to get you both out of here right now. Will you come with me?"

"Sarah said we're supposed to wait for her," Hannah said. "She told us."

"I know, sweetheart, but I don't think she's here right now. The house above you is burning. I think we need to go. I'll get you to safety first and then I'll come back and find your family. Is that fair?"

Ethan was the first to agree. He gathered, with difficulty, a heavy box and approached the ladder. "Here," said Latham. "Let me carry that for you."

Latham went up the ladder, carrying the family strongbox. Ethan and Hannah followed.

Now he was faced with a dilemma. The horse could carry him, and it perhaps could carry the two children as well. That box wouldn't survive the journey.

"We're going to have to leave this," he said. "Let's go."

"No, we have to take it," Ethan said. "Father said it has the family's entire fortune in it."

"I understand. It's papers and files?"

"I think so," said Hannah.

"Then we're going to open it and put everything in my bags. But we've got to be quick. The bad men who did this could be coming back any minute. Fair?"

The children agreed, and Latham looked around for something to break open the strongbox.

What he found was a hoe standing against the northern wall – that and a curved *Gazol* sword laying in the grass a few feet away.

This was an Udar raid for sure now, he knew. No question left.

Returning to the box, Latham swung the hoe down on its hinges, earning a disinterested *clank!* from the box and no other result. A few more desperate swings and he abandoned that effort, taking up the *Gazol* instead. He noticed that he could just wedge the tip of the curved sword into the crease of the iron box at its back between the hinges, and then with some difficulty worked the box into position where he could attempt to pry it open. The lock at the front would not be budged.

Nor would the back.

But Latham had an idea. He'd use the hoe as a wedge and attempt to break one of the hinges, and maybe then the contents of the box could be retrieved.

It was worth a try, and as he drove the hoe's blade into the crease, he felt one hinge begin to give way. As he leaned in, the other did as well and the box popped open, spilling papers everywhere.

"Quick, let's gather these up. Stuff them in this bag," he said, producing his travel case first to fit half the contents and then jamming the rest into a saddlebag.

Latham then mounted the horse, and brought first Hannah and then Ethan aboard – the girl behind and the boy in front. He carefully navigated through the gate to the road, and set off slowly to the north for fear of jostling the children too much as he attempted to take them to safety.

So far, there was no sign of the Udar or anyone else, but looking to the west Latham could see more smoke.

"That's your neighbor to the west, right?" he asked.

"Right," said Ethan. "Grayvern Farm. The Forlings live there."

"It's burning," said Hannah. "They're all burning."

"Was it burning before Hilltop Farm," asked Latham," or do you know?"

"I don't think it was," said Hannah. "They must have come to us first and now they're killing our neighbors."

"We have to go," Latham said. "Hold on tight. I want to get away from here as quickly as we can."

He set the horse to a trot and made a quick exit from the ruined manor, without knowing the fate of the Stuart parents or older siblings who may have been on the estate at the time of the attack. Latham was loath to speculate as to the outcome of what he'd seen.

Either dead or carried off, he thought. *The former is better.*

Latham knew from experience. He'd seen the Udar in action.

...

THREE

In the South of Dunnan's Claim – Noon (first day)

She came to slowly, with the sensation of blood running across her cheek and a scorching headache occupying her entire consciousness.

As Sarah strained to open her eyes, what she saw was the ground passing beneath her and what she felt was the intense pressure of having her head at the lowest elevation of her body. Her hair, which she'd pinned up while dressing that morning, was now a jumble and hung all about her face.

She was tied, bent and slung across a horse, and painfully jostled as it traveled at a full gallop. The Udar rider just next to her, she surmised, was the same demonic man she'd shot before her lights had gone out.

He murdered my sister, she thought, *and the Lord of All knows what he's going to do to me.*

Sarah tried to scream, but couldn't, not with the rag stuffed in her mouth. She tried to struggle, but bound as she was, she could hardly move. Her ankles had been tied together and bound to her thighs, her arms had been bound in a painful folding position behind her, and a rope passed from bindings between her knees under the horse to…

Was that a collar around her neck? It was. A leather collar. As though she were a dog.

And Sarah wouldn't budge off that saddle. Not with ropes binding her at the breast, waist and thigh to it. She was firmly secured and she was going wherever the Udar was taking her.

He was going there quickly, something she felt with every painful bounce as the horse galloped its way away from her home.

She worked out that they were traveling south, since it appeared the sun was on the opposite side of the horse and it was, she thought, still morning. She was heading for *Uris Udar*, the enemy's territory, and a fate described in books she'd read.

The Udar, she knew, had evil designs on Ardenian women. Tales of sexual slavery, forced impregnation and even human sacrifice to their god Ur'akeen had been told to Ardenian girls as cautions against reckless behavior as long as there had been an Ardenia. And now she would be the subject of one more of those tales.

It was enough to make Sarah go to pieces as she not-so-silently wept. She'd done what she could to keep it together after seeing her parents and sister killed and her home destroyed while fighting for her life, but now, in her helplessness and agony, she was completely dispirited. The will to fight, to live, had left her. All she wanted now was for the end to come as quickly and painlessly as possible.

They continued quickly south, Sarah jostling near the horse's rear as the Udar took her further and further from Hilltop Farm, for what seemed an eternity. Finally, the horse, rider and unwilling passenger slowed and Sarah heard voices. She turned her head and saw what looked like a camp, staffed, it appeared, almost exclusively of Udar women.

While the men of the enemy nation were typically stocky, frighteningly muscular and carried long jet-black hair in tight braids down their backs covered by headdresses made of various shapes, sizes and species of bone, what Sarah saw as the horse made its way into the camp was a different sight altogether. The women of the camp had their hair cut almost to the scalp, and they went around bare-breasted, their necks festooned with rolls of beaded necklaces. They wore knee-length britches of some kind of fur or leather and sandals tied at the ankle. While the men were bearded, the faces of the women were covered in tattooed markings – lines, dots and shapes beginning on their foreheads and spreading to their cheeks and chins.

Her captor dismounted, grunting as he limped on the leg Sarah's bullet had wounded. He hobbled into a tent, followed by two of the women. Three more approached the horse babbling in a language Sarah couldn't understand.

She was then untied from the saddle, her bent legs set free, and hauled off the horse. One of the women yanked the rope attached to her collar, leading her forward and stumbling into the camp.

Sarah saw what had to be 200 women in and around at least as many tents. The Udar had set up the camp on a slight rise giving way to a plain running south to Watkins Gulf, and she knew roughly where she was from having made past excursions here with her father. This was the unclaimed land, but it wouldn't be for long – at least that was the plan. Somewhere near here, according to the word among her father and his colleagues, was where the new county seat was to be built, and her father was to have had a seat on, if not the presidium of, the new county council.

All of that was gone now, of course. It appeared as though the county seat belonged to the Udar, and for the rest of what life she had left, she expected, so did Sarah.

The tears which had flowed freely during the ride returned. She felt light-headed as she was dragged along a few more yards, and then made to sit.

Sarah turned and saw she was not the only captive Ardenian in the camp. Far from it. Several dozen others were sitting in tight lines mostly of 10 prisoners – all gagged with rags in their mouths, all tied as Sarah was with collars around their necks. All had been stripped down to their cotton shifts. Most showed signs of having been brutalized.

She was forced down in a line of five captives, one of whom she knew. That was Hester Blaine, from Landsdowne Farm thirty miles to the east. Hester was older than Sarah; she was 20, and had moved to Landsdowne just a few years ago with her family. They were from far to the north – Greencastle, near the capital, if she remembered correctly. They'd bought Landsdowne from the Olivers, who'd sold it after building the manor house and moving home to Aldingham with a tidy profit in hand. Hester had been friends with Sarah's cousin Josey.

Hester looked in bad shape. Her shift was torn at the front, which exposed an angry welt over her right breast; the bloody wound on the top of her head was dressed with a shred of cloth; and she was covered in scratches. She looked as if she'd been in a fight. She had no shoes, unlike most of the captives, and one of her stockings was gone.

But as Sarah took stock of her own situation, she wasn't any better off. She knew she had at least a deep bruise on the back of her head, and she could feel and smell the blood drying on her face from where that wound had bled while she was upside down over the horse. Her clothing – her shawl, bodice, skirt and cap – had been removed, with only her shift remaining, and other than her stockings, which drooped to her ankles, she was also barefoot.

Not much of a presentation. This was a nightmare.

A female captor approached and tied a rope to a ring in her collar. Sarah stiffened.

"You come," the captor said. "Tent there."

Sarah refused to move, paralyzed by fear.

"Come now," said the woman, as she yanked on the rope, jerking her by the collar. "Tent. You need."

She shook her head.

The blade of the woman's *Izwei* appeared at Sarah's throat. "*Avoy!*" said the woman. "Come now. You die else."

Sobbing, with the vision in her head of Tabitha's murder by an identical instrument just hours ago right in front of her, she struggled to her feet and allowed herself to be led into the nearby tent.

The worst of her fears did not prove true when the flap parted. Inside the tent were two women equipped with a large bowl of water and cloth for what appeared to be bandages. Sarah was forced down to her knees, and one of the women began addressing the bump on the back of her head while the other began wiping blood off her face.

"You not hurt," said the one behind her. "You healthy. Make good *javeen*."

Sarah wanted to speak, but she was still gagged. She began shaking her head violently. The other woman recognized what she was trying to signal and pulled the rag out of her mouth.

"Water," she begged. "Please."

The woman brought a leather flask to her lips and she drank.

"Why am I here?" she asked when the flask was taken away. "Why are all these others here?"

"War," came the response from the one who had spoken to her before. Sarah turned to look at her and realized she was only a girl, perhaps no more than Sarah's age.

"We take. You *javeen*, or you *azmeri*."

"What is *javeen*? What is *azmeri*?"

"You *javeen*," said the girl. "You make babies. Much healthy babies. Rapan'na like you. Very."

"*Azmeri*? What is that?"

"*Azmeri*, you die. Burn for Ur'akeen."

"How do you speak the Civil Tongue?"

"I learn," she responded. "*Mazha*."

"*Mazha*?"

The girl thought for a moment. "Mother," she said. "I learn from mother. She *javeen*."

41

With that, the rag was stuffed back into her mouth and the women took off her stockings and drawers, leading her back to the captive line.

. . .

FOUR

Latham and his two charges reached the ferry at noon, dismounting and leading the horse onto the rickety old sidewheeler just in time for its journey across the Tweade. Traffic on the ferry was almost nonexistent. No one shared Latham's knowledge of the apocalypse to the south, which cast, in his mind, a surreal quality to the situation. He told the ferryman of the need for haste, given the threat of a further attack, and they were underway immediately.

The ride across the large river took only a few minutes, and Latham rushed to tell the Marine attendant at the Barley Point landing of what he saw. That created an immediate fury of alarm at the small river port, and Latham and his charges were hustled to the customs house next to the ferry landing.

At the customs house he was met by a Marine officer, a middle-aged portly major named Boyd Irving, per the name plate on the man's blue uniform coat. The Marines handled customs and security on all of Ardenia's rivers, lakes and coasts, and here at Barley Point that meant Irving was in charge of this part of the Tweade.

"What was this you say you saw?" Irving asked, in a characteristically bureaucratic tone.

"An attack. Definitely Udar," Latham said. "These two children are from Hilltop Farm, Hannah and Ethan Stuart. They're survivors. It must have come early this morning. I was on the way there to deliver architectural plans to George Stuart, but I suspect he's gone."

Irving considered Latham's statement, then called in an underling.

43

"Corporal Renford," he said, a bit of adrenaline percolating in his voice, "would you run down Mistress Irving and have her come to take care of these children? We have a situation here."

"Yes sir," said Renford, taking off in a scamper out of the customs house. Latham could hear the bell ringing at the Barley Point Supernal Temple a half-mile away just then, as the town was igniting with the news of what had happened to the south.

"Now," said Irving. "This was a war party? Of what size?"

"I don't know," said Latham. "No one was on the scene at Hilltop Farm but these two, and they were hiding in the cellar when I found them. I saw blood everywhere, though, and found a *Gazol* on the grounds. They had burned the manor house and all the outbuildings. It looked as though they'd taken the livestock as well."

"And they did the same thing to Thistleton Farm," offered Hannah.

"And Grayvern," said Ethan. "We saw the smoke."

"It appeared they'd moved off to the west from Hilltop Farm, from what we could tell," Latham said.

Irving scribbled all this on a tablet, then called another underling to his office.

"Corporal Jones, you will forward this note to Colonel Terhune at the base immediately," Irving barked. "Bring me whatever reply he supplies."

"Terhune was my former cavalry commander several years ago," Latham offered. "He's an old friend. If you like I can deliver the report myself."

"No," said Irving. "Jones will handle that. I need more information from you. Now... you say you didn't see any Udar. Did you see anyone else?"

44

"No one. There was no apparent damage at Stonehaven Farm on the way in, and as best we could tell the occupants weren't around. It appears the enemy came only as far north as the Stuart manor."

"No evidence of captives?"

"I don't know."

Irving winced. "Casualties?"

"My sister Sarah said she'd come for me in the cellar," Hannah said, sobbing quietly now. "She didn't come. I think she's dead. They're all dead!" Ethan wrapped his arms around her, tears escaping his eyes.

Latham dropped to one knee, embracing both children. "I know, I know," he said, doing his best to comfort them. "But we're not sure what happened yet. These men are going to go find your sister and your parents. They're going to try to make it all right."

At that point Renford shepherded a figure clad in a bonnet and cape, who appeared to be Mistress Irving, into the outer office. Irving left the newcomers to converse with her in the other room for a few seconds and then returned. He told the children, "This nice lady is going to take you to her house, and you can stay there as long as you want. She'll feed you and give you whatever you need, all right?"

Hannah and Ethan looked at Latham, seeking direction. "Go," he said. "I'll bring your things as soon as I can."

Renford and the woman led the children away. Irving then circled back behind his desk and pointed at Latham. "You," he said. "You shoot? You were in the cavalry? Consider yourself deputized as a captain in the Ardenian Marine Force."

"Wait," Latham said. "I should talk with Colonel Terhune first."

"No time," snapped Irving. "Go get your horse. You're going back south. You'll be a scout taking my men to the first

45

counteraction. Those bastards won't get across this river alive. We'll take the fight to them now."

He's going to get us all killed, thought Latham. *The bloody fool.*

...

FIVE

Patrick Baker was born with almost nothing. No name, no fortune, not even any parents. He never knew his father, and his mother died in childbirth. She'd been a prostitute in a brothel in South Principia's red-light district until her pregnancy ruined the economic value she could contribute to the brothelkeeper, and he turned her out onto the streets and into the prospect of starvation as soon as she started to show.

She was eighteen.

The nuns of the Sunrise Temple took her in and nursed her through her pregnancy, but Molly Baker's luck had simply run out, and after delivering and naming a healthy baby boy, she died of a postpartum hemorrhage.

Patrick entered the scene as Molly left it, though. When he did, he was remanded to the charge of the Sunrise Temple, which tended to the poor in the grimy, ramshackle tenements of Principia's Ackerton District near to the bustling port where the mighty Morgan River emptied into the Gulf of Prosperity. The Temple happened to run an orphanage along with a shelter, a hospital, a nunnery and a well-appointed and famous, though perhaps declining, house of worship to the Lord of All.

It was to the orphanage that newborn Patrick was deposited, with the idea that he would soon be adopted by some family of better means and fortune than the nonexistent one which had spawned him.

Unfortunately, that didn't happen. Not when Patrick was a newborn, and not when he was a toddler, and not when he was a small child. Patrick stayed at that orphanage for 10 years, under the care of the nuns and the priests who did their best to educate him.

However, while the young boy had no luck in attracting a family, though, in the acquisition of knowledge he was a natural. Patrick was, in the estimation of all in charge of rearing and educating the orphans, the brightest and most inquisitive student they'd ever seen.

At ten, he'd completed the lesson program the orphanage's tutors had designed for a boy five years his senior.

It was at that time Reverend Mother Elizabeth had called young Patrick into her rectory and offered him the first real opportunity of his life. She complimented him on his academic prowess, and told him he had shown real talent and dedication. She further told him that the world would soon be opening its doors to him, and that the Directorate of the Sunrise Temple found his talents suitable to offer him a scholarship to the prestigious Divinate Academy in Bluemont, 250 miles to the south.

With a degree from Divinate, she explained, Patrick would have his ticket punched as a respected cleric within the Faith Supernal and would bring the masses to the Word of the Lord of All. He could choose a parsonage virtually anywhere in Ardenia, with the Divinate pedigree giving him a chance to move quickly into the role of Vicar, or even Bishop. Or he might even return to Principia and join the Faith Directorate, where the clergy interacted with the business and political power in Ardenian society. It was a quiet life of prayer and study, but, Reverend Mother Elizabeth assured him, it was a life which suited young Patrick perfectly.

He remembered her words: "We have directed and shaped you to this point in your life under the inspiration of the Lord of All, and it is He, through us, who has brought you to this moment."

But Patrick's response shocked the Reverend Mother. "Nope," he said.

"I'm going to sea."

Patrick's dormitory room at the Sunrise Temple orphanage was on the fifth floor of that dusty, cramped building, and his window looked out over Principia's South Wharf. There, oceangoing steamers intermingled with Morgan River barges in a fascinating, intricate dance befitting the world's busiest and richest port. In his free time Patrick would wander the port district, hearing bits and snippets of the sailors' stories of Ardenia's other ports of call – Port Excelsior, Gold Harbor, Newmarket, Port William, Maidenstead, even Port Adler and Azuria of the Far West Province – and the foreign ports just opened to trade only a few decades ago.

He spent as much time in the Ackerton public library – and that of the Sunrise Temple rectory – as he was allowed, reading of those faraway places. And Patrick was hooked. He'd lived his entire life in essentially one neighborhood in Principia, and that was enough cloistered time for him. As soon as he could get out and see the world, that's what he'd do.

So when offered a chance to be a pastor or a monk, he couldn't spit on that opportunity fast enough.

This was not well received. The Reverend Mother couldn't force Patrick to attend the Divinate, and she had no reason to punish him for his demurral, but she didn't know quite what to do with him. He was given chores; he did them and then off he went to explore the wharf.

And then one day a few weeks later, Patrick vanished with only a letter addressed to the Reverend Mother in his wake.

In it, he thanked her for everything she'd done for him and pledged his eternal gratitude to the Sunrise Temple for giving him a home and an education – and someday, when he'd earned his fortune and made his mark on the world, he'd return with some measure of effort to repay their kindness. But for now, he wrote, he'd found a ship's captain who'd agreed to take him on as a cabin boy and teach him the ways of the sea.

That captain was Albert Wood of the sternwheeler *Promise*, which made the regular cargo shipping route from Elk's Head in the far north, around the Hard Cape into the Gulf of Prosperity ports of Beacon Point, Port Colby, Gold Harbor, Stableford, Principia and Welvary, south around the coast to

Admiral's Bay and Port Excelsior, and into Watkins Gulf for
Newmarket and Port William. Captain Wood was a humorless,
stern taskmaster of a man, and in taking Patrick on he told him
in his clipped northeastern accent, "You won't like me, boy. In
fact, you may attempt to murder me in my sleep. You will fail,
and I'll regret having drowned you."

Wood, however, was wrong. Humorless and stern was
exactly what the fatherless child craved in a mentor after the
touchy-feely ministrations of the Sunrise Temple. What he saw
in Wood was the masculinity and raw toughness of the Principia
docks – and rather than ignoring him or shooing him out of the
way, here it was demanding he participate in its ways.

Cabin-boy duties gave way to those of boatswain
within a year, though *Promise*'s crew found great amusement in
an eleven-year-old with such a job. But by the time the fast-
learning Patrick was thirteen he had progressed to Sailing
Master, and by fourteen he was doubling as the ship's engineer
having mastered every bolt and screw of its twin engines.

And as *Promise* pulled into Port Excelsior on Patrick's
fifteenth birthday, on the third day of the fifth month thirteen
years ago, Patrick expected Captain Wood to name him First
Mate. The sailor currently holding that position, John Hawkline,
was leaving the crew for a Trenory girl to whom he was
engaged and a 100-acre farm in the new Dunnan's Claim
territory, a place he was planning to call Thistleton Farm. As the
boat inched to its mooring at the Port Excelsior wharf, Wood
called the crew to the foredeck for a bit of a ceremony.

"Gents," he said, "let me interrupt your travails for an
important announcement…a pair, actually, because we have two
of our number to be leavin' us. First Mate Hawkline, an able
seaman for true, is takin' on a new livelihood. He'll be tradin'
the sea sprites and sharks for pigs and chickens down in
Dunnan's Claim, and we have somethin' to send him on his
way." Wood then produced a paper box and passed it to
Hawkline, who opened it to find a small hand-shovel and a
straw hat emblazoned with LANDLUBBER in bright red
stitching.

"I'll keep these treasures at my bedside," the recipient deadpanned.

"Hawkline isn't our only loss," Wood then announced. "We're also biddin' farewell to young Baker…"

Shocked, Patrick glared at the captain, who then smiled at him and continued. "Young Baker here has been admitted on my recommendation and that of the Sea-Captains' Guild to the Naval Academy at Wellhurst just up the coast there – which is why he's leavin' us now."

A roar of congratulatory applause rose from the crew. Patrick was dumbfounded. All he could think to do was embrace the captain, as nobody had ever looked out for him like this man had done.

Patrick didn't finish first in his class at Wellhurst. He finished second, but he graduated a year early, completing a four-year course in three, and earned a plum assignment straight out of the academy as an ensign on *Vanquisher*, a Navy brigantine plying its trade in the Great Sea east of the Ardenian coast. For four years Patrick, who had grown from a skinny, sandy-haired wharf rat to a square-jawed, muscular and handsome sailing veteran, and had even shed most of his South Principia brogue, served on *Vanquisher*'s crew, where he fulfilled all his childhood dreams. He saw the Lerian port cities of Resinan and Arouz, he saw the diamond beaches at Taravel and pocketed five dozen precious stones on shore leave, giving him a not-insignificant nest egg for his retirement even after dropping a dozen of them in the post to the Reverend Mother at the Sunrise Temple with a note of gratitude. There was a reason *Vanquisher* was such a coveted berth.

The young seaman even had an encounter with one of the fearsome Mottled Men of Cavol, during a stopover in the Thosian port of Bergod; the man was nearly eight feet tall and well in excess of 30 stone, considerably more than twice Patrick's weight, with skin so full of birthmarks he was neither black nor white. The Mottled Men were the most fearsome warriors on earth, and this one was in a quite surly mood, so when Patrick happened to bump into the giant and spill a bit of wine on his boot in a quayside saloon in Bergod's sketchy bowery, he made an obsequious apology and a hasty exit with his shipmates.

It was the time of his life, and during Patrick's tenure on *Vanquisher* he advanced his career rapidly. From ensign he progressed to lieutenant junior grade, and from lieutenant junior grade to full-blown lieutenant, and from there to lieutenant commander, even getting some combat experience in a few encounters with Perinese pirates along the Lerian trade routes the Ardenian Navy was in charge of patrolling. He left *Vanquisher* as a lieutenant commander and second mate on the ship, which saw what Patrick thought was a little more-than-healthy amount of turnover through the inordinately frequent retirements of its officers.

Patrick's next assignment was that of Executive Officer of the Ardenian naval ship *Tuttle*, an ironclad gunboat built by the Rackleigh Shipping Works of Port Excelsior. *Tuttle* was assigned to patrol Watkins Gulf and sweep it clear of Udar marauders. There, he saw real combat. While Dunnan's War had mostly made the land safe from Udar war parties, at sea the Udars saw Ardenian shipping as a major source of plunder. With no peace treaty ever signed to end Dunnan's War, not that the Udars had *ever* honored one, the sea was a constant battlefield.

Lacking steamships and operating sail- and oar-powered boats without naval cannons, the Udar relied on guile to ambush civilian vessels. They commonly attacked at night, laying in shipping lanes where small Udar sloops could sail into the path of a sternwheeler or merchantman, and their warriors could use grappling hooks attached to rope ladders to board and savage the Ardenian vessels. Once the attack was over, oar- or sail-powered Udar galleys would move in and whatever cargo or passengers the victim vessel was carrying would be loaded onto their main ships. Whenever a commercial vessel strayed from the convoys the *Tuttle* would often escort, or when one would take its chances at outrunning or slipping past the Udar raiders alone without naval protection, the enemy would all too often lay in wait to do his worst.

Interestingly, the Udar never made prizes of the Ardenian ships themselves. Those they set on fire after slitting the throats of the crew and stripping them of whatever equipment, supplies or riggings they could carry away. Female passengers were commonly taken aboard the pirate ships as plunder, which was why Watkins Bay commercial shipping, unlike the trade along the northern and eastern Ardenian coast, had become more or less an exclusively male endeavor.

On several occasions *Tuttle* managed to intercept those seaborne raiding parties, and the result was one-sided. There is no use attempting to board an ironclad gunship; its decks are empty and its crew is protected inside the plates of metal armor. All boarding such a boat accomplishes is to provide point-blank opportunities for the marines aboard the gunship to pick attackers off through the rifle-slots. On one occasion during an attempt to board *Tuttle* a suicidal Udar did manage to empty a bellows-full of crude oil through one of those rifle slots before being shot down, and another Udar managed to throw a torch through another in an effort to light that crude ablaze, which would have surely been the end for Patrick and his crew. But the torch fell two feet from the puddle of oil made by the bellows and was quickly discarded, and the attack repelled. For days the crew complained of the smell, of course, and the ship got a thorough scrubbing when it pulled into port at Newmarket, but that was the worst of it.

Otherwise, the experience involved a whole lot of shooting at people incapable of effectively shooting back. *Tuttle* was equipped with 10 six-inch cannons firing incendiary shells: casings full of black powder peppered with phosphorous and equipped with pressure fuses lighting the mixture when it hit something, which made for nearly immediate seagoing bonfires of wooden Udar ships. Between the incendiaries and the three spring-loaded chain guns swinging from turrets on *Tuttle*'s foredeck, no Udar ship could match its firepower or weapons range.

But *Tuttle*'s top speed of eight knots wasn't always fast enough to take Udar ships out of the battle space. Because its steam engine, a temperamental contraption requiring the full attention of the crew to keep it from breaking down, trailed a heavy pall of smoke astern, it could hardly sneak up on anyone. The Udar sloops it commonly chased had a top speed of twelve knots. When the *Tuttle* entered the area of a potential pirate attack, it was always a question of landing a lucky shot from a bombardment before the enemy could sail away.

Occasionally, though, *Tuttle* would happen upon the Udar galleys waiting to soak up plunder from the attacks, and in those cases it was pure target practice. The Udar would have as many as 100 oarsmen working to propel their galleys, and at times they might manage to match the *Tuttle*'s speed – for a while. Those galleys couldn't maneuver like the steam-powered *Tuttle* could, and their catapults launching pots of burning crude oil couldn't sink the Ardenian gunboat

Nevertheless, Patrick's duty aboard *Tuttle* was challenging. When Udar raiders did manage to hit civilian shipping, their body count was always at a maximum, and on the occasions when the *Tuttle* arrived too late to stop an attack, the carnage aboard a burning vessel was often highly difficult to stomach. Moreover, the ship's crew seemed nearly unanimous, though the officers were under orders to squelch discussions about it, in thinking politics back home hindered their mission. While the Navy had more than enough firepower to sink the Udar ships when they found them, clearly what they didn't have was enough gunboats patrolling Watkins Gulf to truly control the sea lanes. The older sailors aboard the ship told stories of Dunnan's War, when the Ardenian Navy could amass vast fleets of warships to take the battle to the enemy at will. It was discouraging that while Ardenia was far richer than it had been 25 years before, it demanded the Navy operate with a far smaller navy against what looked like the same determined, if outgunned, enemy.

Also, there were the rules of engagement with respect to Udar pirates; essentially there were none. The official position of the Ardenian Navy was to offer no quarter to the Udar, and so the common practice was to sink every boat and shoot every pirate. Patrick was just fine with that charge at first, but the more he saw of the wanton destruction of the Watkins

Gulf campaigns, the less enthusiastic he was about the wholesale slaughter he and his crew were enmeshed in. It just didn't seem as though there was ever any end to the pointless carnage on the seas, and Patrick wondered more and more if taking prisoners and exchanging them for peace wouldn't be an idea worth pursuing.

At the time, the Excelsior Locomotive Line was finishing its rail corridor between Port Excelsior and Port William, which would all but obliterate the need for commercial shipping along the north coast of Watkins Gulf. Virtually everyone agreed that was a good thing. The safest and easiest way to stop the piracy at sea, if there weren't going to be enough Navy ships to do the job, was to pull the potential plunder out of the shipping lanes.

Despite the frustrations about endless bloodshed and mysteriously scarce resources, Patrick's three years aboard *Tuttle* were profitable career-wise. Twice he earned the Naval Medal for Gallantry during his duty in Watkins Gulf, and when the ship's captain, Commander Victor Marwich, fell ill and died at sea, Patrick assumed command and led two successful combat actions against Udar pirates in a week before the ship put into port at Newmarket. The Admiralty promoted him to Commander and gave him acting command of the ship for his final three months of duty on *Tuttle*.

And from that point, having just turned 25, Patrick Baker commanded ships.

His current command, in fact, was one of the Navy's elite vessels. The newly-built *Adelaide* was a steam frigate supplied by the Markham Maritime Company of Admiral's Bay, 224 feet in length, with dual 625-horsepower steam engines powering screw propellers which could give the ship an astonishing top speed of 22 knots, and it boasted three 100-pounder pivot guns mounted fore, port and starboard, and four chain guns emplaced port and starboard. *Adelaide* had a crew of 120, including 34 marines. It was one of the most advanced naval weapons platforms in the world, and for its mission, to sweep the Udar out of the seas, it was largely overqualified.

Which was fine by Patrick. As was his home port of Dunnansport, a brand-new city at the mouth of the Tweade. Dunnansport had the air of a small town of 5,000 punching above its weight, with new people moving in all the time and construction going on ubiquitously. It was exactly the kind of place a street kid from the slums of Principia making his mark on the world would see as home.

He'd been the captain of *Adelaide* for three years, by far the youngest mainship captain in the entire Ardenian Navy. And during that time the fight against the pirates became significantly cleaner than it was on *Tuttle*. The new ship easily outran the Udar marauders, and its rules of engagement were slightly different. As *Adelaide* had brig facilities capable of holding prisoners, some could be taken, and were.

Patrick was fascinated by what intelligence could be had of the Udar his crew was able to pluck out of the water after sinking their boats. For a society the Ardenians had been warring against, off and on, for 1700 years, less was known about these people than Patrick thought should have been.

That wasn't a particular indictment of Ardenian curiosity, of course. The Udar refused to trade with Ardenia in any manner and they similarly refused any diplomatic contact. To the Udar, Ardenians were simply enemies to be killed or chattel to be exploited. What appeared as wholly irrational, or even inhuman, behavior was explainable, Patrick learned thanks to the Admiralty's bulletins and extensive independent research in whatever libraries he could frequent, and confirmed in the near-fruitless interrogations of the prisoners *Adelaide* hauled aboard, by religion.

The Udar were not worshippers of the Lord of All. They didn't believe in the Faith Supernal or any of its main precepts: that mankind exists to inject reason and order from the chaos of nature, that kindness and cooperation are the Path to the afterlife, and that industry and creation bring one closer to the Lord.

Instead the Udar worshipped the god Ur'akeen, whose name translated roughly to Lord of Us. Udar faith held that

Ur'akeen's people were the only true humans, or at least the only ones who mattered, and the only blessed occupation for his devotees was war against the Others. As Ardenians were the only Others the Udar had any significant contact with, that meant for the 1700 years Ardenia and Uris Udar were neighbors, there had never been real peace, commerce, diplomacy or any other cooperative interaction.

Such circumstances, for a long time, had been greatly to the benefit of the Udar. They had been for most of history stronger militarily, as their entire society was perpetually mobilized for conflict and operated mostly as hunter-gatherers in the wild, mostly mountainous, country of the Great Continent's southern half. The Ardenians had only managed to survive due to distance – most of the continent's northern half went unpopulated for more than a millennium, and it was the eastern coastline, mountains and hills of the Whitlow Peninsula in the northeast and lower Morgan River Valley which was the extent of Ardenian lands. Dangerous wildlife and Udar raids kept that status quo for hundreds of years.

While the Udar were hemmed in by Ur'akeen's admonition that no Udar should die a peaceful death away from his *Afan'di*, or home camp, which kept that society from expanding its landholdings, the Ardenians were a bit more enterprising, however. That was especially true in the past 100 years as the nation experienced a Golden Age.

Technology, something the Udar had never been much interested in, and a mercantile economy had flourished north of The Throat, the mountainous isthmus connecting the two halves of the continent. Ardenians had circumnavigated the world by sea (and just recently by air, in a new innovation pioneered by the famous entrepreneur and adventurer Sebastian Cross) and attempted to open trade with the nations on the other side of the Great Sea, though the presence of dread diseases prevalent in those nations made that impractically dangerous until Ardenian medical science created vaccines to solve the problem.

There was a lot more. Ardenians had discovered gunpowder, steam engines and electricity. Ardenians had built the locomotive network, countrywide, which meant a six-month overland journey from Principia to the Far West port of Azuria on the Sunset Sea could now be made in a mere four days. The two-week sea voyage from Principia to Port Excelsior was now just a day's trip by train. In the last two decades Ardenians now had the teletext, and could send messages coast to coast by wire in mere minutes. Those innovations put Ardenia a vast distance ahead of the other societies across the globe, among whom the Udar lay near the bottom in terms of wealth and advancement.

Mastering the skies was the Ardenian innovation which most inspired Patrick, as only a month before, the young commander had witnessed the docking of the airship *Clyde* at the public field in Dunnansport. This amazing vessel traveled on a row of four hot air balloons inside a dirigible frame with a cabin underneath capable of carrying three dozen passengers, and was powered for steering by a screw propeller similar to the one on *Adelaide*. It could travel at an amazing 48 miles per hour, as fast as the fastest locomotive. The implications, and potential applications, of this new marvel were mind-shattering.

Patrick wondered whether his next command might be a ship like *Clyde*. Or if he should ever consider leaving the Navy, something he had no plans to do, perhaps catching on as a pilot on an airship would be a means of achieving the kind of wealth his current salary wouldn't quite produce.

On the other hand, while Patrick was a believer in the technology of the dirigible airship, he'd read news accounts recently that one of *Clyde's* sister ships the *Justice* had crashed and burned upon takeoff in Principia, and the airship line which owned the dirigibles was in dire financial straits as a result.

That setback saddened Patrick, because the owner of the airship line was that same Sebastian Cross who'd circled the globe in a hot air balloon eight years before, and Patrick was a great admirer of the man. In any event, technology was the order of the day in Ardenia, and it paid to embrace it where one could so as to avoid being left behind.

However, the neighbors to the south embraced nothing but death, depredation and dysfunction, and Patrick was frustrated by the fruitless, violent stupidity he saw from the Udar along the Watkins Gulf sea-lanes.

Patrick had begun to feel differently about the situation in Watkins Gulf now that he commanded *Adelaide*. It was a superior ship to *Tuttle*, for sure, and its engagements with the enemy were infinitely more lopsided. Moreover, they were less frequent, as it appeared the Udar pirates had slowed, though hardly stopped, their activity on the seas in the past six months or so. Patrick attributed that to *Adelaide* and the four other steam frigates now patrolling Watkins Gulf, and he was of the feeling that real peace was finally, after 1700 years, beginning to descend on the region.

At least, that's what he hoped. After six years of blowing pirates out of the water, Patrick was ready for a bit more productive reality to set in.

Similar technological and military advantages on land, proven out in the lopsided result of Dunnan's War 25 years ago, were why Dunnan's Claim was the site of the mad land rush making such quick fortunes in Patrick's new hometown. For the first time Ardenians could come south without mortal fear, and they embraced the adventure and opportunity as only such an intrepid people as his countrymen would.

And today, the sixth of the tenth, *Adelaide* was putting into port at Dunnansport's newly-upgraded naval wharf after a six-week voyage around Watkins Gulf, beginning with a "milk run" mission to deliver munitions to the Ardenian citadel at Strongstead. Strongstead, built in a notch of the Rogers Range along the coast of Watkins Gulf in a bay named for Francis Leopold, the first elected president in Ardenian history, was a bulwark against Udar war parties east of The Throat since Dunnan's War. Its high walls and chain gun and cannon emplacements made it virtually impregnable, and attempts to come through it impossible. Closing The Throat was a national-security imperative, and on that basis four fortresses were in various stages of unfortunately and inexplicably slow progress to go with Strongstead. When all were complete, the Ardenians expected to seal off Uris Udar completely.

After the delivery, *Adelaide* then transported a delegation from the Strongstead garrison to the port at Adams Island, on the north end of Watkins Gulf just off the mainland and south of Dunnan's Claim. From there, Patrick's crew escorted the coal ship *Charles Town*, carrying coal from the Adams Island mines, back to the *Adelaide's* homestead at Dunnansport.

It would be good to be home. Patrick had begun courting a lovely girl in Dunnansport and couldn't wait to see her. Alice Wade, the daughter of a cotton merchant of sizable fortune from Belgarden, was a widow, but she was only Patrick's age. She had a three-year-old son, Joseph, from her marriage to a barrister who died in a carriage accident two years earlier, and while Alice was outwardly standoffish and silent, she secretly possessed a razor-sharp intellect and a wicked, delightful sense of humor which unfurled in the presence of her close associates.

It took some time for Patrick to get to know Alice. Once he had, nonetheless, he'd fallen, and hard. And little Joseph, having lost his father, was someone Patrick felt an obligation to take under his wing. He knew Alice felt similarly about Patrick; she'd been dropping hints about a long-term future for the past four months. Patrick's frequent and lengthy deployments had hampered the growth of the relationship, though, and he worried he'd lose his best chance at building the family he'd never really had.

At some point, he thought, he would want to actually make a home in Dunnansport. Patrick had opted to save his salary rather than to buy property in the new city and was thus inhabiting a pair of rooms at a boarding house near the wharf. Alice chided him relentlessly over that choice, opining that it had been "wrong in every particular."

"You're a naval commander," she said, "and you're not even a full citizen with voting rights because you don't own property. That's a scandal. You've got a dispensation as an officer worth twenty thousand decirans against a real estate purchase, which could buy you that entire boarding house you're living in or easily be enough for a down payment on a mansion in Tweade Landing. And how can you keep the station of a ship's captain without a land-cabin?"

The deciran was the Ardenian unit of currency, so named for its value established as 1/10th that of an ounce of gold.

"I have you for that," he responded. "You're my connection to society on land."

"But you don't have me," she noted. "We aren't married. And even if we were, I'm not moving into some boarding-house."

"Of course not," Patrick said. "We would live at your place."

"Oh, no!" Alice let him have it. "You don't get off so easily. My house is enough for me and little Joseph," she lectured, "but moving in some naval commander and all his globes and maps and trophies from the deep blue will fill it from the floors to the ceilings. And there would be more children besides; if you think I'm going to keep an overcrowded sty like that you have another thing coming!"

He loved her with every ounce of his being, and he knew she was right. But Alice's harangues about his commercial profile made him queasy. Patrick had no experience as a land speculator or householder; he'd never owned much of anything in his entire life, and he'd barely even given it thought. He had a safety deposit box at the Maritime Bank in Port Excelsior containing a cotton bag with 46 sizable diamonds from the Taravel beaches in it, and he had an inkling that bag would make him a fairly rich man were he to convert the stones to currency.

It was his plan to have one of the diamonds cut and set in an engagement ring for Alice when *Adelaide* next docked at Port Excelsior, but he'd kept his mouth shut about that knowing her fondness for surprises and her weakness for impatience. That was a weakness his status as a ship commander, with the frequent and lengthy absences that entailed, did enough to inflame as it was. It was better Alice didn't know what he had planned.

Patrick did think it was time to meet her halfway. If he wasn't ready to buy a house just yet, perhaps while he was in port this time it would be a good idea to sink his dispensation into some property in Dunnansport as an investment. Patrick had made friends with one of the young city's most prominent businessmen David Stuart, whose company stored and brokered commodities of every kind in a complex of warehouses near the wharves, and he decided he'd seek David's advice on buying a strategic piece of property in town that could be rented out or developed into a moneymaking investment. He had his eye on some land on the western edge of town between the train station under construction and the riverbank, because at some point that land might be a good place to store items to be transferred between steamship and locomotive as Dunnansport took its place as a trading center.

At least if he did that, he'd go on the rolls as a voter, which would make Alice happy. Patrick cared not a whit for politics. As far as he was concerned, the Peace Party which had dominated the government in Principia for a decade, had been quite sparing with military expenditures in service to its preference for land giveaways and farm subsidies – sometimes breathtakingly corrupt land giveaways and farm subsidies, from what Patrick could tell – in the country's west and south, wasn't losing power anytime soom. Patrick thought the Peace Party was a collection of fancy boys from the metropolitan north and east, none of whom had ever met an Udar up close or had the faintest understanding of what dangers Ardenia invited by not keeping a proper vigil against that enemy.

Rather than affiliate himself, though, with either the Territorialists or the Prosperitans, two squabbling minor parties which had split from what had been the majority party following Dunnan's War, Patrick had just opted out altogether. Buying property he'd barely see while out defending the sea lanes just so he could choose from among politicians who couldn't or wouldn't do the right things seemed to him a sucker's play and a waste of his resources and attention.

But Alice, who was a proud Peace Party member and in consideration for a spot on the Dunnansport Council of Delegates in the elections the next autumn, was quite political. Patrick wanted to placate her – not to mention he figured if she thought he'd taken enough of an interest to become a full citizen she might actually listen to him when he told her how daffy her party's platform was when it came to national security and the Udar.

Lots to do in port this time, he thought as the ship turned into the mouth of the Tweade and passed the 50-foot bronze statue of Henry Dunnan overlooking the new city from the south side of the river.

Adelaide pulled into the wharf, and as the commander of the ship Patrick was the lead officer down the gangplank by custom. Just as his foot touched dry land, however, he was accosted by a young Marine corporal who hurriedly saluted as he ran to the front of the receiving line.

"Beggin' yer pardon, Commander, but there's a message over the teletext from Barley Point."

The marine handed over a slip of paper. It read…

ALARM TO ALL FORCES ALONG THE TWEADE…UDAR WAR PARTIES ATTACKING FARMS FROM BATTLEFORD EAST TO BARLEY POINT…POSSIBLE ACTION AT FARMS SOUTH OF DUNNANSPORT…MUSTER ALL AVAILABLE FORCES FOR COUNTERATTACK

"Has Port William given a directive?" Patrick asked.

"I don't know, sir," said the Marine, "but the Commodore needs you straight away."

"All right, then. Lead on."

Patrick then turned to his First Mate, Lt. Commander Jack Rawer, an older officer who had served in Dunnan's War before Patrick was born. "I hate to say it, Jack," he said, "but I don't think we'll be doing shore leave this time."

"Agreed, sir," said Rawer, having read the teletext message. "I'll get us back ship-shape and await your orders."

Patrick then followed the young Marine, who scampered toward the Naval Munitions building just off the wharf where the Commodore awaited.

...

SIX

Belgarden – Afternoon (First Day)

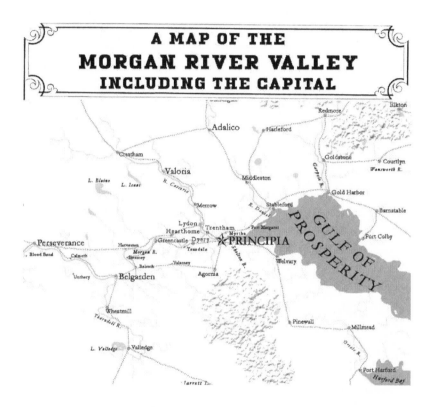

A MAP OF THE
MORGAN RIVER VALLEY
INCLUDING THE CAPITAL

Sebastian Cross was a national hero in Ardenia and perhaps the most famous man in the world, but at present that meant very little to the prematurely-graying aviator and corporate executive.

Cross had the distinction of being the first man to circumnavigate the planet via the skies. He'd achieved that feat by piloting a hot-air balloon from Gold Harbor across the Great Sea to the Lerian port of Arouz, then over the Siverne Sea to the great city-state of Revarcha, then east over the active volcanoes of the Thengreve Archipelago, then drifting past the vast fields of Cavol. It would have been unwise to set down inside that large nation's borders and risk an unfriendly reception from the Mottled Men, so Cross's expedition continued without stopping for the long journey over the Sunset Sea and back to Ardenia, landing at the northwest port of Brenwick. That occasioned a hero's reception which repeated itself at Stelhurst, Crestham and Middleston before the winds deposited him, amazingly, on the rail line just forty miles north of his point of embarkation. The entire journey took him and his partner 35 days and was considered a miracle of technological advancement which set the whole world afire with possibilities.

That journey was eight years ago, when Cross was 30 and his partner, Winford Gresham, was 28. In truth, Gresham was the real innovator of the two. It was Gresham who'd designed the balloon and its revolutionary propulsion/navigation system, which relied on aluminum rocket cylinders packed with sugar and saltpeter. Gresham lacked the persona to carry off the public end of the mission, though; that was Cross' specialty, seeing as though he'd been the captain of the Principia Elks rugby team and had the rugged good looks and easy charisma expected from the scion of a large Morgan Valley estate. Cross' family sat upon 10,000 acres of prime wheatland west of Principia, and as one of the richest clans in all of Ardenia they were able to dabble in whatever commercial and technological fads struck their fancy.

So when Cross took a shoulder to his knee as he scored the winning try to give the Elks victory over the Belgarden Cannoneers for the Landon Cup, he knew it was time to move on to bigger and better things. The knee ultimately healed, though Cross certainly wasn't the runner he'd been. Before he knew it he'd made the acquaintance of Gresham through the latter's cousin Bernadette, a stunning beauty who'd been on the dance line at the famous Helverose theater in Principia's swanky Elkstrand entertainment district.

As Cross was a regular and a chronic invitee backstage, Bernadette and he had struck up a friendship of sorts. While he never thought of her as wife material, owing to her tragically common upbringing – his family would *never* take to her because of that, not to mention her inelegant manners and Ackerton District East Principia brogue – Cross had been desperate to avail himself of her feminine charms.

Bernadette had something else in mind, however, and after one particularly ribald post-party following a performance at the Helverose, she had dragged Cross to a nearby after-hours joint where he'd met her cousin Winford. While Cross' attention was initially much more intently focused on the area between Bernadette's legs, as he made polite conversation with the young scientist that focus began to change toward what was between Winford's ears.

Because Gresham, at the time just 24 years old and a self-taught clerk in the Principia custom exchange with little formal education, was explaining to Cross the ins and outs of how air travel could be perfected and turned into a major international industry worth billions of decirans.

Cross was infatuated with the idea of striking out into financial superstardom, seeing as though his athletic career was rapidly winding down and the last thing he wanted for himself was the languor of life as a Morgan River Valley heir, drinking whisky naturals on verandas while the hired hands worked the land and getting statements of stock dividends via post on the twelfth of each month. He craved far more excitement than that future before him, and as his conversations with Gresham continued, he saw his destiny in the skies.

Cross therefore invested a large chunk of his personal fortune, prevailing on his father to liquidate the trust in his name and having his solicitor deliver a bank draft for two million decirans for the purpose, into Gresham's idea for a hot air balloon that would traverse the planet. Cross's conditions for the investment were that he would be a majority owner, that the endeavor would publicly be his show, that he would do the interviews for the broadsheets, and that he would bear the title of Chief Executive Officer for the project.

Gresham, six inches shorter, dirt broke and cursed with a nose resembling that of a cistern rat, was in no position to demand any public face in an around-the-world balloon ride. He agreed, and the two set up a company to conquer the skies.

The prototype began with the cabin, which was made of a pinewood-plank floor surrounded by a cage of aluminum. Gresham built the walls and ceiling of the cabin with a thick, resin-coated canvas, and for the envelope he contracted with a silk loom in the southern city of Shadegarden for an alum resin-coated taffeta fabric which would hold the air with a minimum of leakage.

The burner, critical to the success of any long-distance air journey, used cannisters of coal dust tinged with white phosphorous – not the safest fuel mixture, but durable enough to heat and lift the envelope over a long duration. Gresham also used the invention of sugar-based steering rockets to keep the balloon on course; those had to be used sparingly, but they were quite effective in short bursts.

It was a phenomenally expensive prototype, burning through three-quarters of Cross' investment. He suspected Gresham was raking off the top of the assembly contracts as it was being built, but didn't ask many questions so long as progress continued.

After nine months of design and assembly, peppered with a few doses of instructive trial and error, the Airbound Corporation's balloon was ready for its initial flight. Cross and Gresham took off from Grand Park on the north side of the Morgan, just across the river from the capitol district in Principia, and flew 45 miles north to Merrow along the Castoria River, landing on the rugby field in the middle of that city's posh Greathaven district. It was a grand public success, and the duo became stars in all the broadsheets for weeks thereafter. The publicity, and the fees earned in flying the prototype from town to town, earned Cross' investment back in the course of only a year.

Shortly after that came the trip around the world, which made them superstars.

Along the way, the vision for this enterprise of theirs became further refined. Gresham had drawn up plans to combine the design of the prototype with the screw propellers that had begun predominating in the shipping industry and figured that the propellers would be a more efficient instrument for steering an airship than rockets, which burned through their fuel too quickly for long-distance navigation. To support a larger cabin, necessary for the transport of passengers, more than one inflated envelope would be needed.

Accordingly, within two years he'd finished plans for a true airship. As Gresham presented it to Cross, this would involve a wood cabin sitting under a fuel source comprised of a different mix of coal, phosphorous and wood chips in four bins underneath balloon envelopes similar to the one from the initial prototype, and that inflated core was encased in an aluminum structure wrapped in a canvas outer shell.

After securing an investment of ten million decirans from four Principia businessmen, Cross and Gresham built three airships – the *Clyde*, the *Ann Marie* and the *Justice*. The plan was to establish regular flights from Principia to Ardenia's next three largest cities, and then grow the company's flight lines as demand and additional airships warranted.

There was a regular line to Port Excelsior, a commuter line to Belgarden and a luxury line to the sparkling city of Alvedorne along the Great Mountain Lake. Each airship was capable of travel at unheard-of speeds: the *Clyde* had been clocked at 48 miles per hour, as fast as the fastest locomotive in service, but functionally faster, since its trips contained no stops.

The small cabins of the three airships filled with customers willing to pay through the nose to complete a trip in 15-18 hours or less, when otherwise it could take as long as three days on a locomotive to access Airbound's destinations. Cross' corporation looked for all the world like the next great disruptive enterprise on the economic scene and the possibilities were endless. Plans and orders for additional airships to open service to more destinations were on the drawing board. Eventually, as the public embraced air travel as safe, Cross expected he'd have a network connecting every city of size via the skies, using the four cities he was already servicing as hubs, and slowly, *too* slowly, he thought, it was coming.

All that had been true until three months ago, when the *Justice* exploded as it took off from the newly-built Pelgreen Aerodrome on Principia's South End. Thirty-four passengers bound for Alvedorne were killed in the blaze, and the *Justice* collapsed and fell into a middle-class residential neighborhood, lighting some four dozen houses afire and destroying millions of decirans in property to go with a grand total of sixty-four deaths. To date no explanation had been found for what caused the explosion. Gresham had insisted it couldn't have been a design flaw, while Cross had lost much confidence in his partner's engineering prowess.

At a prohibitive cost, Cross had the three airships and their flights insured by the Yellowvine Indemnity Company in Principia. Unfortunately, that seemingly-rock solid firm had its foundations tested in paying damages to the victims of the crash, and Yellowvine's liquidity was found wanting. Worse, as the risk associated with such a new venture as air travel couldn't be adequately calculated, the company had been unable to purchase reinsurance to back its coverage of Cross's airships. That meant when the *Justice* crashed a rolling financial disaster followed. Yellowvine had declared bankruptcy as the claims rolled in, leaving Airbound exposed to suit from the victims with no financial protection.

He was going broke, and fast. And after the *Justice's* explosion the passenger bookings dried up on the *Clyde's* Port Excelsior line and even the *Ann Marie's* commuter shuttle from Principia to Belgarden. They were hemorrhaging money with a lot more exposure to come in the way of those pending legal claims, and Cross saw little future.

He attempted to stanch the bleeding by taking the *Clyde* on a cross-country public relations tour, charging small amounts to put them on display as exhibits in towns where an airship was a never-before-seen exotic curiosity. They were a particular success in the bustling little hayseed town of Dunnansport at the mouth of the Tweade, for example. Cross knew, nevertheless, that charming the rubes out of a copper or two was anything but a sustainable business plan for what was supposed to be a high-end passenger airline. If he couldn't put his airships to use as a means of carrying loads of swells from metropolis to metropolis, there had to be some better way to survive than becoming a traveling carnival.

In the meantime Cross was forced to cut costs whenever he could, and today that involved piloting the *Ann Marie* back from Belgarden himself, having laid off the line's regular airship pilot along with halving the frequency of the commuter service. He had a rare full cabin today, the product of a special call to Parliament at the Societam due to some national security development in the south. Belgarden's delegation knew that the *Ann Marie* could make the trip to Principia a lot faster than could a locomotive or steamship.

Maybe we'll turn a profit today, he thought. *Maybe if enough todays stack up we can get out of this mess.*

Cross knew that was a foolish, desperate fantasy. Soon he would have to go to his father and make the dreaded request for a bailout from the family to either save the company or wrap up its affairs and consign himself to the status of failed scion of a dynastic Morgan River Valley house. It was the last thing he wanted to do; as the third son of Preston Cross VII, Sebastian had always been treated as little more than a playboy. Asking for help this time would be a surrender beyond what he could bear.

"Please, everyone, take your seats," he said with false cheer as he made his way through the *Ann Marie's* posh cabin, greeting the even more posh passengers: the men in their silk peacoats, embroidered vests and leather knee-high riding boots, as was the style among the Ardenian upper class, and the women in fur stoles over lace-encrusted shirtwaist blouses and flowing ankle-length skirts, their ears, necks and wrists dripping with sparkling adornments, along the way to the cockpit. "We'll be departing for Principia in short order."

"Cross," barked a voice from the front row. He recognized the gruff little white-haired man as Delegate Horace Harms, Peace Party, for 25 years the member of Parliament

71

from Belgarden's working-class northeast district and currently the chairman of the powerful Defense Committee.

"Why aren't you taking this gasbag down to Dunnan's Claim?" Harms demanded, waving his oaken walking stick at Sebastian to punctuate his utterances.

"I don't know what you mean, sir," he replied. "We did take the *Clyde* to Dunnansport on an exhibition last month. Are you suggesting we do that again?"

"No, dammit," Harms fumed. "Don't you know? It just come over the teletext. We're at war again. The savages have plundered Dunnan's Claim, and we're to Parliament to attend a levy for the largest military force ever sent south. You ought to mobilize what's left of your airship line for the effort."

Now that isn't a bad idea at all, thought Cross, who quickly recognized that a military contract or two might just be a lifeline for Airbound's failing fortunes. When he got to the capital he and Gresham would have to have a talk, and then he and his family's solicitor Madison Gregg, who handled parliamentary matters at the capitol for the Cross clan, including Airbound, would have to have a similar one.

"May we have a conversation on that very subject when we arrive, sir?" Cross answered.

"I am ever at the service of one of Ardenia's great entrepreneurs and celebrities," Harms gushed in false obsequiousness. "Get your people in touch with my people."

. . .

SEVEN

Port William – Afternoon (First Day)

Robert Stuart was just seventeen and in his first year away from Hilltop Farm, the place of his birth and his childhood home. He had only matriculated at the Defense Academy at Aldingham in the fourth month that year; the six months away were, to put it mildly, difficult for him.

He missed his mother. He wasn't ashamed to say it. He wasn't the only one. His longings were perhaps a little worse than those of his peers among the first-year cadets, but it wasn't something to be teased and bullied over.

Sadly, though, to bear the brunt of teasing and bullying was Robert's experience. He wasn't the smallest of the cadets at the academy, but he wasn't quite average – at 5'9" and a little less than 11 stone, Robert was too small for rugby and was a low juniorweight boxer. And the bigger boys saw him as a figure of fun. Rob the Knob, they called him, due to his emotional state and the limitations of his size in making their torments end. He'd spent too much time locked in closets and steamer trunks, and he'd endured too many cruel pranks and been subjected to too much humiliation to have made his transition to living away from home a good one.

Things got so bad that after the first three months, Robert wrote a letter to his father asking to be relieved of tutelage at the academy. He'd suggested something else as part of his future, something he thought was a perfectly well-constructed compromise. Rather, Robert requested in the letter, than pursue military service through the early part of his adulthood before going into commerce, as his father and uncle had done, couldn't he simply start his real career? He would take an apprenticeship in Dunnansport with his Uncle David's commodities storage and brokerage business, he would learn its ropes and he would then help build the family's commercial fortune from there. He promised to make his father proud as a businessman, and he suggested everyone knew his talents would best be served in that line of endeavor.

The response did not come by post. It came in person.

Two weeks after Robert sent the letter, his father appeared at the academy. Having so august a presence as Col. George Stuart, hero of Sutton Hill and Rogers Rock, on campus set off quite a buzz, so much so that morning classes were canceled and the cadets were summoned to the auditorium, where a hastily-arranged lecture starring Robert's father had taken place. Rob found himself seated prominently in the front row for what turned out to be quite a spectacle; his father regaled the assemblage with true stories of horror and heroism in Dunnan's War a generation before, describing in detail the fearsome and diabolical enemy they'd faced, his crude but deadly weapons and the never-ending threat of aggression by the Udar hordes.

And then George Stuart had a message to the crowd which, it was quite obvious, was intended for one particular cadet.

"You are here," he reminded them, "because you are the toughest, bravest, slickest little bastards we have." The cadets laughed.

"I'm serious. You're our best," George pressed. "And while the vast majority of you are destined to be captains of industry and commerce, or great intellectuals, healers, inventors or statesmen, all of which don't require a military background, what we are asking of you is five to ten years of service to your country to keep those demons to our south at bay.

"You are here because the motherland needs you to put your talents toward protecting your sisters and mothers, brothers and nephews. And even washed-up old horse soldiers like me."

That earned a chorus of guffaws and a loud standing ovation, and George gave a short bow before exiting the lectern.

Robert then saw him in the mess hall, as the academy had scrambled together a luncheon reception.

George handed him his letter of two weeks before and gave him a tight, loving embrace. He then stood off, gently put his hands on each side of Robert's head just below the ears, looked him square in the eyes, and said, "We'll have no more discussion of what's in that letter. You will satisfy your obligation to this country which has given you so much, and then you will make of yourself a grander success in business than either I or your uncle could ever dream. Do you understand?"

"Yes, father," Robert said, and meant it.

George then clutched his son tightly. As he departed, he ran into Robert's old friend and Dunnan's Claim neighbor Will Forling, whom Robert hadn't had much interaction with at the academy to date. Robert saw his father and Forling having a short conversation, and then off the old man went, bound for Hilltop Farm and home.

Things did get slightly better from there. Some of Robert's tormentors approached him with gestures of respect. "Didn't know you were one of *those* Stuarts, Knob," said one. "Maybe there's hope for you yet." And while he'd struggled to make any close friends with his own classmates, following his father's visit he'd renewed acquaintances and become much closer again with Will – who had made a sincere effort to take Robert under his wing over the last few weeks.

It was a difficult first year, but Robert was hopeful and determined to finish it better than it began.

And while he'd been miserable, at least to date he wasn't a miserable failure.

His academic marks were average, but passing. For soldiery, he was better. As a farm boy and a hunter, Robert was an expert horseman and a crack shot with both pistol and rifle. Physical combat was not quite his strength; he could somewhat hold his own with a sword, but in bare-hand combat and dagger-fighting, he flopped. Robert's best marks came in military tactics, which was a gift from his father. George had educated him thoroughly in the history of Dunnan's War and kept a board of war-chess constantly open in the study at Hilltop Farm. Before leaving for the academy Robert had even beaten the old man once or twice. When he had the chance to play among the students at Aldingham, he was a terror at the game.

And now Rob was looking forward to putting those refined strategic skills in another classic matchup in the study with George in a day or so as the locomotive carrying him from Aldingham click-clacked its way to Port William, the last stop before the Dunnansport station where, after an overnight stay at his uncle David and aunt Rebecca's house, they would board a riverboat for Barley Point and then home. They'd be there soon.

"What are you reading, Will?" Robert asked his travel mate.

"*The Last Days of Abraham Wise*," was the answer. "I'm getting a start on the history course for the next session, but this is a hell of a read. I'll be done by the time we get to Dunnansport and I'll let you borrow it if you want."

"I've heard of Wise," Robert said. "Father had me read about him. He was the first of our people to locate the source of the Morgan River."

"He was. 200 years ago. Mapped the whole thing. His whole party got wiped out in a raptor attack in the Venseline Hills, but he managed to survive and he made it back to civilization with his maps and notes before he died."

"Glad that horror is in the past," said Robert, meaning the deadly avian monsters.

"No kidding. You ever see one of those things?"

"I have. We did a family trip to Trenory when I was 10 and went to the Museum of the Wild. They had a stuffed one and a skeleton of another. Scared the hell out of me."

"Little man, everything scares the hell out of you," said Will, jokingly. "But you're right. My grandfather back in Lake

Valledge has a stuffed one in his library. Raptors are no joke. I don't want to see a live one."

"Speaking of nasty, predatory birds, are you going to make another run at my sister at the ball this weekend?"

"That's what you're going to ask me?" said Will. "After everything I've done for you?"

Though he suspected it had taken a plea from his father to reinvigorate the friendship, Robert and Will had been close friends since both were small, though "small" had never been an apt description of Will. At 6'4" and sixteen stone he was a mountain of a young man, and at twenty, with two and a half years of training at the academy, he'd matured into the very model of a budding cavalry officer. Will had won the academy's seniorweight boxing title in his second year (and had won a not-small amount of coin as a prizefighter in the saloons of Aldingham in his off-hours), he was the captain of the rugby team and the best swimmer in his class, and he held the highest rank – First Lieutenant – of all the third-year students.

To Robert, he was still the gangly, stuttering oaf he'd chased puppies with back in Dunnan's Claim, but he couldn't hide his envy of Will's amazing transformation at school – and his frustration at not making similar progress. Needling Will over his unrequited love for Sarah was Robert's best revenge, and he used it often.

Besides, Robert had always thought his sister's behavior toward Will was dreadful. He wanted Will as a brother-in-law, after all. Keeping those fires lit was a good tactic, and Robert knew tactics. He'd convinced Will to restart his regular letters to Sarah and had even contributed a few ideas for him to include in order to win her attention. The inner workings of the female mind weren't precisely a specialty of Robert's, though he did claim to hold a certain popularity with the girls at the Barley Point Society Hall during his younger years prior to matriculating at the Defense Academy.

Rob knew Will was less accomplished in the consortial arts, which made sense. After all, Will had six brothers, each of whom was at least ten years older than he was and most of whom had been gone to seek their fortunes by the time he was old enough to pay attention to girls. His mother had been the only female resident of Grayvern Farm, and Lillian Forling was a stern, unapproachable woman whose constant admonition to her youngest son was that he must make something of himself before considering a dalliance with other people's female children.

To this, Will's father, who was a crusty, declining man past seventy years old, heartily agreed. Though Old John, as the neighbors all called him, had quietly, earnestly suggested to Will that Sarah Stuart was his best bet at marital bliss, as well as the fortune he wouldn't otherwise have. Grayvern Farm, after all, was mortgaged to the hilt and Will's inheritance was only one-seventh of it when his parents were gone. The lack of society among people his age growing up led Will to spend much of his childhood as a tag-along at Hilltop Farm with the Stuarts, and it was Rob and Sarah he spent most of his time around. Being the oldest, Matthew's time was mostly occupied with George, rather than the other children, as he learned the ropes as the eventual landholder of the Stuart Estate.

Therefore, Robert's affinity for Will was mutual. The older cadet had in the last few weeks become Robert's principal defender from the bullies and smart-alecks at the academy, and had beaten some decency into more than a few of them. That included a brisk throttling he'd given just last week to Alexander Keane, a particularly nasty heavyset second-year ogre who insisted on trapping Robert on his stomach and then sitting on his head while flatulating vigorously.

Sadly, boys of that age are difficult to control, and it bothered Willy greatly that as a third-year student Will wasn't able to serve as Robert's bodyguard at all times. While he had hoped the adversity would toughen Rob up a bit, Will was starting to believe he'd need to step in personally and mentor his friend in the art of self-defense. Will had a story to tell in that regard, He also had some highly productive suggestions he thought would pay dividends to the younger boy.

"At some point we're going to have that talk I mentioned, Rob," he told his friend. "You're not a little kid anymore. And I can't keep beating the shit out of every hellion who whips up on you."

"I know, Will. Maybe I'm just not cut out for all this."

"Pigshit. Pigshit. You're George Stuart's son. Hell, you're Matthew Stuart's brother. Everybody at that school knows exactly who you are and that's why they give you so much trouble. They know the standard your family sets."

"What if I can't meet it?"

"Wrong attitude, little man. You meet it by being you. Or maybe a little tougher version of you. Hell, you're taller than your brother, and he's a bad sonofabitch. I understand he's a captain at the garrison in Strongstead now. Not even 22 years old."

"He is. Made rank last month. Not sure how he did that; all they do over there is tan at the beach, drink brown ale, and play war-chess."

"Well, you're about to pull into the second half of your plebe year. You might *want* to be a mama's boy, but that's all past you now. You know what I'm saying's true."

"Yeah, I know. I don't want to think about it right now, though, all right? We're goin' home for the harvest and a month's vacation. Can I just do that for a while?"

"Suit yourself," Will shrugged as he returned to his book. The locomotive slowed as it approached the Port William station. In three hours they'd arrive in Dunnansport, where Robert would be spending the night at the palatial Stuart house. Will had been invited as the family's guest, and he'd enthusiastically accepted.

. . .

EIGHT

The Camp – Evening (First Day)

Made to kneel in an uncomfortable spread-kneed position in the patchy grass of the Udar camp, Sarah had little to do but watch as riders came in ones, twos and threes to deposit additional captives throughout the warm early-autumn afternoon. It seemed business was lively for the raiders, and the Udars had a fairly intricate system for gathering Ardenian prisoners. Each were slung across their captor's horse behind the saddle, exactly as Sarah had been. Tied down so well, the gagged captives were safely, if uncomfortably, secured to be transported at a high speed – and that's precisely how they were delivered by the Udar.

Upon arrival, they would be untied at the legs, though their arms would still be tied down, painfully folded behind their backs, and put in the lines of ten. Each one had arrived stripped of her clothes, wearing only her shift. Most did have shoes, unlike Sarah.

I guess it was a mistake to wear clogs today, she thought, then instantly defended that choice to herself with the admonition that neglecting to prepare for abduction by the Udar when she'd gotten dressed was no evidence of carelessness.

At times, the captives would be injured when brought in. As they'd done briefly with Sarah, the Udar women in charge of the prisoners would drag the new arrivals into a tent to offer them medical attention of a very rudimentary fashion.

As for the captives sitting in their lines, every so often the captors would pass through with leather canteens of water, and one by one they would remove the gags from each prisoner's mouth and allow her a sip of hydration. Other captors would come through with canteens of something else, a rather viscous dark liquid which tasted of blackberries and produced a calming, out-of-body effect on Sarah. There were no bathroom breaks for the captives, something that should have been the source of no meager inconvenience and emotional trauma, but Sarah noticed she hadn't had to go all day, and it didn't appear that any of the other women in her line of fellow captives had to, either. She thought that a bit odd. In any event, as the holding area was in the center of the camp, there wasn't really anywhere any of them could escape to. So mostly, the captives were left alone.

Near sundown, the deliveries of female captives petered out. By then Sarah had counted – she'd had lots of time for counting – 38 lines of ten prisoners each in the holding space in the middle of the camp.

380 of us, she thought. *I've never heard of so many in one raid.*

There was no particular pattern to the identity of the Ardenian captives. Many were girls in their teens like Sarah, a few were younger, perhaps half or more were adults. She didn't see any old women, though. Perhaps that was because Dunnan's Claim was a new area largely settled by younger families...

...Or perhaps they don't want the old women, she thought, fearing what might have happened to Will Forling's mother who was nearly sixty years old.

Assisted by that blackberry drink they kept giving her, she surmised, Sarah was beginning to calm down from the trauma of her capture and seeing the loss of her family. She knew – could feel – that her father, mother and sister were now in the embrace of the Lord of All, and His peace was emanating through them. She remembered her lessons from the Supernal Word, particularly those regarding unjust suffering. The most blessed path was to resist, she knew, but if that were not possible the next blessed path was to bear all with dignity.

She could hear her mother's calming voice. *You have resisted*, it said. *Now you must bear.*

Not that she'd accepted any of this. Sarah was devastated and still just wanted to lay down and die after what she'd seen that morning.

Worse, her mind was still tortured with the uncertainty over what had happened to Hannah and Ethan. Had they survived in the cellar? Had they been taken? Killed? Sarah knew that leaving them in the hiding space was the only thing she could have done, but that was no comfort given the result at Hilltop Farm. She could only pray they'd made it out alive and unhurt, and that someone would find them and take them to her aunt and uncle in Dunnansport where they'd be safe.

As dusk settled, the Udar warriors began to arrive at the camp in full. Sarah noted it was considerably more than just female captives they'd been after.

It appeared as though the enemy had sent an entire *Anur*, a mobile warrior village, to Dunnan's Claim, and as the warriors made their way into the camp, they led a great mass of trophies. Hundreds of horses, as many cattle, dozens of wagons full of valuables scrounged from the farms they'd plundered. Sarah estimated there were a bit more than 250 men leading the train of booty back to the camp, and several of them looked wounded, some seriously. They'd clearly taken some casualties from the farmers they'd attacked.

Good, Sarah thought. *I hope they paid as dearly at the other farms as they did at ours.*

She noticed that none of the riders appeared to be female. This didn't surprise her, as it corresponded with what she knew about the Udar from books she'd read and stories her father had only recently begun to tell her. George had said she'd been too young to be given details before, but earlier this year after a large social event at Hilltop Farm when all of the neighbors had come and the men had gathered to themselves for a discussion of some serious nature Sarah wasn't privy to, he'd begun telling her of the Udar.

One of the things her father had imparted to Sarah was that in the *Anur*, which was the basic unit of Udar society and the closest thing to an Ardenian family, the men were the warriors and the women were, more or less, everything else. That made a certain sort of dysfunctional sense, in that the Udar were a society of hunter-gatherers whose economy consisted in large measure of killing people and stealing their things when they weren't out slaughtering bears and great mountain goats in the jagged badlands of Uris Udar. Something else her father had told her was that unlike in every other society on the planet, the Udar didn't take husbands and wives. An Udar man would couple with a different woman of the *Anur* every night as he pleased, and the *Anur* would collectively raise the children issuing from those nocturnal encounters in the tents.

But Sarah hadn't noticed any Udar children in the camp, and she also hadn't noticed any pregnancies among the women captors. Did this *Anur* leave the pregnant women behind with the children when they set off on their current adventure? She didn't know enough about them to hazard much of a guess.

And truth be told, she wasn't in much shape for objective analysis. Having spent most of the day in a haze as she kneeled in the holding area of the camp in a line with nine other women with whom she wasn't allowed to communicate, still reeling from what she thought might be a slight concussion from when she'd been tackled and captured, and in decreasing agony due to the unnatural position her arms had been tied in a painful folded wrist-to-elbow position behind her, Sarah was increasingly straining to keep her wits. The effects of that berry liquor her captors were supplying her were making things infinitely more difficult.

As she looked around her fellow captives she knew she wasn't alone. The fear, mortification and sadness on their faces appeared to equal that of hers; some already had the gray pall of those who'd given up hope – unless that was the effect of the dark liquid the captors were passing around.

We've all been through hell, she thought, *and it's just beginning.*

At the head of the incoming procession was the hulking man who'd captured Sarah that morning, the one she had shot after he'd slashed her sister's throat. His bandaged thigh still appeared to be bleeding, but descending from his horse he looked none the worse for wear.

"Rapan'na!" cried the Udar women of the camp as he approached.

The man gave the reins of his mount to one of the women, then made for the large tent nearest the middle of the camp. A woman, naked other than a pair of ankle-tied sandals and a roll of beaded necklaces around her neck, exited the tent and kneeled at his feet.

"Rapan'na," she said softly, and bent down to kiss his boot.

Sarah noticed this was not a typical Udar female. Udar men shared a similar physical appearance: they were almost universally thickly-built, with jet-black hair, long beards tied into a point below their chins and rough features. Many of the Udar women, though, were more varied in skin tone and hair color. But this woman had what looked like it had been blonde, almost white, hair and her complexion was far fairer than anyone else's.

Sarah also noticed that unlike the other women in the camp, whose faces were covered with tattoos containing lines, dots and shapes from forehead to chin, this one had no markings. She was very clearly an Ardenian.

I really hope that's not the life these people have in store for me, she thought to herself as her heart sank with dread, *but it's a very good guess that's exactly what's coming.*

The man placed his hand atop her stubbly head. He took her hand and led her into the tent. And then two women came and dragged Sarah in that direction.

. . .

NINE

Barley Point – Evening (First Day)

Latham had managed to extricate himself from Irving's grasp for a short time by promising he'd return to the customs house and join the captain and his contingent for their sally south. That gave him an opportunity to return to the inn for a few items – his personal sidearm, a more practical pair of boots, his Thurman rifle, a map of the Dunnan's Claim territory he'd obtained from Col. Terhune at the army barracks the day before, a pair of field glasses, and a leather hunting jacket – that he figured would suit him better than whatever kit the marines might have for him. It was sadly an article of universal understanding that the weapons and equipment the government was currently issuing to its defense forces were of secondary quality at best.

Latham had another errand to run. After emptying his carrying case of architectural plans and leaving those in the innkeeper's safe, he filled the case with the papers they'd rescued from the Stuart manor that morning. As he did so he noticed several of the items among those documents and quickly understood why they had to be saved. Included were not just the deed to Hilltop Farm, but also stock certificates in large denominations for several of Ardenia's most blue-chip concerns. Also, he noticed, certificates indicating major holdings in banks in Trenory, Dunnansport, Barley Point and Port William, title deed to tracts of land in Barley Point and Dunnansport, and several other items of compelling value. The Stuart children who survived that morning's ordeal had certainly lost much, but they hadn't lost their wealth.

On his way back to the customs house Latham stopped at Mistress Irving's house located down the main drag from the inn, to check on Hannah and Ethan and make his delivery. Latham rang the bell at the front door.

85

"May I help you?" asked the angular, effete older gentleman who answered it.

"Hello. I'm H.V. Latham. I'm here to see Mistress Irving and to check on young Hannah and Ethan Stuart who I understand are here. I'm the man who brought them back from Hilltop Farm."

"Yes, sir, right this way." said the man, waving Latham inside. "I am Firestone, the chamberlain of the house. Please call on me for anything you may need. You will find the lady of the house within. Follow me."

Firestone led Latham through the central hall of an elegant home, turning him to the right in the middle of the first floor into a very large, well-appointed study. "May I present Mr. H.V. Latham," he announced, and then departed.

"Mr. Latham," said Mistress Irving, seated on a sofa with three other ladies.

Latham hadn't really gotten a look at the mistress when she'd come to retrieve the children at the customs house. That, he thought, was an awful shame. Before him was one of the most exquisite specimens of human femininity he had ever beheld. He guessed her to be about 25, with perfect skin, luscious dark hair in well-appointed curls and a face from one of the Great Masterpieces at the Palace Museum – an angular chin, magnificently high cheekbones, a pert, dainty nose and a pair of shimmering green eyes he thought he'd get lost in.

"Mistress Irving, I presume," he half-stammered. "I'm sorry to barge in like this, but the circumstances seem to demand it. I've brought some papers the Stuart children will need for safekeeping."

"Of course," she said. "May I present my friends Miss Edith Carruthers, Miss Ann Penright and Mrs. Felicia Gwynn. They have heard of your misadventures across the river from Corporal Renford, who initially summoned me at your arrival. Such a terrible day."

"Indeed," said Ann.

"You must be in quite a state," Edith added. "To see such horrors!"

"Thank you, ma'am," Latham said. "But what I witnessed was property destruction, mostly. I fear what I didn't see was far worse."

"Surely we are safe on this side of the river," Felicia said. "The savages wouldn't dare attack a town with a military cantonment such as this one."

"I hope that's true," said Latham. "But I would prepare for the worst nonetheless. Have you all safe places to weather this storm?"

"Actually, we're all staying here," Mistress Irving said. "Felicia's husband is in Trenory on business. We don't know when he'll be back. Ann and Edith are houseguests from Port William."

"You all picked a fine time for a visit," said Latham. "I can sympathize. I'm from Port William myself."

"We know," said Ann, somewhat wickedly. "Your reputation precedes you."

Ouch, Latham thought as he grimaced. *I don't think she's just being familiar with that remark. What are the chances these two women are friends with the ex?*

He really didn't want to find out.

"Well, it was good to make your acquaintance, and I hope you all fare well amid the trouble," Latham blurted, as he politely made for the exit. "I'm bound for the customs house where Captain Irving has dragooned me into service to scout for the Marine Force."

"Let me walk you out," said Mistress Irving as she rose from her seat.

At the door, she stopped him.

87

ANIMUS

"I want you to know, my brother can be very reckless," she said. "He missed Dunnan's War – joined the Marines just as it ended. He's been a customs clerk with a thirst for glory ever since, and I fear he might be leading you all into some terrible danger."

So she's the sister, he thought. *That's some useful information if I can make it back from this adventure alive.*

"Well, I'll be careful, Mistress. I promise."

"Call me Helen."

"I will, Helen," he smiled. "Are you sure you'll be all right here? Can I get you anything before we depart?"

"I have everything I need," she said. "Don't do anything stupid out there. We'll take good care of the children. The poor darlings are upstairs asleep. I'll tell them you looked in on them and brought their documents."

"Thank you. Their uncle is David Stuart," he said, "in Dunnansport. You'd be doing me a huge favor if you could get a message to him that Ethan and Hannah are safe."

"I will do that," she said, "and I will also arrange to bring the children to him. You have done a great thing saving them – I shudder to think what would have happened to them if you hadn't come along."

"It was nothing," he said. "I wish I could have done more. Of course, I was alone and unarmed – had I shown up a little earlier at Hilltop Farm things might have been even worse."

"That's true," she said, wincing. "But I will do what I can to help, so you can focus on coming back from the battlefield in one piece."

You're a saint," Latham said, and meant it. "I hope to see you soon."

"I do as well," she said, with a peculiar gleam in her eye. "Be careful, especially with my brother in charge!"

88

Latham left, retrieved his horse and trotted back to the customs house whereupon he found himself amid something of a controversy. The army had mustered along with the Marines, and there had been some pushing and shoving over access to the town arsenal, located next door to the customs house, where there were far too few Thurman rifles for the men being mustered. What remained were the standard-issue Benchfords no serviceman wanted to be caught on the battlefield with; their propensity to jam and their lackluster muzzle velocity made them unreliable and ineffective weapons of war. Latham thought it was a scandal for such a rotten weapon to be the main rifle of his nation's military and suspected politics was the reason the Thurman, which was the best rifle on the market, was no longer the one the military used. He wasn't alone in that view; his old commander had been adamant in sharing it at dinner the previous night.

Latham worked his way through the unruly crowd and soon found Irving and Col. Terhune, his old cavalry commander, in something of a heated discussion.

"I wonder if I might help," he said.

"Latham. I heard you'd made it back, dear boy," said Terhune. "You'll be with our detachment as we head south."

"He will not," said Irving. "He's joining my contingent. That was already arranged."

Terhune shook his head. "You're not in command here and you have no contingent. I am the ranking officer in this military district, and I will arrange the composition of my battle force."

"You won't if you're going to raid my arsenal for weaponry, and you won't if you're going to use my ferry to move your troops," Irving said. "The Marines protect the river, and we'll do that by routing out the enemy and driving him back where he came – and with our weapons that we had to beg, borrow and steal to stock that arsenal with."

Terhune's eyes narrowed. "You have no authority here. Stand down or I'll have you court-martialed."

"You can't court-martial a marine officer, Terhune."

"Gentlemen, this isn't going to get us anywhere," Latham offered. "Has anything come over the teletext from Army headquarters in Trenory?"

Just then an Army sergeant came forward with a slip of paper. "Orders, sir."

Terhune read the message, then gave it to Irving. The latter read the sheet and shrank a little.

"With me, Latham," the colonel ordered. "Irving, take fifty men, you'll garrison the city. Watch the river, but don't neglect the east and west. They might cross upstream or down and attack from your flank or rear. Muster what militia you can to bolster your force. And put the town under martial law."

"Aye," said the captain, shrinking.

"The rest of your men are coming with me as a supplement to my force," Terhune said. "Give them supplies for three days' ride. Beyond that we'll either send for more, or we're either victorious or dead. And you have my permission to commandeer what weapons and men you can find to kit out your garrison, though I would *suggest* you ask for cooperation first."

"I'll do it, sir," Irving said.

Terhune nodded at him, then turned. "Latham, a word."

Terhune took the architect into a side room.

"You saw the lay of the land this morning. Can you lead us down there now? Am I misplacing faith in you by taking you with me?"

"I'm no combat hero," came the reply, "but I can still shoot, I know the area and I have some idea what's out there. If you want me, I'm ready."

"Fine. Welcome back to the army, Lieutenant. You're with me, in the lead element. We're for the ferry, now."

Terhune then hastily gave orders to the other members of his regimental staff as to the provision of the expeditionary force, which Latham noted contained a good deal of pre-arranged scrounging from the community.

No wonder he raised so much hell last night, Latham thought. *He's got a tiny force equipped with a bunch of old rifles, and he's borrowing equipment from all the dry goods and hardware stores in town that he ought to have ready at the base.*

How on earth was a frontier garrison in such a state of neglect in a rich country like Ardenia? Latham's recollection of his time as a soldier more than a decade ago, when Dunnan's Claim was still largely wilderness, was a whole lot different than this.

A little under an hour later, as the sun started its descent over the horizon, two hundred and sixty men departed with their horses across the Tweade on the Barley Point ferry toward an uncertain fate at the hands of an unknown and unreconnoitered enemy force. Latham was among them, nursing memories of past Udar encounters he'd hoped to forget.

. . .

TEN

Pelgreen – Evening (First Day)

The sun had disappeared from the western sky behind them an hour earlier as the *Ann Marie* touched down at the end of a four-hour flight from Belgarden. Cross's ground crew raced to secure its moorings as he powered down the engines. The 38 passengers, a collection of politicos and well-connected swells, were collecting their things and waiting for the cabin doors to open.

Cross made his landing announcement. "Ladies and gentlemen," he called over the clamor, "we've now made our landing at Pelgreen Aerodrome, and this concludes our journey. I hope you've enjoyed the voyage, and I'd like to thank each of you for traveling with us to our capital today. The Airbound Corporation wishes you a successful visit to Principia, and we hope you'll choose us again."

He was ecstatic that none of the passengers were heckling him at those remarks, knowing the foul odor his company enjoyed with the public at present.

However, as Cross moved from the cockpit into the passenger area in hopes of helping the customers to debark, he found himself accosted by no less than five of his passengers, led by the dumpy white-haired politician from the front row.

"This might be your lucky night, Cross," said Harms, as the four others nodded. "We might have a proposition yer in no position to turn down."

Cross shot him an inquisitive look, his eyes widening.

"We believe we can deliver a majority vote at the Societam to have the Army purchase Airbound at a suitable price," interjected Delegate Mortimer Vines, a Peace Party member from the well-to-do Settleton district of Belgarden, who currently sat as Vice-Chairman of the Treasury Committee. "That is, if you have interest in such an arrangement."

"Certainly we would wish to insure your participation in the continued progress of this aeronautical endeavor," blurted a third politician, the notoriously verbose Delegate Ralph Gray of Jerrison, the middle-class suburb across the Morgan from Belgarden, who sat Third Chair on the Improvements Committee. "This would be important in selling such a transaction to Parliament and the government."

"And there are some truly outstanding partnership opportunities waiting that your company might find useful to its future," added Oliver Pleasance, who had an executive position of some kind with Foreman Technologies, a manufacturing concern in Belgarden which had a corporate account with Airbound for shuttling its personnel back and forth to Principia. Cross had shared a bottle of whisky with Pleasance in a Principia evening club once or twice, but he didn't know the man well or exactly what he did.

They were all looking at him.

Cross gave a nervous chuckle as he spread his hands wide. "That sounds a very attractive offer, fellas," he stammered. "Of course, before we'd commit to any arrangement I'd have to confer with my partner, and we'd want to make sure the particulars are sufficient to everyone's benefit. But I'm quite willing to listen."

There were knowing smiles all around, and heads nodded.

The fifth member of the impromptu parley, a rotund middle-aged man in a top hat and a golden vest named Winston Gregory, had said nothing. Cross knew why. Gregory was the Peace Party's political boss in Belgarden Province; he was the intersection between money and votes in the bare-knuckles political swamp the nation's fourth-largest city was known to be, and Gregory was also the man behind Belgarden Province's governor Thomas Cole, who stood to be the Peace Party's presidential nominee and almost certainly Ardenia's president at the next election.

It was Gregory, Cross knew, with whom any deal would need to be struck. Otherwise it wouldn't be possible to get the support of uber-powerful Belgarden delegation, without which nothing got done in the Ardenian Societam.

And Cross knew that whatever deal was presented to him would almost surely be the product of Gregory's quietly pulling levers and making moves that he would never see.

. . .

ELEVEN

Dunnansport – Evening (First Day)

To call the locomotive terminal here a "rail station" would be charity on a scale straining credulity. The Aldingham & Port William Line's southernmost reaches ended in a short loop in a grass field some 500 yards from the Tweade on the western outskirts of the new city, with wood fires burning in iron braziers atop six-foot poles for what illumination existed as the locomotive slowed into Dunnansport. The city had yet to be wired for light, and unlike the fine houses of Tweade's Landing and the business district to the east, the station lacked its own electrical generator. A wooden frame which would, presumably, soon be the skeleton of an actual building but was now covered with canvas served as a makeshift station house, while the muddy field astride the tracks was dashed with planks that would in time become a platform.

"Lot of progress since we left," Will said as he stepped off the train. He wasn't kidding.

"Master Robert!" came a voice as the smaller cadet followed Will off the locomotive. "It's good to see you, sir."

"Jefferson!" Robert answered. "Thank you for meeting us here. It's good to see you too."

"Come, sirs," said the manservant, dressed in the uniform of the well-to-do Ardenian male: knee-high riding boots, woolen britches, an embroidered waistcoat and a thigh-length frock coat over a high-collared shirt with a necktie in a floppy bow. "Your uncle is home and must see you straight away. There has been important news which I fear will not meet you kindly."

"What news?" asked Will as the two loaded their bags on Jefferson's carriage.

"An attack by Udars," answered the man. "Your uncle has the details. We'll be there in minutes."

They boarded the carriage hastily. Jefferson took the reins, and the team of horses was off. Will and Robert shared nervous looks at the man's news.

A few minutes later, Robert and Will strode through the front door of David Stuart's Tweade Landing mansion – perhaps the most opulent and palatial house of the district. Uncle David, dressed not in his usual business suit but a brown leather cavalry jacket, sleeve pinned at his left elbow, over a waistcoat made with copper mesh above a woolen lining, and sporting tan riding pants and black leather boots, wasn't in an entertaining mode, though. When the two arrived, he gave his nephew a short one-armed embrace and then commanded, "Sit, both of you. I have something to tell you."

They sat in the living room chairs David indicated. He remained standing, and began as he paced nervously.

"This morning H.V. Latham – he's the architect from Port William your father had commissioned to do the expansion at Hilltop Farm..."

"I met him," said Robert.

"...right. Latham was on his way down to the farm to deliver the plans and go over them with your dad. But when he got there the whole estate was aflame and everybody was gone but Hannah and Ethan."

"By the *saints*," gasped Robert, tears forming in his eyes. "Are the children all right?"

"They are. Latham got them out. But, and I regret to tell you this, Will, but Grayvern was also burned."

"Bastards," Will said, his eyes narrowing.

"We don't know whether anyone got out at your estate, Will," David continued. "There's a military detachment leaving this evening from Barley Point to sally south and meet the enemy. We're putting together another here from Dunnansport to sweep the eastern farms and then meet up with them. A third force is mustering at Battleford. The plan is to locate the enemy and then trap him, in hopes of rescuing what captives he's taken."

"Do we know…"

"Robert, we don't know who they have," David's voice rose just a little. "We don't know who's alive and who's dead. We know there are a lot of families – maybe hundreds – who were blown apart today. Every one of them needs our help. I'm the captain of the militia here, and I need to draft both of you to join my contingent."

"I'm in," Will said in a somewhat emotionless voice Robert hadn't noticed before. "When do we leave?"

"Shortly," David said. We'll have a quick bite to eat, so Robert can at least say hello to his aunt, and we'll give you two a chance to change into something useful to a military expedition. Then we're riding down to the ferry where the militia will meet up with a few of the marines the *Adelaide* was able to part with, and that'll be our detachment. We need to try to get south and save what people we can."

His head reeling with the news, Robert strode into the kitchen, where his aunt Rebecca had been supervising the cooks, and the two embraced. "I'd thank the Lord of All you're here," she whispered in his ear, "but you'll be gone in a flash of lightning. It's all I can do not to weep."

"I'm terrified I've lost Mother," he said quietly. It was beginning to dawn on him that Judith had been taken from him before he could even say goodbye.

"I know, darling," she said, the collar of her shirtwaist blouse betraying small stains where her tears had earlier deposited residue of her eyeliner. "Such evil. And that you must face it at only seventeen years."

Robert and Will stepped away, as the meal was ready to be set out. The four sat at table, and Uncle David offered the benediction.

"Lord of All, you have graciously given us your Word and summoned us in your presence this evening. Nourish our souls as we nourish our bodies, for our hearts are broken at our most current news. Lord, grant us the courage to face the terror we meet in the south, and grant us the will to defeat that terror. And Lord, let us be mindful of the need to help those innocents we may. We pray, Lord of All, all this in your name."

"And grant us vengeance on those who have wronged us, Lord," muttered Will, his eyes strained shut.

They ate quickly. Will and Robert dragged their bags to the upstairs guest rooms, where they changed out of their cadet uniforms and into combat attire: leather cavalry jackets, canvas-covered aluminum helmets, riding britches and heavy combat boots. The three men then departed the mansion and met a similarly-dressed Jefferson, who had four horses at the ready in the barn next to the house loaded with weapons and supplies.

Robert was fighting off a numb feeling of loss, like an appendage, a leg, perhaps, had been cut from his body. If the Udar had come, his father had fought. And if his father had fought, they'd killed him. The last interaction he'd had with the man had come prompted by Robert's having let him down, and George had blown into Aldingham to put on a show for the cadets and bail him out by appointing Will as his bodyguard. Robert had neglected to write him a note of thanks, figuring he would do so in person. That opportunity was now, presumably, lost to the afterlife, taken from him by a horde of sub-human scum.

And Robert knew of the Udar depredations where women were concerned, which meant something horrible had happened to his mother and his sisters Sarah and Tabitha as well. With him at the academy and his older brother Matthew at the garrison at Strongstead – *and what about Matthew if the enemy had come this far north?* – the women would have had to assist in defending Hilltop Farm. That meant the Udar would have likely killed them too.

He didn't want to process it. Robert decided that until he knew the final score of the day's horrors, he would maintain faith that somehow, his parents and his sisters had made it.

But deep down, he knew that wasn't true.

And as he looked at Will, who'd had very little to say since getting the news about what had happened back home, he could tell Will knew it wasn't true as well.

The four then mounted up and rode for the Dunnansport ferry landing as the sun set in the west.

...

TWELVE

Principia – Night (First Day)

Cross' rented carriage covered, laboriously, the seven miles from Pelgreen Aerodrome to the Airbound Corporation headquarters on Broad Street downtown, as the bustling streets of the capital were jammed with traffic of all kinds–pedestrians, bicycles, horses, carriages and even the new steam wagons and motor sedans (of which he'd regretfully sold his, owing to Airbound's financial exigencies and the need to create appropriate appearances). Traffic would be especially challenging in a mid-evening hour such as this, when the prosperous denizens of the world's most opulent city were venturing forth to enjoy their nocturnal entertainment.

Principia was a city of six million, spread out over a large area centered around the massive port where the Morgan River emptied into the Gulf of Prosperity. A bit upriver from the port, separated on the south side of the Morgan by a reviving residential area and the smaller Shelton River which flowed into the Morgan, was the Capitol District. At its center was where the Presidential Palace, Hall of Justice, the Societam and National Temple formed a diamond around a massive, 100-foot statue of Fletcher Belgrave, who 400 years ago led a rebellion against the dynastic monarchy which had governed Ardenia for two millennia, and established a republic to replace it. The Capitol District was the foremost tourist destination in the world, and it drew throngs of people at all times of the year to gawk at its majestic buildings and other landmarks. Just south of its parks, museums and halls of power was the Elkstrand, an entertainment district filled with theaters, restaurants, cafés, saloons, a high-class brothel or two and some of the priciest apartments on the planet.

Cross would be on the Elkstrand scene shortly enough, as he made his home in a seventeenth-story penthouse along

Courtlyn Avenue and would be entertaining some of his new political friends at the Oleander Club around the corner on Selwyn Street. But first, he and his partner had to have a heart-to-heart, and Gresham, having received a teletype message from Pelgreen upon the *Ann Marie's* landing there, was at the office waiting for him.

Where Cross was going was the Business District, located west of the Capitol District and just up the river from the government buildings, in which Airbound's fate would likely be decided in the next few days. Broad Street ran along a slight ridge three blocks from the Morgan River, on a natural embankment; that location meant a north-facing office in one of its stately brick commercial buildings afforded a fabulous view of the city and the river.

Such a panoramic view was precisely what Cross had on the fifteenth floor of Airbound Corporation's headquarters, and it was to that office that he hustled as his carriage exited Broad Street to the portico in front of the Harrow Building. Cross blew through the lobby, jumped into the elevator and barked, "Fifteenth," to the operator.

"Yes, sir, Mr. Cross, sir," the man obeyed. "It's good to see you home, sir."

"As opposed to what?" Cross snapped, which was uncharacteristic of him. He made it a practice to pour on the charm with everyone he met, as it never hurt to befriend people in every walk of life with whom favors could be traded.

The operator shot him a frightened look. "Oh, Mr. Cross, I didn't mean nothin' but that you're a famous man we all like havin' around, and…"

"All right, all right," Cross held up his hand. "I'm sorry. It's been a bear of a day and it isn't over. Didn't mean to bark at you."

"Yes, sir," the man said. "No offense taken at all, none whatever."

After an awkward silence as the elevator neared the fifteenth floor, finally the ascent ended and the operator threw open the folding gate. "Fifteenth floor, sir, and might I say may the Lord bless and keep ye."

"Much obliged," he said, depositing a twenty-deciran note into the operator's jacket pocket. "Take care of yourself."

Cross' secretary Theresa met him in the reception area, the office mostly deserted thanks to a fresh round of layoffs just the day before. Airbound once had 112 headquarters employees before the *Justice* explosion; now, they were down to twenty-eight. Theresa was likely one of the next round, as the company's hemorrhaging finances indicated Cross and Gresham both probably wouldn't have secretaries, and Theresa's husband was a physician who earned a solid living, while Gresham's secretary Mary was single, had come from Ackerton south of the port and was barely hanging on financially. A layoff would be a crippling blow to her, so she'd be taking on both partners as the company continued to shrink.

"I've got nothing but bad news," Theresa warned him. "Bills, demand letters, warnings from the investors and now we've got some accounts receivable trouble."

"People can smell blood," he lamented as the two walked to Cross' corner office. "And they smell it on us."

"Charrington Coal sent a man this afternoon," she said. "They can't offer any further credit, and by Monday we are cut off from fuel. Do you want me to line up a conversation with Fanwood in the morning?" Fanwood was a competing coal supplier to Charrington, and their prices were considerably higher.

"Dammit," he fumed. There was just no end to the troubles.

"And Stephen Bell was here from Hendle and Reese. He says we need a conference with the *Justice* claimants by the end of the week or else he won't be able to settle the passenger damages before they file in Justice Court."

Cross grunted, briefly considering the irony of the ill-fated airship's name, considering where it was leading him.

"All right, fine," he snapped. "Go on home, Theresa. We'll start tackling these one at a time in the morning before I have to pilot the *Ann Marie* to Belgarden and back in the afternoon."

The *Ann Marie's* Belgarden shuttle had been a twice-daily line a month ago.

"Yes, sir," she sighed. "Get some sleep tonight, will you? You look like death."

I imagine I do, he thought.

Cross blew through the doors of his office and found his partner Gresham sitting with a pile of files in his lap on one of the visitor chairs in front of the desk. He circled around to his "throne," as the office jokesters had termed it and memorialized the joke with a small gold plaque screwed atop its back. He sank down as he reached for the decanter of whisky and two glasses on the service table aside the desk.

"Hooch?" he asked Gresham.

"No," came a disapproving response.

Cross gave Gresham an uncomfortable stare. "You went and got religion now?" he asked him.

"I don't see a need to inebriate myself when we're in crisis," admonished his partner.

Cross shrugged, poured himself four fingers into a wide glass and guzzled down the golden lubricant.

"So I may have a way through," he exhaled, as he let the whisky burn its way down his esophagus. "Had some interesting passengers on the run from Belgarden this evening."

Gresham tossed the pile of files onto Cross' desk. "We're bust," he said. "We're out of business by the weekend. The only way through is you doing what you said you were going to do and go to your father. You've been lying about that for a month while we've bled out, and now it's the end. Will you finally swallow your pride and do what you should have done from the start of this mess?"

Cross stared at Gresham, and Gresham stared back.

Then he filled his glass again, and slugged back another four fingers of the good stuff.

"Unbelievable," shrieked Gresham.

"Can I talk now?" said Cross.

"Please!" Gresham said, exasperated. "Anything out of your mouth would be an improvement after the last four weeks."

"What do you think about the Army?" asked Cross.

. . .

THIRTEEN

Hilltop Farm – Night (First Day)

Night had fallen on Dunnan's Claim, though purple streaks of the gloaming were still visible in the sky. Terrestial light, as one would expect from burning buildings, was reaching its dusk as well as the Terhune contingent approached the Stuart estate.

"All right, boys," said Colonel Terhune. "B Company, reconnoiter Grayvern Farm to the west. C Company, you have Idlewild Farm to the east. We're going to do this systematically and evacuate those we can. Use your bugles to raise alarm on any enemy activity you see.

"D Company, you're south to Thistleton Farm, and E and F, you're with them and then split off to Nairne and Easterland, respectively. Like we drew it up on the ferry. A Company, we start here."

Latham expected he'd be helping to scout for one of the companies heading further into Dunnan's Claim, but Terhune had changed that along with his mind on the way in from Barley Point. "You're with me," he'd said. "I'll not have you killed in the middle of the night by some savage when I have better soldiers for that purpose."

Instead, torches and lanterns in one hand and pistols in another, they combed the Stuart property for signs of life…or death. And shortly those were uncovered.

The body of George Stuart was found aside the road south of the property. His head was missing.

Judith and Tabitha Stuart's corpses were found burned when one of Terhune's men climbed a stone column to peer at the charred wooden balcony on the second floor of the house.

And twelve bodies of Udar warriors were found laid out in ceremonial style behind the house, hands on their *Gazols* and heads turned to face south toward Uris Udar.

"Looks like one hell of a fight took place here," said Terhune. "Hell of a fight. Old George was a hero of the last war; he may have been the first hero of this one."

Just then a rider approached from the west.

"All dead at Grayvern Farm, Colonel," he announced. Two bodies in front of the house; looks like the farmer and his wife."

"That's the Forlings," spat Terhune. "All their children are grown and gone. Did Old John take any of the bastards with him?"

"We saw one Udar body, sir."

"All right. Continue west to the next farm, then work your way south. Send me dispatches of your progress."

The Terhune contingent went that way systematically, spending as little time as possible at each property once they assessed whether anyone was alive and how many had fallen in that day's attacks.

"I don't want to keep this up too far past midnight," Terhune confided to Latham. "There will be a battle coming against these sons of bitches, and I don't know how many we're up against. I want rested soldiers for what we face."

But the grim work went on. By midnight the contingent had visited three dozen properties, each one hit by Udar raiders. They had rescued four survivors – three young boys and an old woman, all of whom had managed to stash themselves in cellars and other hiding places. The death toll had mounted.

It was obvious that this was a more involved Udar operation than the army had usually encountered since Dunnan's War had petered out twenty-five years earlier. The frontier with the enemy hadn't been totally pacified, but most of the Udar raids had been one-offs with perhaps one war party of thirty or forty raiders hitting the odd property far out on the perimeter of Dunnan's Claim or the farmland southwest of Trenory, close to The Throat. Most of those in Dunnan's Claim were warriors on foot who had made an amphibious raid after slipping past the Navy's gunboats in Watkins Gulf. To inflict this much carnage meant this had to be an entire *Anur*, or even more than one. Terhune knew his 260 men were probably outnumbered if they attacked the enemy's camp at their estimated strength.

That wasn't too much of a problem, Latham thought. After all, with rifles (most of them Thurmans, after a late surge of donations from the people of Barley Point before the departure across the Tweade) and pistols issued to every man here, and two chain guns they could set up in the event of a pitched battle, the Ardenians would have a sizable advantage in firepower they could leverage so long as they weren't in a close-combat situation with the Udar. But in the event of that circumstance, the enemy would give as good as he got. Or worse.

"These war parties, they carry a supply train of sorts," Terhune told Latham as he nodded, having seen this himself in his slightly younger years. "There's a woman camp follower for every warrior in a tent-camp. They cook, they mend wounds, they guard the prisoners, and they tend the livestock. We hit that camp, we'll get our people back and then we can fight these warriors on our terms."

"Like at Stone Lip, back in '42," agreed Latham.

"The Throat," Terhune said. "You remember."

"Never will forget that. Keeps me up at night."

"Well," Terhune chuckled, "Your memories are going to be a good bit worse after I'm done with you."

The contingent reassembled and camped around midnight on the far south end of the Barley Point road, nineteen miles south of the Tweade. Latham knew somewhere between here and the Watkins Gulf coast, probably a bit to the west, was the enemy camp. With so many captives and so much loot to carry, though, the Udar would be moving slowly in comparison to the pursuing cavalry. Further, as Terhune noted when outlining the battle plan in the headquarters tent, the Ardenian force would be stronger when the Barley Point contingent met up with the smaller ones from Dunnansport and Battleford.

"I want a maximum force when we hit them," he'd said. "I don't want to try cutting them off. Not when we don't know what's between them and the border."

"Strongstead is between them and the border, sir," said a young captain named Pelham. "Maybe if we drive them westward along the coast we'll smash them against that wall."

"Udar has a better plan than that," replied Terhune. "There's something here we don't yet understand. How they got here, for example. They couldn't have come through The Throat without raising an alarm. They couldn't have come by sea; not at this kind of strength and not with horses they've obviously got. We control Watkins Gulf. And how could they get through Strongstead?"

"They haven't, sir," said Pelham. We're still in communication with the garrison at the citadel over the teletext. They report all is well."

That earned him a frown from Terhune, who cocked his head at the man. Pelham shrunk away a little.

"Something isn't right," agreed Latham. "It's almost like this is a provocation. They want to suck us in."

"We go carefully in the morning," Terhune decided. "We go ready for action, and we'll give these bastards hell when we find them. But no mistakes. If they aren't trying to lay an ambush I'll be a sonofabitch. Expect it. Prepare for it."

. . .

FOURTEEN

South of Dunnansport – Early Morning (Second Day)

The Dunnansport expeditionary force commanded by David Stuart was made up of 98 militiamen and 12 Marines from *Adelaide*, and it was the product of a meeting in the early afternoon between himself, the young Commander Baker of the Navy ship and the Commodore in charge of the naval wharf in the new city, an elderly man named Barstow.

At that meeting it was decided that *Adelaide* would steam along the coast from the mouth of the Tweade south to Cotter's Point, then west along the Watkins Gulf Coast in the strait between the mainland and Adams Island with a sharp eye out for the Udar force, which was seemingly on or near that coastline. Upon fixing their position, *Adelaide* would communicate with Baker's Marines attached to the Dunnansport contingent by use of heliograph (signal mirrors and lanterns the Marines would carry with them), and hopefully link up with the other two expeditions to offer a battle with naval support. *Adelaide's* twenty-two other Marines would be available to put ashore for additional manpower.

Additionally, Barstow had engaged Port William by teletext, securing the services of a sidewheeler – the *ANV Yarmouth* – for evacuating the captives by sea; *Yarmouth* had already provisioned with food, blankets and relief supplies and was underway. It would be a day behind *Adelaide* and hopefully close the distance in time to assist the operation. Two other frigates, *Castamere* and *Louise,* were due to make port in either Port William or Dunnansport within the next 24 hours; both would be dispatched to the Watkins Gulf coast at full speed.

David had invested a not-insignificant sum out of his personal fortune in order to keep the Dunnansport militia exceptionally well-provisioned. Each man, which also included Will and Robert as well as the *Adelaide* Marines, was equipped with a Thurman rifle and a Bearingdale pistol, the best on the market, with an extra supply of ammunition, and their horses were saddled with custom-made rigs. David took pride in the fact the Dunnansport contingent would be the best-armed force of the three meeting up somewhere in the south of Dunnan's Claim. The lack of men with any combat experience, though, was a limiting factor in his expectation of how they might do if they faced a serious enemy out there.

What they most lacked was intelligence about the enemy, and perhaps most pressing, the origin of this Udar force. It should have been detected before reaching Dunnan's Claim– either at one of the forts along The Throat, at Strongstead or by ship somewhere along the coast if it were an amphibious expedition. Baker said he saw no sign of the enemy when he put in at Strongstead a few weeks earlier, and the citadel there was in good order at the time. It was hard to believe Strongstead might have fallen, though that was the most plausible explanation for a raiding party large enough to do such damage to have appeared behind the front lines.

But the garrison was communicating with the Army base at Barley Point via teletext and reporting no Udar activity. The pieces simply weren't coming together.

Solving that mystery was of crucial importance, because the enemy had clearly exploited a weakness in the Ardenian defenses. And hundreds, perhaps thousands, of their countrymen were now dead as a result. It was a military disaster on a grand scale, and they were reeling.

No point in denying it, but at least there was an initial plan to respond.

Robert had joined Will and four other riders in a small company working the far eastern farms along the Tweade south of Dunnansport. None were hit by the raiders, and the farmers had seen no evidence of attacks. The riders offered assistance, but the farmers turned it down. "Stay in your homes, then," advised Will. "Protect your property. But be smart – if they come, and you can get away, then get out across that river."

The ferry was still running. Uncle David and Commander Baker had discussed evacuating the area. Ultimately that idea had been suspended–for now. In case of a hot battle, the evacuation would commence with all possible speed.

When the riders got just south of the riverside farms, the horrors surfaced.

At a log cabin on a farm named Sunnyside five miles south of the river, a man, a woman and three children had been staked out on the ground and their skin stripped off. Two miles south of that, at Howarding Farm, they found three headless corpses. Three miles west, at Gilvary Farm, they found a survivor – of sorts. The relatively young man lay bleeding, an *Izwei* buried in his stomach. Before dying, he told his horrific tale.

"It was forty of the bastards," he wheezed. "They come before sunup and broke down the door. My Mary and me wasn't even awake. I ran for my rifle, but one of 'em got me with this dagger. I can't pull it out, see…the barbs on the side'll rip out my guts."

"Mary, they took her. And the two young'uns in their cribs…" he cried, unable to finish. Robert stepped through the ruins of the cabin and saw what the man was referring to: a pair of toddlers, dismembered and hacked beyond recognition. He'd vomited up his dinner, thinking of his own family.

When he returned to the victim, the man was dead.

"We can't help him, Rob," said Will. "Let's go."

In all, Will and Robert and their platoon had looked in on nine farms. Each one was a similar story. But some of them – many, in fact – weren't just the resting places of Ardenian settlers. The invaders had taken casualties as well. Turtlehead Farm was the scene of a fierce battle at which five Ardenians – four men and a woman – had perished and been skinned, but had taken no less than 10 Udar with them. The dead raiders were laid out in a ceremonial style holding their *Gazols*, their heads turned toward Uris Udar.

111

"Good on you all," said Robert. "Send the bastards to hell. Resistance is the blessed path."

"Damn right," Will mumbled.

Perhaps the worst of that awful experience, though, came at Landsdowne Farm, the furthest east of the estates the scouts surveyed. This was the home of the Blaine family, who were dear friends of Robert's aunt and uncle; their daughter Hester had been childhood friends with his cousin Josey.

Hester was gone, but the rest of the Blaines were not. Richard Blaine, the father, had been impaled to the front door by a spear through the side of his head and Mary Blaine, the mother, lay in the front yard with her skin stripped off. The charred corpses of Hester's three younger brothers hung from the flagpole in the side yard, and the Blaine's Ardenian flag had been taken down and was covered in manure.

Robert's worry about his family, and the panic about their fate, was no longer the only thought in his mind. Not anymore. As he saw the carnage and the horror at homestead after homestead, what welled up in him was rage. Rage and vengeance.

He knew this night had changed him. All he wanted was to kill Udar, and he didn't care whom. The scared boy missing his mother was gone forever, and someone else—something else—had taken his place.

Rob sensed Will had a somewhat similar reaction to his own sudden grief, but his friend, who had always been fairly easy to read, was giving off a different air than he'd seen from him before. Normally quite outgoing, Will had nothing much to say about anything that night, and along the ride Rob had tried, without success, to engage him in conversation.

And the more death and destruction they'd seen south of Dunnansport, the quieter Will had gotten. He was in charge of the scouting party, and he gave orders with a professionalism that impressed Rob, given that Will's only experience in this sort of thing was in mock training battles in the woods adjoining the academy, but he could sense that his friend was a lot more affected than he let on. Will's facial expression had turned blank, and the carnage he'd seen didn't move him at all anymore.

For Robert, it was different. His fires were burning close to the surface, and while Will was keeping a poker face Robert could feel himself losing control. His fury was eating him whole, having already consumed the grief he'd expected to feel.

Shortly before dawn, after working to the farthest southern edge of the Dunnan's Claim homesteads and turning west toward Barley Point, Will and Rob's group met up with the main Dunnansport contingent and compared notes. The damage had been severe. Of twenty-nine farms the men had examined, all had been hit. Bodies of their countrymen had been found at twenty-seven, many more than 100 dead. But thirty-four Udar corpses had also been found, seemingly a fairly high casualty rate. When they caught up with the savages they might have an advantage. And there would be hell to pay.

The contingent set up a couple of campfires on the Dunnansport side of a slight ridgeline which trailed north, giving them a bit of cover from the view of any Udar scouts who might otherwise see their fires, and pitched a quick makeshift camp.

"Let's put out a sentry and get a couple hours of rest," said David. "After dawn we're going to sweep south to the coast and then west, and we'll catch up with the Barley Point group tomorrow."

His uncle pulled Rob aside with his good arm as the men tucked in for a short bit of shut-eye. "What you saw out there," he said, "I know you haven't seen that before."

"Yeah, well," Rob answered. "I've seen it now, haven't I?"

"Rob, we don't know that's what happened to your parents and your sisters."

"Yes we do, Uncle," he said. "I've carried that pigshit around with me all night. Oh, they're fine, they made it out. But they didn't. All those farms we looked in on? Four survivors. *Four*. Ethan and Hannah got out, which is a miracle. But everybody else? Let's not be deluded. And Uncle...the Blaines. I can't even describe it."

"They took prisoners, Robert," David shook him by the lapel of his leather jacket. "That's why they came up here. It's how they work. Stay in this fight, and we still have hope that we can see Sarah, Tabitha and your mother again. You get me?"

"Oh, I get you, Uncle," Rob said. "I'm in this fight. Don't you worry about that. Only thing keeping me moving is I want a good damn kill, and then I want another."

"Well, we can use that. What about Will? How's he holding up?"

Rob looked over at his friend, who had prepared a sleeping berth with his bed roll and saddle but was just sitting by the fire with that same blank stare as he gazed at the flames.

"I don't know," he admitted. "Outwardly, he's fine I guess. He's functioning. But he's not right, Uncle David. He's distant. He's a talker, but he isn't talking now."

"Well, it's understandable," said David. "War does that to a man. But I want to know if either one of you can't handle it. You're both under more strain than anyone could expect right now, and it's indecent neither one of you can properly grieve. I shouldn't have dragged you two out here, and I'm sorry for that. By the saints, you're not even eighteen yet and what you've seen tonight..."

"No, you need us," Rob said. "And I'll be all right. I'm eighteen in two days; I'm not some little kid. My engine is running. I'm sure his is, too," he said looking at Will, who had slumped onto his back next to the fire.

...

FIFTEEN

Elkstrand – Early Morning (Second Day)

Cross brought Gresham with him to the hastily-arranged confab at the Oleander Club, an exclusive hot spot on the north end of Principia's entertainment district where he'd been told to expect a delegation of political and military grandees and to be at his most charming and agreeable. He'd been told that by Madison Gregg, the Cross family's solicitor and hired political insider, who had known about Harms' overture to him even before Cross had sent him a message upon landing at Pelgreen. Gregg, in fact, had set up this late-night meeting.

So when Cross and Gresham arrived at the Oleander Club, Sebastian's old gal-pal Kimberley Swain, the club's hostess with whom he'd had many a late evening of lubricating liquors and various levels of intimate interactions, led them up to the VIP lounge on the third floor, and Gregg met them at the top of the stairs.

"Delivery for you, Mr. Gregg," she said flirtatiously. "You don't even have to sign for them."

"You're the best, Kimberley," the solicitor said with a familiarity which surprised Sebastian. He gave her a glance, which was returned with a slight shrug before she turned around and departed, her sleek golden dress shimmering in the electric light as her matching high heels carried her back down the club's red-carpeted staircase.

The three paused at the scenery. Cross was broken out of his reverie when Gregg grabbed him and dragged him and Gresham into a nearby anteroom.

"All right," he instructed the pair. "Showtime. We've got some big fish in the net in there, and this is a big moment for

ANIMUS

both of you. You both need to keep a cool head, don't get offended by anything that's said and for the love of the Saints keep your bloody mouths shut unless you get asked a direct question. Get me?"

"What's going on in that room?" asked Gresham with an air of suspicion bordering on hostility.

"That is entirely the wrong attitude, boy," Gregg answered. "What's going on in there is you getting to end up rich with a chunk of a business they trade shares of at the Havener Street exchange, no more lawsuits, no more damages and a hell of a lot better product to sell than two airships that could blow to blazes at any time."

"Hey, sod off," Gresham bristled. "I'm not going to…"

"Shut your damned mouth!" Gregg hissed. "You pop off one more time and I'm sending you out of here and we'll deal with him" – he pointed at Cross – "and you can go back to that shithole in Ackerton you come from."

"Let's just hear these guys out, all right?" Cross said, soothingly. "I think this might turn out to our satisfaction. Come on, old boy."

Gresham glared at him, whispering "We're going to lose the company to whatever is going on in there, and if you'd done what needed to be done a month ago, we'd have *options*."

Cross wanted to respond. He wanted to jump down Gresham's throat, frankly, as he'd held his tongue about how Gresham had built airships that were flying bombs and killed sixty-four people with shitty, crackpot engineering, about how he was now piloting one of those flying bombs every damned day while trying to run what was left of the business with no sleep, no respite from the constant flow of bad news and no prospect of it getting better, and about how he'd lost his fortune backing a business that was down the tubes despite all his best efforts to save it short of debasing himself in front of his family, which he would sooner die than do.

And he also wanted to tell Gresham that he knew about his kickbacks and graft, and that maybe if he'd put Cross'

116

personal resources and those of the company's investors, all of whom were Cross' family friends, into engineering and materials instead of his greasy pockets, they wouldn't be in such dire straits.

But he didn't.

Because Sebastian Cross was not the guy who tore people a new posterior orifice. He let the hotheads do that. And Sebastian Cross was no hothead. Sebastian Cross was the guy everybody liked, and therefore would do things for when he asked them. And Sebastian Cross didn't show anger, because showing anger always made things worse.

So instead, he kept his mouth shut like Gregg told him to. Because when they entered the lounge he knew that opportunity was knocking in that room, and loudly, and anger and recrimination would be expensive commodities they couldn't afford.

He knew that because the codgers sitting on the plush chairs and couches of the lounge, puffing on cannabis pipes and swigging from tumblers of Beacon Point whisky, were some of the heaviest hitters in all of Ardenia.

There were Harms, Vines, Gray and Gregory, who'd been part of his conversation as the *Ann Marie* had landed at Pelgreen. There was John Elmore, the Minister of Defense. There was Paul Porter, the Chief Delegate of the Societam. Delegate Carlton Raines, twirling his handlebar moustache, chaired the Parliament's Treasury Committee. Michael Todd was in the center of the room; he was the presiding executive of the Ardenian Transport Commission, the regulatory agency supervising locomotive, river and coastal ship transportation which had not yet claimed jurisdiction over the new airship industry Cross and Gresham had pioneered–a miracle Cross figured was existing on borrowed time. General Abraham Dees was there; he was chief of the Army-Navy Office of Special Warfare. Jonah Barnaby, Director-General of the Peace Party, was pouring himself a strong one at the courtesy bar. Cross saw Victor Phelps, the Admiralty's chief of staff, making notes as he sat on the far couch.

117

And then there was Maynard Stone, chief of staff to President Catherine Greene. Stone was the second most powerful person in the country, eyeing Cross and Gresham as they entered the lounge.

"Well, hello gentlemen," Cross announced. "I'm surprised and humbled to see such a distinguished assemblage."

"Sit down," Porter ordered, pointing to two chairs in the middle of the room. Cross and Gresham complied.

Dees then piped up. "You two might be the luckiest bastards who ever lived, you know that?"

. . .

SIXTEEN

The Camp – Early Morning (Second Day)

It was a little after dark when the women came again for Sarah. She didn't resist, as by now she was fairly sure she wouldn't be killed.

Bear it with dignity, she thought.

They led her into what she by now had recognized to be the commander's tent, and the commander was the man who abducted her and killed Tabitha. When she was led in, she saw the naked woman she had deduced was Ardenian kneeling in the middle of the tent. And the commander, who was lounging on a cushion half-covered by a horsehair blanket while glaring at her with a lewd and intimidating expression Sarah didn't like one bit.

Four small iron braziers were laid out near the corners of the tent with small piles of wood burning in each. That made the tent into something of a sauna, something Sarah didn't really understand given the increasingly pleasant air outside that Sarah's fellow captives, clad only in their shifts and stockings, sat comfortably in. Relatively speaking, given their circumstances.

"Please, kneel in front of me," the woman, who Sarah gauged was in her mid-thirties, said. The guards pushed Sarah down facing the woman. Her gag was removed.

"Water?" the woman asked. Sarah nodded. She produced a leather canteen and poured a mouthful past Sarah's lips. Sarah noticed the woman's lips were tainted a dark shade of purple, and her pupils were dilated a little bit more than you would expect from a normal person. And Sarah noticed that she didn't have hair *anywhere* on her body–not even on her head.

Earlier when she'd seen the woman she'd had some almost-white stubble on her head, but that was gone now.

"I am Shori'zel," she said.

Sarah cut her off. "That's not your real name."

"It is," she answered patiently, but firmly. "What you mean is that I was formerly named something else, and you are correct."

"You're Ardenian. Are you a prisoner like me?"

"I was. I am originally from Welvary. Do you know where that is?"

Sarah nodded. Welvary was a city of 200,000 three hours east of Principia by locomotive. She'd never been there. Or Principia, for that matter. She'd always wanted to see the capital, and it dawned on her that the chances of that were fading, rapidly.

"Where were you taken?" Sarah asked.

"At Strongstead."

"Strongstead has fallen?"

"It fell. Yes."

"*How?* How long ago?"

"I don't know. What is the date?"

"Tonight is the sixth of the tenth."

"A month. By the Saints, it seems longer." The woman trailed off for a moment.

"What *was* your name?"

"Charlotte. Charlotte Naughton. My husband was the commander at Strongstead."

Matthew! Sarah thought. Her oldest brother was stationed there. *If the Udar had the commander's wife...Lord of All!*

"How did it fall?"

"They came from above. Raptors. In the night. None manning the Citadel out of doors survived. And from below, the men. They tunneled under the Citadel and then attacked through the basement and sewers. Eight hundred men of the garrison dead."

"Ohhh." Sarah shut her eyes. She couldn't process the loss of another sibling. *Not Matthew as well. He's gone a month and we didn't even know. None of us could even say goodbye.*

"The Udar are here in their millions," Charlotte said. "They have come to finish Ardenia. All is lost. I see that now."

"They've made you their slave."

"I have chosen this. My loss was great. My husband, gone. My son, gone. But when Rapan'na," she waved at the man behind her, and Sarah now knew that was his name, "offered me the benediction of becoming his *javeen*, I agreed. I have saved three of my daughters in doing so."

Sarah gave a horrified look, which the woman brushed off. She continued.

"I am faithful to Rapan'na and his *Anur*, his tribe that you see in this camp. In return he keeps my daughters safe."

"He'll let them go?"

Charlotte shook her head. "He has spared them. He has bestowed upon them the high honor of conveying them to the capital at Qur Udar to live under the protection of the *sa'halet*. And when they are old enough they will also serve the Udar as *javeen*."

"That's insane. You let him sell your daughters to the king? You chose this over death and that's all you got for it?"

121

"I am following the Blessed Path. I will bear with dignity the unjust suffering."

"I don't think I could do that if I were you."

"But you can," she said. "And you will. It is the only way."

"You want me to be this…this *javeen*?"

"All of you will. It is why you were taken. I know now, it is the life the Lord of All has chosen for us."

"No. I don't believe that. This is not holy, it's a crime and an atrocity. This did not come from the Lord of All."

"It is what is, my dear. It is the way of war. What we make of it is what determines our fate in the afterlife."

"They've brainwashed you. I'm sorry for you. I can't believe any of this."

"Listen to me," Charlotte said. "There are 380 of you out there. Do you think the Udar would have the slightest hesitation in cutting every throat in those lines? They would not."

"I don't care. Cut my throat now. They've killed my family. You've told me they killed my brother."

"Who is your brother?"

"Matthew Stuart. He was at the citadel. He was a captain in the garrison there."

Charlotte closed her eyes and paused for a minute.

"I knew Captain Stuart." Tears welled in her eyes. Then she straightened.

"It is an unjust thing," she declared quickly. "He was a soldier. He died for his cause."

"*Our* cause. And you're telling me he had his guts torn out by a raptor. You can make peace with that? And how was he killed in a raptor attack, anyway?" Sarah nodded toward the Udar headman. "They coordinate with deadly predators now?"

"They do," said Charlotte, as Sarah detected a faint sparkle in her eyes. "This war, this endless war – it will end soon. You have a choice to be on the side of life. You may lead those others to that side."

"To the enemy side? None would follow if I did choose what you've done. Not that I ever would."

"You're tired and you're hungry. I understand your emotion. Here. Let me nourish you."

Charlotte dipped her finger in a bowl full of some sort of gruel, and then stuck it in Sarah's mouth. It wasn't awful, though she surmised almost anything might be palatable after having had nothing to eat all day. The woman fed her several more bites from the bowl, then a few blackberries from another. She then gave Sarah a drink of that familiar dark liquid in a goblet. It tasted very sweet, and her head began to spin a bit.

"Let me untie your arms," Charlotte offered. She stood and walked behind Sarah, bending to untie the knots binding each of her wrists to her elbows. Sarah unfolded her abused arms and rubbed her wrists and then stretched, her hands above her head, the circulation returning and fiery tendrils of pain spreading from her elbows. Charlotte gave her another sip of the liquid. Her head spun a little faster and the pain subsided.

"What's in this?" she asked.

"It is *marwai*, a liquor made of the *gibor* berry," Charlotte answered, "which grows in the Ur'akeen Valley near the capital. Similar to belladonna, which you had in Ardenia, but less toxic. It is infused with the extract of the *aniwa'di* cactus. You will find it allows you to see things with a clearer mind."

Sarah didn't think her mind was clearer at all.

What was closer to the truth is that she was getting drunk from having this stuff poured down her throat all day. But it wasn't really like getting drunk. She'd had enough wine or

123

whisky on a couple of occasions to catch a buzz, and this was *very* different. She felt as though little lights were dancing all around her and she felt a warm sensation bubbling up from her insides. And Sarah knew her elbows and her head ought to be absolutely throbbing, but at the moment she was barely feeling any pain at all.

And she felt a weird impulse to listen and accept what Charlotte was telling her about her future–an impulse she was determined to reject completely.

"So a *javeen*'s job is to do what? Get pregnant?" She pointed feebly at Rapan'na. "Be his whore?"

"It's far more than that. As *javeen*, you are wife and mother to the entire *Anur*. It's a position of leadership, to an extent. You serve the *Anur* as others cannot."

"They need Ardenians for this? What about all these other women?"

"They are not *javeen*. They are members of the *Anur*. They keep the camp running, and they couple with the warriors to make children. But only *javeen* may couple with a *Var'asha* – a leader of the *Anur*. And her daughters will also be *javeen*. Only those from outside Uris Udar may do this. It is the will of Ur'akeen. You must choose such an honored life. It cannot be forced upon you."

Sarah knew some of what Charlotte was saying from the quick education his father had given her in the past few weeks, but it was beginning to make sense why the Udar kept mounting raids when reason dictated they should have stopped a long time ago. *They need a steady supply of sex slaves for this* javeen *thing*, she thought. *I really don't want to be here.*

"And what happens when we say no to all this?" Sarah asked, her brain going numb from fatigue and the *marwai*.

"You must not say no." And Charlotte gave her another swallow of the liquid.

"Or what?" Sarah asked, her eyelids getting heavy.

"Or they kill you, and sacrifice you in the sanctified fire."

"I think I'd prefer that," she said, reeling. "I'm not letting that *man* have his way with me."

"You don't have to decide tonight," Charlotte said, smiling sweetly. "But you will sleep in the tent with us where it is warm, and you may consider your options in the morning."

Sarah no longer had the power to resist. Charlotte embraced her and slowly led her to lay down on a cushion near where Rapan'na was lying. She kissed Sarah lovingly on the lips, which produced a short purr from the captive girl, and then a look of alarm as Sarah recognized the unusual attention she was getting in a last burst of lucidity. Charlotte gave her another sip of *marwai*, and then drew a blanket over Sarah. Then Charlotte downed the rest of the liquid in the goblet before turning to Rapan'na.

Charlotte then climbed onto the commander's bedding, and got on her knees. He rose, and pulled the blanket covering himself away, and Sarah saw that he was naked save for the new bandage on the thigh where she'd shot him that morning.

Rapan'na came behind Charlotte, and she spread her knees. He massaged her private area from behind, and then he mounted and entered her. With a gasp, she began pushing back against him. As the two began a vigorous sexual encounter, Sarah passed out.

. . .

SEVENTEEN

Principia – Morning (Second Day)

Cross arrived early to the Airbound Corporation's offices on the morning of the seventh of the tenth, exhausted from a lack of sleep and a very late night of discussions with the assemblage at the Oleander Club the previous evening.

But for the first day in three months, he came to the office with real hope that things were actually going to turn out all right. Maybe even better than that.

It had certainly not been a pleasant meeting, and Cross had been terrified throughout that his partner's mouth would leave them destitute with the lawsuits from the victims of the *Justice's* crash still hanging over their heads. But after a protest or two Gresham, upon having been told by the Chief of Staff of the entire Ardenian government that nobody in the room gave a pile of turds about whether he cooperated or not, had piped down and kept quiet.

Gregg did most of the talking for his clients, and the contours of a deal Cross found acceptable–to say the least– began to take shape. The long and short of it was that the Army, or more specifically the Army-Navy Office of Special Warfare, wanted the *Clyde* and the *Ann Marie* as weapons platforms, and they wanted the two airships refitted with chain guns mounted on all four corners of the cabins, and they wanted them today.

And the full resources of the Ardenian government were available to make that happen.

Of course, the military wasn't willing to deposit a pot of gold on their doorstep just for a couple of airships. Not by a long shot.

In fact, the deal on the table was that Cross and Gresham would sell the two airships to the Office of Special Warfare for a grand total of...one deciran.

But the next afternoon, the Peace Party would push a bill through Parliament appropriating 14 million decirans to a special relief fund for victims of the *Justice* disaster left unpaid following the bankruptcy of Yellowvine Indemnity Company, with a statutory declaration that the crash was an act of the Lord of All and no blame could be assigned to the Airbound Corporation for negligence or malfeasance on the part of its officers or employees.

In the meantime, Airbound would be sold to Foreman Technologies of Belgarden, a maker of train and riverboat engines, for 10.2 million decirans – enough to make the company's outside investors whole and give Gresham and Cross 100,000d each for their trouble–and an assumption of its current operating liabilities. Foreman had a job standing by for Gresham as its Chief Aeronautic Engineer, and he was moving to Belgarden. That city, owing to its outsized political stroke as the site of the Peace Party's founding, the likelihood of its provincial governor being the nation's president in a year's time, and its delegation's influence in the Societam, would become the new center of the Ardenian aviation industry. A pair of Foreman engineers had perfected something they were calling the internal combustion engine, which was a significant improvement over the steam engines that powered virtually everything in Ardenia and ran on fuels other than coal, and that engine was going to replace the burners and propellers on the *Clyde* and *Ann Marie*.

As for Cross, he was getting drafted into the Army, something he would never have expected in a million years. He was going in as a major, though, and the executive officer of the brand new Special Air Force to be set up under the Office of Special Warfare, which was going to be headquartered outside a little town on the Tweade called Barley Point, in that area close to the frontier called Dunnan's Claim. There was no sense in having an air force if it wasn't going to do business with the

Udar, Dees, who was going to be his boss, told him. So he'd better get used to the idea of sharing space with the enemy.

In the final tally Cross had lost 1.6 million decirans, all but 400,000d of his initial investment, in Airbound. The last eight years was thus a thorough waste of his time from a financial standpoint. And he was moving from a sumptuous bachelor pad in the Elkstrand to some dusty craphole in Dunnan's Claim, where he could easily expect to catch a *Ba'kalo* in the chest as he slept. He'd be giving up his lifestyle, sharing Vinland red and the cannabis pipe with theater and dance-line starlets each night, and replacing that with, what? Tilts at cards in a barracks with a collection of farmboys? And yet they had told him this was a good deal for him.

Even stranger, he agreed.

Earlier in the day Cross was the corporate executive who'd killed sixty-four souls with an irresponsible contraption built for disaster and the sad clown who'd set not just his own fortune ablaze but ten million decirans from some of the most prominent citizens in Ardenia, all of whom were friends of his mortified father, who was barely speaking to him.

At the end of the night, though, he was all set to be the hero who'd circumnavigated the world and then turned his budding, cutting-edge civilian enterprise into a weapon against the hated Udar with a patriotic commitment to bring his technology to bear in subduing that intractable enemy once and for all.

Call him shallow, sure, but from a pure public relations standpoint this was the kind of comeback all the money his family would ever have couldn't buy.

None of it was his idea, of course. Gregg and Gregory and those big shots in that room last night had more or less dictated it to him. But against what he expected he'd be getting? Cross wasn't about to look this gift horse in the mouth.

And thankfully, neither was Gresham. Most of the deal he didn't like, and some he could tolerate. But what made him go along with it was the engineering. He was fascinated with those engines Foreman was working on, and he couldn't wait to have a look at them. Gresham was having breakfast with Pleasance, who it turned out was that company's vice president of operations, ostensibly to chisel out a few choice perks for himself while negotiating on behalf of Airbound's remaining employees. Cross planned to bring some aboard the Special Air Force as civilian contractors; others were going with Foreman.

Which meant today, Cross was in the office to sign over his company and wrap up its affairs. Tomorrow, he was catching the first locomotive out of Belgrave Station to make the all-day trip to Dunnansport, and from there he was catching a steamboat to Barley Point to make preparations for the Special Air Force's new headquarters with a refitted and armored-up *Clyde* and *Ann Marie* to follow three days later.

One hell of a last 24 hours, that was for sure.

Cross wasn't sure he was cut out to be a military man, and he definitely had misgivings about that aspect of the plan. But as Dees had explained, the Udar didn't have anything they expected would be a counter to the Ardenian air power the *Clyde* and *Ann Marie* were bringing to the battlefield, so he'd be relatively safe in the air. And on the ground, he was assured that shooting the enemy was easier on the nerves than he'd expect.

"It's like hunting," the general said, patronizingly. "You've been hunting, certainly."

"Of course I have," Sebastian had said, determined not to become flustered. "Hasn't everybody?"

He'd hunted elk several times before back in the Morgan Valley. Never, ever had hit a single one.

Nevertheless, there was something about the general that Cross found reassuring – a certain cavalier confidence and general badassery that made Sebastian want to follow him. And Cross really, really liked the idea of becoming a war hero.

Theresa poked her head through the door of his office to find him hard at work on a stack of papers. "Come on in," he said cheerfully. "I've got a whole lot of news, and I don't know how much of it you're going to like."

"Don't worry about me," she said, even more sunnily. "Last night I got hired to work for the President's Chief of Staff. I'm just here to help you close down the company."

. . .

EIGHTEEN

The Rendezvous – Morning (Second Day)

At eight of the clock, the Dunnansport contingent was mounted and spreading out along a line stretching from the small rise at the south end of the settled farms to within sight of the coast. With only 110 men in twenty-two platoons of five riders apiece, they were far too dispersed for combat effectiveness, but as Uncle David said this was far more about reconnaissance than battle. Their theory was that the enemy had set up one camp, and it was to the west somewhere. So rather than engage the Udar, the aim was to mark the enemy position and get the hell out of there without getting killed.

They would then join up with the larger Barley Point contingent, without which David was loath to press an attack in any event. He'd figured the Udar had to have well in excess of one hundred men out here somewhere, virtually each one a battle-hardened killer. David's militia were certainly well-equipped and provisioned, but other than a handful of their older members and the dozen Marines from *Adelaide* who were included in their number, they had precious little combat experience.

It had struck David on the way south that they were grossly, criminally unprepared for what lay ahead. Taking risks without having linked up with the larger and more experienced Barley Point force, made up as it was of regular Army cavalrymen and Marines, was simply not in his plan.

The riders worked quickly, processing the area and noting that clearly there had been Udar through this ground recently, as there were reasonably fresh horse tracks through the muddy grasslands. But the action was west. By noon, a bugle call on the north end of the Dunnansport line, relayed team to team along the loose formation, summoned the riders together, where they found the Barley Point group.

"Colonel Terhune," David greeted the leader as he rode up. "I bring you the 110 men of the Dunnansport contingent. Ninety-eight militia, including these two cadets from Aldingham, Lieutenant William Forling and my nephew, Lieutenant Junior Grade Robert Stuart. We have with us also twelve Marines from the *Adelaide* commanded by Lieutenant Charles Wells here."

"Good to have you, Mr. Stuart," said Terhune, who then turned to Robert and Will. "And Mr. Stuart and Mr. Forling, I am truly sorry for those you've lost. Last night we passed through your homesteads, and I'm afraid the news is not as you'd hope."

"Colonel, do I have any parents left?" Rob pleaded.

Terhune gave him a pained look. "We found your mother and father, son. They've passed. And we also found your sister Tabitha. She's gone as well. I'm so sorry."

Robert shut his eyes as they welled up with tears, the finality of what he'd suspected coming home to him. He sagged in his saddle and leaned to one side, expecting to vomit. Uncle David, who'd rode next to him, reached out and put his good hand on his nephew's shoulder.

"Son, I'm very sorry," Latham interjected, "but I do want you to know you haven't lost all of your family. I'm the architect who had the plans for the expansion of your home. It turns out yesterday I was to review them with your father. I got there too late for the fight, but I did manage to get Ethan and Hannah out."

"I thank you for that, sir," Robert answered, eyes still shut. "You're Mr. Latham then."

Latham nodded. "You are welcome, Robert. Your brother and sister are in Barley Point, staying at the home of Mistress Helen Irving. She's an excellent hostess, as best I can tell. We managed to salvage some important valuables and commercial papers as well, which are also safe there. And Mistress Irving will by now be making arrangements to deliver

Ethan and Hannah to your aunt in Dunnansport, so we're doing what we can to facilitate that reunion."

Robert nodded. His eyes, now open, carried a glassy, far-off look. "Did you find any dead Udar at Hilltop Farm?"

"We did," Latham said. "Twelve of the bastards, in fact."

The cadet was motionless. Latham thought he almost detected a faint smile of satisfaction amid his tears.

"I'm sorry about your mother and father, Forling," Terhune said, turning to Will. "If it's any consolation, we found a dead Udar there as well."

"They lived a good life," Will replied in a monotone. "They raised seven of us. I was the youngest. Mom was so damned proud when I left for the Academy."

Then he went quiet, staring ahead blankly.

"All right, men," Terhune spoke up. "I know this has been the worst you've all seen. Many of you have suffered great losses. Inconceivable losses. It's war, and war is loss.

"But war is also vengeance. And while we suffer, and while our hearts are broken over what these savages have done to our families, our friends, our communities, our country, it's our responsibility now. We are the hand of that vengeance. Are we going to go gently at the bastards?"

"NO!" came the loud retort from over 300 men.

"Will we let them get away with what they've done?"

"NO!" again.

"We going to get justice for those they took from us? We going to bring hell on 'em?"

"YEAH!" they roared.

"Good. Let's ride."

. . .

133

NINETEEN

Cotter's Point – Morning (Second Day)

Adelaide steamed as close to the shore as she dared, with Patrick's crew taking soundings almost continuously to match their nautical charts. Running aground was not an option on this mission.

But the ship was not running at its full speed of twenty-two knots. Patrick knew he had to wait on *Yarmouth*, which had gotten underway a little earlier than planned yesterday and was steaming its way at a fourteen-knot clip. Patrick had *Adelaide* moving at twelve knots, which was a happy medium enabling him to lend sea cover to the expedition, should it find battle close to shore, in a reasonable time while also having *Yarmouth* soon on hand.

What he didn't like about this mission, although he commanded the bridge of the meanest, nastiest gunboat in Watkins Gulf, was the uncertainty. What was needed–though it wasn't worth risking the lives of the cavalrymen combing Dunnan's Claim for the Udar and their captives–was for someone to run down to Strongstead and find out what had happened there.

I wish we had that airship for this mission, Patrick thought. *The* Clyde. *That thing would be the perfect reconnaissance craft and you'd get a whole lot better signaling range using it as a relay up in the sky. Hell, you'd be able to relay signal communications for 50 miles with that thing on station. Can't help but wonder how useful it could be if we mounted a half-dozen chain guns on it and made it a weapons platform, too.*

In fact, Patrick and the Commodore had that exact conversation back in Dunnansport. The Commodore had agreed to run the request up the line all the way to the Admiralty in

Principia, though he couldn't promise they'd have the asset in theater by the time the mission reached its critical point. It wasn't even known where the airship was; someone would have to locate it and then requisition it for the Navy's use. By the time that could happen, well…you go to war with the weapons you have, and they didn't have the *Clyde*.

A familiar refrain in this man's navy, he thought.

Another thing Patrick didn't like was the inability to coordinate. *What we also don't have is communications*, he thought. *We've got signal flags and the heliograph mirrors, and we can deliver messages to ships or shore via line of sight. But what we need is teletext that's wireless to communicate over longer distances. I need to be able to talk to Yarmouth, and to Castamere and Louise. Maybe then we could keep this mission from cocking up.*

Again, it sure would be nice to have a damn airship to use for that purpose.

Soon, as he surveyed the shore with his field telescope, Patrick saw riders close to the shoreline ahead of *Adelaide's* approach. That was the Dunnansport contingent; he'd caught up to them. He slowed his speed to eight knots.

We're coming together, he thought. *Just need my landing craft in position and this fight will be on.*

Adelaide continued plying its way along the coast. Per his maps, Patrick estimated they were just forty miles east of Strongstead.

The battlefield is close, he thought. *I just hope these savages are dumb enough to get within my cannon range.*

. . .

TWENTY

From The Camp, moving southwest – Morning

(Second Day)

Charlotte had woken Sarah before dawn.

"Darling, please rise," she'd said sweetly. Sarah, feeling the aftereffects of whatever drug she'd been given in that *marwai* she'd had the night before, sluggishly opened her eyes.

"It's time to prepare you for the day," Charlotte said, kissing her on the cheek.

"Prepare me how?" Sarah mumbled as she struggled to lift her head off the cushion.

"I want to explain to you what will happen today," said Charlotte, "because it will be difficult and made worse if there are surprises."

"Surprises? What does that mean?"

"You will see something this morning that will upset you," Charlotte said. "I regret that you will see it. But I want you to know that this is the way, and it will have been necessary in order to save the larger whole. Do you understand?"

"No," Sarah said, though she had an inkling of what Charlotte might say from what her father had recently been telling her of the Udar. "I don't understand. What does that mean? Is somebody going to die? You're going to burn somebody in the fire? Is that it?"

"Such a perceptive girl," Charlotte complimented. "You are very intelligent; this is clear. I want you to be wise, for me. Can you do that? Do you believe that I want what's best for you?"

136

"I don't know," Sarah said. "I do think you don't want to hurt me. But I'm sorry–I don't trust you. I think you're doing what you think is right, but I think they've so traumatized you that you can't judge that anymore."

Charlotte's expression became much less loving. "You are in no position to question my *judgment*, girl. I am trying to help you, because I believe you are worth helping…"

"We are *all* worth helping!" Sarah was fully awake now. "None of this is all right! How can you tolerate it?"

"Because it is the will of Rapan'na," she answered sternly. "He is the *Var'asha*, and this is his *Anur*. You are under the mistaken belief you're still in a republic where all the great men and women get together and debate, and have tea and cakes while making their corrupt deals. Well, it isn't."

"Clearly not," said Sarah. "Though it sounds like maybe you're happy about that."

"You know nothing, girl," she said. "The Udar are many things, but they don't sell out their own."

Charlotte's voice rose. "You weren't at Strongstead. You didn't see the badly-engineered chain guns that became useless because the defective ammunition jammed them. You didn't hear the screams of the men made defenseless by rifles that barely even wounded the raptors which ate them alive. You couldn't feel the foundation of the citadel as it gave way when the Udar tunneled under the flawed construction by a politically-connected, crony contractor, and you couldn't smell the blood running in the corridors as the Udar *baz'ahi* warriors raced through the barracks building in a killing frenzy."

Sarah's eyes grew wide as Charlotte's voice became even more shrill.

"I know of these things, because I was there. I saw my husband slaughtered in front of my eyes because the government of the people he was there to protect cut corners and hung him out like beef to be aged, and I saw my son's throat cut as I pleaded for his life. And the people who allowed that horror call themselves the Peace Party." She spat.

"You may find these Udar to be savages, and what was done yesterday was savage," she said. "But that is their way, which I am learning to accept because unlike Ardenia, Udar has honor and conviction. And when Rapan'na swore to me that if I would learn the ways of the Udar and serve as *javeen* to his *Anur*, he would give my daughters a life, we made a lasting bargain. That is more care and respect than the *weasels* in Principia ever showed."

She clapped her hands and two Udar women entered the tent.

"You should consider these things, and your future," she fumed. "You have an opportunity to join a nation that will care for you, and cherish you. Or, you can throw your life away on a failed dream of a doomed, corrupt empire. It is your choice."

Then the women were on her, gagging her and once again binding her arms behind her back in the usual miserable folded position before dragging her out of the tent. As they returned her to her line, she saw that the women were now attaching the frightened, miserable captives' collars to a long pole.

Coffles. They were being transported. This was really happening now.

The captor women were coming through the lines with more *marwai*, and Sarah noted most of her fellow prisoners were accepting the liquid eagerly. They were becoming increasingly docile, and there was considerably less weeping and visible distress than she noticed the previous evening.

Sarah accepted her own dose of *marwai* when it came. And her head began spinning slightly again.

Is there really no rescue coming? she thought. *The most advanced, strongest country on the planet and we're inside our own borders and the cavalry isn't going to come? We just all get to die or be whores for these savages, brutalized and brainwashed like that poor naked woman? Was she right that Ardenia doesn't care?*

She considered what Charlotte had told her the night before. *In their millions*, she'd said. Were there really that many Udar warriors? She guessed there were. Nobody knew the population of Uris Udar; it wasn't exactly a modern state like Ardenia, so they didn't do a census and publish it. And the Udars had a huge country. It wasn't as big as Ardenia, to be sure, and they didn't have a lot of big cities–they didn't really have cities at all, as Sarah understood it, other than the capital at Qor Udar. What they had was lots and lots of *Anur* like this one, which were basically mobile army camps where the whole population spent their days training for exactly what they were doing now. That the entire Udar nation, or a big chunk of it, had just up and decided to invade Ardenia, with its locomotives, and cannons, and chain guns, and big ships and even bigger cities where everybody had a rifle or a pistol, was unexpected in the extreme.

Insane, she thought. *It can't actually be. How could they possibly win?*

On the other hand, if what Charlotte had said about Strongstead was true, the current situation was pretty scary. If what was supposed to be the greatest fortress in all the world was armed with defective weapons and not even built correctly, maybe her country's might was an illusion. She'd heard her father and uncle talking politics on a couple of occasions; neither man was a Peace Party member. Territorialists, she thought they were. Both had agreed the corruption of the Peace Party was a national scandal, and they'd been very concerned with the low priority the military was getting from Principia. That was something they both thought, as Army veterans living close to the frontier, was irresponsible bordering on treasonous. Sarah started to realize that her father's sudden decision to inform her about the ways of the Udar, which he had previously refused to do, might have had something to do with the increase in his political discussions with the other landholders of the territory.

The Dunnan's Claim land rush, after all, followed a successful war that happened before the Peace Party took power. The Stuarts and their neighbors had all moved down to this part of the country when the military was conducting regular patrols and actively rooting Udar out of Dunnan's Claim.

When Sarah was barely more than a toddler, though–in fact, she guessed it must have been when her mother was still pregnant with Ethan–the Party of Enterprise, which had been the majority party, had split basically in half between the Territorialists and the Prosperitans, and that had led the Peace Party to power in a landslide. Their platform was headed by a plan to roll back the money being spent on the military and invest it in the Ardenian people, they said, and they greatly reduced the number of military bases and enlistments. The military had been an institution that almost all boys joined at nineteen, but those recruitments had dried up to a large extent. Both the Army and Navy had also retired a large number of their officers, and particularly the ones who had fought in Dunnan's War; many of them were farmers now, having been given generous land grants in the South and West. The Peace Party had said they were going to complete all the fortresses in The Throat to go along with Strongstead, and they'd have an iron defense along the border, but only Strongstead had ever been finished. The four forts in The Throat were still, ten years later, only half complete and barely manned with soldiers.

And they've probably all fallen, she thought.

And while Udar attacks had been rare, they'd happened. Just last year there had been a raid on one of the farms in the hills south of Battleford, and an Udar war party had killed a farmer and one of his sons. The rest of the family had managed to escape, and the neighbors rode out with rifles to drive the Udar away. Then the Army showed up three days later and did a few patrols, assuring everybody it was all right.

But it wasn't, and the Udar probably knew there was this easy prize to be had in Dunnan's Claim. It was *provocative*. And now there was the disaster she'd gotten herself caught up in, with 380 women from all these farms they'd been promised would be safe, prosperous places. Instead of that promise being honored, they were being dragged off to slavery or worse.

And most of her family were dead.

She was starting to see why Charlotte had turned on Ardenia like she had, and honestly, if she had to be with these people for a month after what had happened to her, she could understand how maybe she'd adopt a similar attitude. *If you know you're not going home and you don't have anybody to go home to,* she thought, *then I guess you start thinking of the people you're with now as home.*

Not to mention what it would do to her if they kept giving her the *marwai,* which made her resolve progressively weaker with every sip. A month of constant doses of that drug every day and she'd probably be addicted.

That made her sad…and scared. It was as though she was starting to feel she'd lost her country and her identity.

Then there were the raptors. For a long time, centuries in fact, the raptors had been the reason Ardenia was only really settled in the northeast and down the east coast. Venturing into the interior for any length of time was more or less suicide because of those giant birds.

She'd seen one, or at least she'd seen a stuffed one. When she was a little girl her parents had taken the whole family to Trenory for the winter holiday, and while there they'd paid a visit to the Museum of the Wild, which had exhibits of every beast in the Ardenian wilderness. It was far too dangerous to carry a live raptor, of course, and thankfully they'd been more or less eradicated over the past hundred years, which opened up the interior and the Far West for settlement. The museum's stuffed raptor, and the skeleton of another raptor they'd had on display, were more than enough to show her all she needed to see of those winged monsters, though.

For the raptors were pure killing machines. They had a wingspan typically at least fifteen feet in length, with a torso half again as large as a man's. Their talons were two feet long with a razor-sharp ridge at the bottom which could tear skin like

141

paper with little effort. The raptors also had two-foot spines on a tail which protruded from their hind feathers; those spines emitted a liquid which had the effect of keeping blood from coagulating. If you were attacked by a raptor, it would rip you open with its talons and then inject you with that poison to insure you'd bleed to death.

Then came the worst part. The raptor's beak wasn't a mouth like a normal bird. Instead it was more like a pipe with curved teeth on the end. It would insert its beak into the hole it made in you with its talon, after it injected you to make sure your blood would flow, and then it would just suck you completely dry. People or animals who'd been killed by raptors were left as nothing but a loose bag of bones. There might not be a worse way to go in all the world.

And that was how her brother Matthew had likely gone.

Charlotte said the Udar had somehow figured out how to use these demons as weapons. That made Sarah shudder. A month ago they'd been at Strongstead; with so much time since then the raptors could be almost anywhere right now. They could be in Trenory. Or Port William. They could even be attacking Principia. Sarah considered that and found it awfully ironic. She'd never been to Principia, and maybe raptors would get there before she could.

It wasn't the end of the world, though, she knew. Ardenians had eradicated the raptors, at least within their borders, through technology. Sarah knew the story of Arthur Thorne, the man most credited with ending the threat of the raptors in Ardenia. Six decades ago explorers had picked their way through to the Great Mountain Lake where Alvedorne currently sat, and reported back that the area was rich in silver, iron, coal, something called bauxite and Blood Oak timber, all highly prized commodities. That area had to be settled, and a locomotive line laid in. But to do any of that, the raptors which dominated the area had to be eliminated.

Thorne, a retired general in the Army hired by the locomotive company, found a brilliant way to get the job done.

He mounted several of the then newly-invented chain guns on train cars, and used those trains as a base while the railroad workers laid the tracks. The workers would come out and lay tracks, and the locomotive would inch along behind them as they were laid. When the raptors came, the workers would jump aboard the armored locomotive cars and wait while Thorne's chain gunners would open up on the birds as they swooped in. They got very, very good at shooting raptors and killed them hundreds at a time.

And what was interesting was that an evolutionary feature of the birds really aided in killing them off. Raptors had two fleshy pads hanging near the bases of their tails, and when they got excited they'd shake themselves to make those pads slap against their bodies, producing a loud *thump-thump-thump* sound. That was the signal for a raptor feeding frenzy, and the birds would come from miles and miles around when they heard it.

But from a distance, that noise was a lot like the noise a chain gun made when it was firing. So when Thorne's guns would open up on a few raptors with a *thump-thump-thump* sound as they started shooting, by the time they were done they'd killed hundreds of them, or in one day fifty-seven years ago, more than 2,000. The raptors were accustomed to descending on large herds or horses or cattle, or collections of people; but with Thorne's men and their chain guns, it was the avian attackers who were suddenly the prey.

And Thorne's men knew that the massive birds were more than just predators that had to be destroyed. They knew what they had were probably the most valuable trophies on earth. So, since they were at the end of a rail line they brought up locomotives to come to the scene where the dead raptors lay, and they loaded the birds onto flatcars and brought them back closer to civilization. The city of Perseverance, which now had close to a million people, grew up largely on the raptor trade. It was where the locomotives would deposit the raptors to be stuffed and mounted, and then sold to rich people all over the country for thousands of decirans each. Thorne more than financed his operation selling stuffed raptors. He bought the entire rail line and financed its completion, and ended up founding the unbelievably rich city of Alvedorne, which at this point was apparently almost as prosperous as Principia, though only about a third as big.

At the time of his death Thorne was the richest man who ever lived, and the Thornes of Alvedorne were still probably the wealthiest family in the whole country.

Sarah had seen pictures of their estate along the shore of the Great Mountain Lake. It was the most beautiful thing she'd ever seen. When she was a child, she dreamed about living there.

Nothing like that is in my future now, she lamented silently.

The raptors could be wiped out, and probably would be, if they tried to attack a populated area, Sarah figured. That was true only if the Ardenians were ready, though; if they weren't, a whole bunch of people would die. And she had no way to warn anybody about it, something that was *killing* her.

Not that it ought to come down to me, she thought. *Maybe if they'd done a better job of having the army ready, the raptors would have never gotten to Strongstead, or maybe Matthew and the garrison would have been able to defeat them.*

Her oldest brother was dead because of some crappy politicians in Principia who didn't give him the support he needed while he was standing at the border defending the country. Wasn't that something?

She wasn't going to join the Peace Party if she did make it home and became a full citizen. That was for sure. In fact, she would make it her mission in life to see them permanently out of power.

The camp was a whirlwind of activity as the sun poked out of the horizon to the east. Tents were being broken down, packs being rigged to tent poles which were then attached to saddles to be dragged behind. Captured horses were being tied together, cattle herded, horses mounted and the prisoners made to get up.

Before the *Anur* broke camp, though, there was an item of business to take care of that Sarah had been warned about. A captive woman had attempted to flee overnight and had been caught by one of the Udars. She was brought to kneel by the large bonfire at the northern edge of the camp, with women holding ropes attached to either side of her collar. Rapan'na emerged and walked near to the fire.

"*Abascat!*" he called. "*Abascat, Ur'akeen! Daheyu at'lo savalyay!*"

A cascade of whoops came from the members of the *Anur.*

"*Besoul, mavat at'lo savalyay!*"

Louder, more intense whoops.

"*Kaw'at besoul, mavat at'lo savalyay!*"

"*Aaaawhalat!*" screamed the Udar.

"*MAWANI MAVAT AT'LO SAVALYAY! UR'AKEEN, SO'AS AZMERI!*" howled Rapan'na.

The two women began dragging the captive forward. She struggled, but it was clear she hadn't the strength to resist them. Forward she went, into the fire.

And she was soon engulfed by the flames. Within seconds, she was dead.

Sarah looked around among her fellow captives and saw complete terror on every face. Many looked away; some couldn't.

The captors then dragged their prisoners to their feet by raising the poles their collars were attached to. The Udar broke camp, and the procession headed southwest toward Strongstead. Scouts were sent in each direction.

...

145

TWENTY ONE

On the Small Rise – Noon (Second Day)

Once again Will and Robert were together in a small group of riders, this time as part of a detachment of seven sent as advance scouts. Their orders from Terhune were to make visual contact with the enemy, but not to close and destroy. They were to avoid notice if possible.

After three hours of nothing south of the rendezvous, though, it turned out that avoiding notice was not possible. The seven had come upon what had clearly been the enemy's camp. Hoofprints were everywhere, as was refuse, and the remnants of small campfires and a very active bonfire were unmistakable.

"By the Saints!" said Will, in the first real show of any inflection in his voice since he'd heard about his parents. "That's a dead body in the fire."

"Human sacrifice," Robert agreed. "It's what they do. Wonder if it's someone we know."

"Really, Rob?" said Will.

"I'm just saying. This is personal. These are our friends, neighbors, relatives. We probably do know that poor woman. Or we did."

"We're close," Will said. "It's not a good idea to be here on our own. We should report back to the command line."

But just then one of their number, an enlisted man from Barley Point named Athcart, grunted in pain. He was struck through the stomach by an arrow. "Shit!" Athcart said, and then he slumped off his horse.

"Scatter, men!" ordered Will. "Find that savage and mow him down!"

It was Robert who encountered the Udar first. He'd taken a sniping position behind a pile of rocks about fifty yards away from the bonfire, but the Udar was dismounted, and Robert spotted him as he rode past to the left. He wheeled his horse around and closed on the man, his Thurman at dead aim. And at fifteen yards Robert shot the Udar in the throat.

He dismounted, and approached the wounded sniper, slowly. The Udar attempted to crawl away on his back, clutching his hemorrhaging neck with one hand, an *Izwei* in the other.

"Oh, no," Robert said. "Where are you going? You are not running away from me."

Will and two other members of the team rode up from the man's other side.

"You just shot my friend there," Robert said. "Your people killed my parents and my sister. For all I know you might have gotten my brother and my other sister too."

"Sausoway," the Udar stammered. *"Ibebleen."*

"Do you think I'm going to let you crawl away from me, you sodding animal? *Do you think that?*"

"Just finish him, Rob," said Will.

"Not so fast," Robert said, as the Udar feebly waved his *Izwei* in Robert's direction.

He glared down at the Udar. "My name is Robert Stuart. Son of George Stuart, hero of Dunnan's War. He took twelve of you bastards with him when he died. And *I'm going to send you with them.*"

Slowly, Robert drew his sword. The Udar attempted to stand, but lacked the strength.

"This is going to hurt," Robert said, as he slashed at the Udar's right leg. A wound opened with a torrent of blood.

"Rob, finish him," Will said. "You can't torture him all day. We have work to do. We have to report back to command."

"I'm not done. He's going to *feel it* before he goes."

"Do it, Rob," said another of the riders. "Finish him."

"You want me to finish him? I'll finish him." And Rob then drove the tip of his sword into the man's crotch, ripping to his stomach.

The Udar went limp almost immediately.

"Go to hell, you fucker," Rob said.

The riders returned at speed to the command line to make their report. Athcart attempted to ride with the team, but fell off his horse within half a mile. When Will doubled back to assist him, he was dead.

. . .

TWENTY TWO

Principia – Afternoon (Second Day)

Cross had spent a busy day at the headquarters of the Airbound Corporation, with personnel interviews, papers to sign, follow-up meetings and letters and memoranda shuttling back and forth via courier. All the while, though, he was frankly amazed at the speed and smoothness of the transition of his company from a small passenger airship line to…whatever it was that Airbound was becoming. It felt as though some invisible arm was moving pieces around to clear his path. Of course, he was unspooling in a day what should have taken three months.

Around lunchtime Gresham came back to the office after his meeting with Pleasance, the man from Foreman Technologies, who was supervising the corporate merger. He plopped down in one of Cross' visitor chairs. "You interested in going somewhere for a tipple and a luncheon?" he asked in a friendlier voice than he'd offered Cross at any time in the past three months.

"I can't," came the response. "I need to get through this stack before I get out of here tonight. My train's leaving for the sunny south and a hail of arrows and spears from half-naked savages in the morning. If you're thirsty, by all means help yourself."

Gresham did, and then returned to his seat.

"Well," he said, "I can't really say all this worked out like I would have wanted. But what I can say is I can live with Foreman."

"Good," Cross said, scribbling his signature on yet another document. "I'm coming across a new regret every five minutes as I go through all this, but at the end of the day I think this is a good outcome."

"The things we coulda done," Gresham held up his glass, and then took a sip of his whisky.

"I think you're going to do all right in Belgarden," Cross said, giving Gresham a friendly look. "It's a nice town. The west side is a little like the Elkstrand."

"I love the possibilities with these engines," Gresham said. "You're going to see–the whole concept of how we're going to do the burners is going to change. Essentially what Foreman's going to do is run a liquid fuel they're going to refine from coal through one engine that will make four blast furnaces to inflate the envelopes with hot air, so the altitude will double. And the propellers are going to be a lot bigger and turn three times as fast with these new engines. The ships are going to do 80 or 90 miles an hour when they're refitted."

"Makes you wish we'd pursued this tech earlier," Cross said wistfully.

"I know," Gresham said. He took another swallow of the whisky.

"Anyway, it's exciting stuff. And the work was always what turned my crank."

"Yeah it did, buddy," Cross said. "I'm happy you're happy."

"So what about you, huh?" Gresham changed the subject. "Gonna be a big Army hero?"

"You know me," Cross said. "Born glory hound. I can't help myself."

"I would think an airship would be a pretty safe place in a war against the Udar," Gresham assured him. "I mean, what are they gonna do, shoot an arrow at you when you're a thousand feet up?"

"I'm a little more worried about what happens when I'm on the ground," Cross said, "but that was more or less my thinking. We go down there, kick some savage asses and make Ardenia safe for civilization again, and then I get to go back to being Sebastian Cross, The Great National Hero. Who knows what happens from there."

"Maybe politics," Gresham said, taking another pull from his glass.

Cross glanced at him. Then he shrugged.

"Vote Peace Party, one and all," Gresham said, giving the two-fingered victory sign as he finished his drink. Then he stood, and extended his hand. "Seriously, though, it has been a pleasure working with you. Ups, downs and everything else. You're a gentleman and an aviator, sir."

Cross stood and returned the handshake. "You take care of yourself, Winford. And if you need anything, ever, you just say so."

Cross' inner self felt a good deal less warmly toward Gresham than he let on, but that's the way he wanted it. *At some point he'll do me a favor*, Cross thought. *And I bet I'll need it, no matter what I think of him.*

Never burn a bridge. Burned bridges are useless, even if the people they lead to are also useless. Which Winford, despite some of his questionable choices, was not.

A bit later, he'd finally plowed through his stack of documents, and said goodbye to some of the employees and "See you down south" to others. His last day as CEO of Airbound Corporation had come to a close. Cross hadn't had the slightest opportunity to let his "wolfpack," as he called them– the cadre of boozehounds, party girls and other assorted swells he usually made the rounds of the Elkstrand playpens with in his off-hours–know of his circumstances and that this was his last night in town for the foreseeable future, and he was about to summon a courier to deliver a message or two to circulate that word.

151

He never got the chance, though, because as he was tidying his desk and stacking his papers for what remained of the secretarial staff to process the next morning as Foreman's wrap-up team came in to assume control, he heard a rap on his office door.

"We don't seem quite so busy in here," a voice Cross recognized said.

And when he looked up, he saw he was in the presence of the mighty Preston Cross VII, the very man he'd been avoiding for the past three months. His father was resplendent in a gray felt derby hat and had a fur jacket draped over an arm, his gray woolen suit immaculately tailored from his collar down to his oxford shoes – an appearance nearly the opposite of Sebastian's rumpled collarless shirt with no tie under a pair of suspenders.

"Hello, Papa," he sighed. "What brings you down from paradise?"

"You do, boy," said the old man. "Are you out of business yet?"

Sebastian gave his father an ugly look.

"Relax," Preston said. "I'm just giving you the rear. Gregg has told me all about your troubles, and I want you to know that I understand what you've done and I respect it. You are a man of honor, and for that I'm proud of you."

That earned his father a different reaction. "I appreciate that, Papa. I really do."

"Are you occupied at present?" Preston asked. "Care to take a walk?"

That stopped him in his tracks a bit, as Sebastian couldn't remember the last time he and his father had a low-key interpersonal encounter. It would have had to have been before Mother died, he thought, and that was when he was still playing for the Elks. Back then his father had been his biggest fan and his worst critic, and rugby was all the old man would talk about.

But then came Airbound, and Preston Cross VII was a lot more critic than fan of that enterprise. The effect therein was a downward spiral in their relationship, and most of the communication between the two generally came via Sebastian's older brother Preston VI, who ran a brokerage firm that traded on the Havener exchange a few blocks away from Airbound's offices. Press, as everybody called him, was the family workaholic and infinitely more successful than his younger brother, and he was also married to a plain, and dull, mega-wealthy heiress from Winterstead he'd met in business school. Press had supplied his father with four grandchildren and a fifth on the way, which solidified the old man's disapproval of Sebastian's more hedonistic and less family-oriented social life.

For someone who had so prized his ability to keep his interpersonal relationships on a friendly level, the estrangement with his father had been a source of deep angst for Sebastian. And yet here was all that strife, that stress, melting away before his eyes.

"A walk sounds all right, Papa," Sebastian said, fighting back a bout of emotion. "I'll get my coat."

· · ·

TWENTY THREE

Watkins Gulf – Noon (Second Day)

Patrick ran into an excellent stroke of luck just after dawn as *Adelaide* surged ahead of the cavalry's sweep west in search of the Udar camp. Namely, his crew spotted a pair of telltale sails only a couple of miles off the coast as *Adelaide* steamed west. He ordered a detour to the port side to investigate and shortly came within sight of an Udar raiding sloop.

"Sons of bitches out looking for a coastal packet to or from Strongstead," said Rawer at Patrick's side on the bridge. "We know what to do."

"We do," said Patrick, "but I think we want some prisoners here. Let's not just stand off and sink this one–we'll see if we can get in close and grab a few of the bastards."

Rawer scowled – to the *Adelaide*'s First Mate there was only one good kind of Udar, and that was the dead kind, but he knew an order when he heard one.

"Aye, commander."

Adelaide left the coast for the bluer water of Watkins Gulf, and in under an hour was bearing down on the fleeing Udar. The frigate hailed the sloop by way of its steam whistle, but the hail was ignored.

"Put a shot across the bow," Patrick ordered. The pivot gun on the port side carried out that directive in short order.

The sloop continued its course, heading south away from the coastline. *Adelaide* quickly closed the distance between the two vessels.

"Commander, should we just steam over the top?" asked Rawer.

"Yes. Make it so," said Patrick. "They've had their opportunities, and I'd just as soon not show the enemy a fireball on the horizon."

A few seconds later, the *Adelaide*'s crew could feel the crunch of the larger ship's iron hull shattering the Udar vessel's wooden frame. Some two dozen Udar sailors jettisoned haphazardly away from their wrecked sloop, splashing into Watkins Gulf and furiously attempting to swim away from *Adelaide*.

"Lasso a few of 'em!" Rawer ordered to the *Adelaide*'s crew. "Might as well go fishin' this mornin'."

What followed was a facsimile of sport, as the Ardenian sailors took their turns attempting to loop their hemp ropes over the escaping Udar swimmers – the ropes commonly landed in position to find purchase, but mostly the Udar in their clutches craftily made escapes before those ropes could be pulled taut.

As the sportfishing commenced, Patrick nodded to Ensign Joseph Broadham, who had joined the command team on the bridge. Though fresh out of the naval academy at Wellhurst, Broadham was a great catch as the *Adelaide's* Udar translator. His mother had been captured by the Udar at the beginning of Dunnan's War and spent six months as a prisoner of a particularly nasty *Anur* who made their *Afan'di*, or home-grounds, along the Watkins Gulf coast to the south of where Strongstead currently stood. She was rescued when a naval armada, plying the coast, put ashore a thousand Marines for an amphibious assault. That was the Battle of Bak Jayen, and it was one of the bloodier encounters of Dunnan's War. Only half the Marines made it back to the landing ships, but some 20,000 Udar lay dead under their withering cannon, chain gun and rifle fire. Bak Jayen was heralded as a grand victory despite its cost – especially given the rescue of forty-three Ardenian women held captive in that tent city.

That included Broadham's mother, a professor at the women's finishing school in Newmarket who'd been captured in a pirate raid befalling a ship she'd been on as it traveled to

155

Port William. An expert linguist, in her six months of captivity she'd mastered the Udar language. It took several months of mental and emotional recovery after her rescue, as the shame of her having objected to being taken away from the *Anur* left a deep psychological scar, but once she'd regained her faculties Georgia Broadham wrote the definitive treatise on spoken Udar. She then took a position at the Admiralty in Principia as an instructor to naval officers as to the enemy's language and customs. Her book describing her experiences as a captive of the Udar and her rescue and road to recovery was considered one of Ardenia's greatest literary masterpieces.

Having the son of the great linguist as his ship's translator was a significant asset in Patrick's mind. From having served several years in Watkins Gulf, though, his own knowledge of the enemy was considerable. So far, the opportunity to interrogate Udar aboard *Adelaide* had yet to yield much intelligence value; the pirates they'd captured rarely knew anything interesting outside of the typical "see prize, take prize" directives. In Patrick's experience these people weren't very complicated.

But today felt different. Today there were Udar sea-raiders operating in close proximity to war parties pillaging farms in Dunnan's Claim.

This was unusual. The common understanding was that the Udar operated independently on land from on the water. Put another way, there were land-based *Anur* which spat out war parties to hunt and raid, and there were sea-based *Anur* who, though they originated from harbors on the coasts, operated with galleys as mother ships and used sloops like the one *Adelaide* had just crushed under its hull to conduct pirate raids. If there was coordination between the two, it was evidence of a change of some kind.

That's why the prisoners were worth having, even though Udar at close quarters in any context rightly made Patrick uncomfortable. These were superb warriors with impressive skill in hand-to-hand combat–something the crew of *Adelaide* had not been selected for. His sailors were able seamen, boilermakers, navigators, heliograph operators, gunners, and the like; other than his Marines, of which he had only twenty-two thanks to his having detached a dozen to the Dunnansport expedition, his crew couldn't be expected to take on Udar with fists or knives. If combat broke out on the deck of *Adelaide*, there would be casualties–and he couldn't afford them.

Accordingly, the prisoners were brought aboard one by one, and marched at gunpoint into the ship's brig where they were manacled and gagged, and then carefully locked in the cells. The first two hauled aboard were a burly middle-aged warrior and a quite comely female who couldn't have been a day older than eighteen. The sailors continued their efforts, taunted by the swimming survivors of the wrecked sloop. Several more were ultimately lassoed; more chose drowning in the choppy waters of Watkins Gulf as they attempted to swim away from *Adelaide*.

Broadham translated the utterances of the prisoners as they came aboard, mostly to laughter and applause from the *Adelaide*'s crew. If anything was true of Udar warriors, it was that they ranked among the most verbose and rhetorically gifted of the world's braggarts and taunts.

"He says you should take your little worm out of your dungarees and put it in the water," Broadham informed one crewmember hauling the first Udar aboard. "He says you might catch a minnow for your dinner in that way." Laughter erupted.

When the man was spilled onto the deck and forced to his knees at riflepoint, he continued his rant. "Now he says you'll have to line up neatly," Broadham translated. "He can only sodomize you one at a time."

"Get that savage belowdecks," an irritated Patrick ordered. "I want to know everything he knows."

He retired from the bridge, leaving Rawer in charge of the fishing operation. Patrick did linger for a minute as the woman was hauled aboard, particularly when, rather than shriek in Udar, in the Civil Tongue she thanked her captors for saving

157

her life. He ordered that she be brought to his ready room; he'd interrogate her himself later.

Adjacent to the cells of the ship's brig, on *Adelaide*'s mezzanine deck, was an interrogation chamber with a two-way mirror opening to an observation room. Patrick and two of his officers took seats in the latter, while Broadham readied himself to query the powerfully-built Udar male captive.

Three *Adelaide* sailors dragged the man into the interrogation chamber. He was dressed in the usual fashion of an Udar pirate, which is to say he had very little on: a loincloth and a pair of ankle-length boots of some sort of animal skin were the extent of his uniform. Bound at the wrists, he was kept docile by two pistols held to his head courtesy of a pair of the crew members. The man sat in a chair, glaring furiously at his guards.

"Aaliu," Broadham greeted him cheerily.

The man shot a vicious look in the ensign's direction, and told him something apparently unpleasant in the extreme. Broadham blanched a bit.

...

The interrogation was clearly going to take some time, and after a few minutes Patrick's irritation with the combative and uncooperative Udar warrior overcame him so he left Broadham to his work. The commander returned to the bridge as *Adelaide* steamed back to the coastline. Normally he would prioritize the sinking of the Udar galley this sloop was attached to, as doing so would eliminate a pirate threat, but sadly, today there were higher priorities.

Upon returning to their former position near the coast a couple of hours later, the naval charts indicated that *Adelaide* was forty-two miles east of Strongstead. Somewhere between here and there they were bound to run across the enemy. The Udar had to have come to Dunnan's Claim via the coast, because otherwise the high mountains of the Rogers Range would serve as a barrier to their escape home. If their route of egress wasn't along the coast through Strongstead, it would have to be considerably further to the west, through the narrow mountain pass of The Throat, which amounted to a gauntlet of four half-constructed Ardenian fortresses along the way. And had they come through The Throat, it was more likely the farms to the south and west of Trenory would have been the first ones hit. The first attacks came from well east of there, though. The Udar had either come by sea–and if they had, how did they have horses in the numbers they reportedly did?–or through Strongstead.

He had a hard time believing the latter possibility. How could Strongstead have fallen? The weapons and equipment the Udar had couldn't possibly have overcome its cannons, chain guns and high walls. What was more, the base at Barley Point was still communicating with the citadel via teletext, so obviously the garrison was still extant.

Patrick meant to put the Strongstead mystery to rest, even if it meant breaking off from the coastal escort for a few hours to lay eyes on the citadel, and he'd tasked Broadham with getting what information was possible on that issue from the prisoners as he interrogated them.

Broadham came to the bridge after about an hour of his queries to make his report.

"How's your savage, Joey?" asked Patrick.

"A rare specimen, Commander," said Broadham. "Has nothing to say and lots of words to say it."

"He gave you nothing?"

"A few choice references to my manhood and the usual boasting. He does demand you match daggers with him in single combat."

"Of course he does," Patrick said. "They always do."

Single combat was an Udar specialty. In a society essentially of hunter-gatherers made up of *Anura*, which were essentially mobile communal tent villages ranging in population from a couple of hundred to as many as thirty thousand or more, there was nearly constant internecine warfare. But the Udar

159

avoided killing each other off in large numbers, largely through the practice of *Kawes'kin*, or challenge. Once a battle between *Anura* had been joined and warriors had died on both sides, one *Var'asha* would declare *Kawes'kin* to the other and the battle would pause upon which time the two headmen would agree on champions and stakes. *Kawes'kin* was a kind of trial by combat– whatever the object of the battle was would be put on the table and the outcome of the combat between champions, usually equipped with *Izwei* daggers, would determine which side would get what. Sometimes the stakes would be safe passage or grazing rights on disputed land, sometimes they would involve the exchange of desired captives or slaves, sometimes horses or cattle would be paid.

Udar single combat was always to the death. It was serious business, and the Udar were therefore quite frighteningly good at it.

The first prisoner hauled aboard *Adelaide,* the one with all the combative insults and sexual references, had several iron rings circling his left wrist, which Patrick knew meant he'd survived multiple bouts of *Kawes'kin* combat.

But there would be no *Kawes'kin* aboard *Adelaide*. This was a naval vessel, not a damned savage horde.

"He also says that refusing his challenge marks us all as cowards and reflects the dishonor of the Ardenian race," Broadham added. "Didn't really want to talk about anything else."

"I could give a shit," Patrick said. "Nothing about the disposition of forces? Coordination with the war parties in Dunnan's Claim? Strongstead?"

"All I got for my trouble was indignity and vituperation when I broached those subjects," Broadham shrugged.

"Fine. He's the strong, silent type. Any of the others have anything to add?"

"Not so far."

"All right, then. Keep at them, standard interrogation protocol. But first we'll see if our special guest is more cooperative. Lieutenant Commander Rawer, you have the conn. Keep us on a heading of two-nine-zero, following the coastline as closely as safety allows. And look out for land forces, ours or theirs."

"Aye, sir," said the First Mate.

Patrick took Broadham with him to the ready room, where he found the female Udar tied to a chair with a pair of marines watching over her from opposite sides of the small chamber.

"Hello there," he greeted her. "My name is Commander Baker. You are aboard the Ardenian naval frigate *Adelaide*. Welcome."

"My name is Edyene," the prisoner responded. "Thank you for...what is word...rescue me."

"We're delighted to have you, dear," Patrick beamed courteously, sitting across the small conference table from the prisoner. "As you might imagine, I do have some questions I'd like answered before we determine what to do with you. If you cooperate, we do have some options to offer you..."

"I help you," she said, her brilliant blue eyes wide. Patrick noticed she was truly an exotic specimen of Udar beauty. Female Udar were very much a mixed bag, the opposite of the strikingly similar facial and physical characteristics shown by their male counterparts. That meant you'd sometimes see some very beautiful women among those you ran across, as well as others who looked every bit the part of half-starved savages.

Edyene was the former. She wore britches of some kind of animal skin and a roll of necklaces made from various media–sea shells, shark teeth, and small stones among them–and nothing else other than the blanket draped over her shoulders. Her hair wasn't in the typical close-cropped or shaven style of Udar females; it had grown out into something that resembled the bob style currently in fashion in Port Excelsior and

161

Newmarket. And while the sun and sea air had made their mark on her, giving her a very tanned complexion from head to toe, she didn't have the leathery skin of most Udar Patrick had made acquaintances with while doing battle in Watkins Gulf.

"You know Udar coming for war, yes?" she began.

"We know there are war parties taking captives and plunder in Dunnan's Claim," Patrick responded.

"Is more. Ur'akeen send vision to Ubel'la," she continued. *"Enafan'di* no more."

That was significant. Ubel'la was the current *sa'halet*, or king, of Uris Udar. But he was more than that; his position also conferred upon him the function of high priest to the Udar god Ur'akeen, and in Udar tradition that meant the god communicated with him by means of dreams and visions.

And *Enafan'di* was the only favor the Udar had ever done for Ardenia. It was a religious tradition holding the force of law among the Udar which held that none of their warriors should ever die a peaceful death outside of his *Afan'di*. Functionally, that meant while the Udar more or less constantly raided Ardenia when they could in search of slaves and plunder, they very studiously avoided conquering and occupying territory and they always went home. If *Enafan'di* was to be lifted and the Udar were making war, what had happened in Dunnan's Claim was the beginning of something much worse.

It was time to solve the mystery that had bothered him since the current crisis began.

"Before you go any further," he asked her," can you tell me what happened to Strongstead?"

"Udar have your Strongstead," she said. "Thirty moons ago."

"How?" Patrick asked.

"Vitau'hi," she responded, meaning the raptors no Ardenian had seen live in decades. "They come at night and kill soldiers on walls. Warriors come from tunnel, under. Kill rest."

"Udar are using *vitau'hi*?" he asked incredulously.

Edyene nodded. "They train. Since I was little girl. Now there are thousands, like warriors. They kill you, not us. More training all the time."

"You were there when Strongstead fell?"

She nodded again.

"How is it the citadel is still communicating with Ardenia?" he asked.

"They keep soldiers to work machine, act like no Udar there."

"Shit!" Patrick banged his fist on the table. "How many Udar are at Strongstead? How many further into Ardenia?"

"More than can count," she responded. "Is war. All *Anur* moving. Through citadel, through *lepon'hin*, over water." *Lepon'hin* was the Udar name for The Throat.

That meant the Udar were bringing virtually their entire country to war, and the raiders in Dunnan's Claim were a mere taste of what was coming. Worse, those raiders were retreating and sucking in the small Ardenian responding force, who could well be heading into a trap.

"Where are the *vitau'hi*?" Patrick asked. *If they hit Strongstead a month ago, they could be anywhere, ready to wreak havoc on our people.*

"I no know. They attack soldiers, feed on bodies at citadel, then fly off over mountains."

"Where is the main body of the Udar force?"

"Be march from Strongstead now," she said. "Along coast to big river." That meant the Tweade.

"And the boat you came from? What is your home?"

163

"*Afan'di* of Bak Jayen," she responded. Patrick saw Broadham stiffen, as that was the place his mother had been held captive, and Edyene had come from the people who took her.

"What about your friend we brought aboard just before you joined us? What can you tell us about him?"

"He no friend," she said, vigorously shaking her head. "He bad man. Danger."

"Is that so?" Patrick asked. "Who is he, then?"

"Ago'an," she answered. "He *Var'asha* of Bak Jayen. Older brother of Ubel'la."

This was a truly fascinating development. Among the 20,000 Udar casualties of the Battle of Bak Jayen had been the enemy's *Var'asha*, or headman, and when he was taken out by a Marine sniper during the battle, things had fallen apart very quickly for the Udar. There was an Udar custom which held that an *Anur* could not conduct operations beyond the day-to-day variety without its commander, and most of the time, given the usually-chaotic succession plans those mobile villages had in the event of their headman's death, it would take some time for a new commander to be chosen. There would be a series of physical measurements taken among eligible male candidates, and several tests of athletic and martial performance given among the members of the *Anur*. A successful candidate for the status of *Var'asha* was one who could meet a set of highly rigorous standards; the larger the *Anur*, the more difficult those standards were.

So far as Patrick knew, the Udar king had been from the capitol, not far up the coast along Watkins Gulf. So if his older brother was the headman at Bak Jayen now, that had meant he'd been sent all the way from Qur Udar to take command of these pirates.

And with his loss, they might have neutralized a significant pirate force, at least for a while. Perhaps.

"And how long has Ago'an been the headman of your *Anur*?"

"Two hundred moons," she said.

Six and a half months or so, he thought. That was about the time he'd started noticing a ramp-down in Udar activity in Watkins Gulf. He wanted some more information on that.

"Was he the one who stopped the pirate attacks for the last six months?"

She nodded. "Said must come all at once, not few, few, few. Hit harder, more Udar."

"So a concentrated attack."

She nodded again. Patrick knew Udar strategy was all of a sudden far more advanced than it had been.

"Who was Var'asha before him?"

"Lawa'ya," she said. "From since big battle. He old and die. Ubel'la send Ago'an to be *Var'asha* after. Two warriors from Anur say no, they *Var'asha*. Ago'an kill."

Sounds like fun times, Patrick thought. *What bloodthirsty savages these people are.*

"So how many motherships are out here?"

She shook her head.

"Not here," she said. "South. They come soon."

"Then what are you doing here?"

"We scout," she said.

"With Ago'an on the boat? They wanted to risk that? Us taking him?"

"He talk with Udar on shore," she said. "We pick him up, take him back to army."

165

That proved the coordination Patrick had suspected all day. Miss Edyene had been a quite helpful little prisoner.

He looked at Broadham and the two shared a knowing glance. Broadham could now re-interrogate the Udar headman by letting him know his identity wasn't a secret, and that might lead to something more in the way of information from the so-far-uncooperative brute.

"And why do you say he's a bad man?" Patrick asked.

"He kill women," she said. "He enjoy."

"As in, he murders them? With a knife?"

She nodded. "Make *Anur* watch. Punish for anything. He smile."

"He killed someone you were close to? Is that it?"

She nodded. "Mother," she said. "She *javeen*." Tears began flowing from her eyes, which was striking in itself. Udar *never* cried.

"All right," Patrick sighed. "And you're telling me all of this why?"

"I want be you," she said.

"I don't understand. You want to be me?"

"Come with you. Be Ardenia."

"You're defecting? Is that it?"

She tilted her head. She didn't understand the word.

"You want to live in Ardenia? As an Ardenian?"

Edyene smiled. She nodded. "I through with Udar life. Ardenia better. If my words help you win war I join you?"

"Well, this is a hell of a time to want that," he exhaled.

Edyene's wish wasn't one that would be easily granted. Ardenia had some experience with Udar immigrants, and at one time there were more than a few of them in the country's western areas. A century before, however, an Udar immigrant named Kose'ya, who had adopted the Ardenian name Cosey Southman as a day laborer in the then-frontier town of Trenory, led an uprising of Udar immigrants all over Ardenia. Blood ran in the streets through Ardenian cities as Udar laborers and domestics turned on their employers and neighbors, and for two weeks terror reigned throughout the country. The Udar even set fire to the Societam, the Ardenian parliament building in Principia, though the blaze had been extinguished before it could fully engulf the seat of the legislature. At that point the army was called out to exterminate all Udar in the country – an emergency measure which had been debated as either an atrocity or a necessary evil ever since.

But from then on Udar were not permitted to immigrate to Ardenia. They had tried, to be sure, and there was a mechanism to facilitate Udar who wanted out of their country: if an Udar asked for refuge, they'd be taken to Adams Island to work in the coal mines as an indenture to pay for their travel across the Great Sea, whereby they could then settle in Leria, Thosia, Taravel or one of the other countries in the vast archipelago on the other side of the ocean.

That was probably the best anybody could do for Edyene. *But what a waste!* Patrick thought. She was a staggering beauty. He could tell Broadham, who was about her age, heartily agreed.

"Your mother was a *javeen*," Broadham pressed. "Was she Ardenian? She was captured and brought to your *Anur*?"

Edyene nodded.

"What was your mother's name?"

"Ann," she answered. "Ann Ludlow. She say she from May-den-stead."

Maidenstead was the southernmost city in Ardenia, an equatorial port on the Charles Peninsula which jutted southward at the far eastern end of Watkins Gulf. In years past the Udar had been very bold in attacking not just shipping to and from that city of 100,000; at times they'd actually come ashore there to take women as slaves.

Patrick shook his head at the brutality. *I'm sorry for what they did to you, Mrs. Ludlow,* he thought. *And I'm sorry the Navy allowed it.*

Her heritage meant Edyene was half Ardenian, though, which made her prospects for immigration a little different. Legally anyone who was half Ardenian or more was eligible for Ardenian residency, so they could put Edyene together with a judge-advocate when they next made port and, with a letter of recommendation from Patrick, she stood a fighting chance of being allowed to immigrate.

Another effect of that information was that Patrick now could charge Ago'an with murder under the Ardenian Naval Code and, after a brief shipboard trial, hang him from the observation tower.

Which he desperately wanted to do.

He doubted that having Broadham relay that desire to the man when he sat back down to re-interrogate him would produce a deeper level of cooperation, but if nothing else, Patrick thought, letting the sonofabitch swing might just intimidate some of their other guests into a friendlier, more collegial attitude toward Broadham's inquiries.

He was also inclined to help Edyene. But Patrick wasn't about to let her know that. Not yet.

"Find out if she knows anything else that can help us, Joey," Patrick said.

"Aye, sir. Thank you, sir," beamed Broadham.

. . .

TWENTY FOUR

Principia – Afternoon (Second Day)

Preston Cross VII and his son ambled out of the Harrow Building and down Mercantile Street toward the Morgan River three blocks away, making small talk about the super-rich neighbors of the Cross estate about thirty miles up the Morgan. The river valley west of the capital was the scene of stunning, fabulous wealth built up over centuries of highly-successful farming, and then later, land development and investments in Ardenia's industrial and technological Golden Age. The families controlling the Morgan River Valley, of which the Crosses were one, were the closest thing remaining to an aristocracy which had been abandoned when Fletcher Belgrave had led the revolution deposing the Ardenian monarchy some 400 years earlier. The Morgan Valley elite didn't possess their status because of any titles conferred on them, though; these were aristocrats of a commercial and capitalist stripe.

Sebastian had grown up around the Morgan Valley gentry and taken them more or less for granted in his youth, but after the just-concluded experience of his entrepreneurial endeavor in aviation, he was certainly forming a new perspective on what it took to achieve and hold that exalted status.

When they reached the river, Sebastian regarded perhaps the most beautiful thing he'd ever seen. It was a boat–a yacht, to be more precise, though his usual definition of such a craft would include rigging and sails, of which this vessel had none. Instead, the 100-foot craft had only one mast just aft of its bridge, on which were strung bulbs for electric light, and its steel hull sloped gracefully to the waterline. Aft, Sebastian could see what looked like twin screw propellers under the waterline and below the transom in the afternoon light, and noted the name "SEBASTIAN" painted across the transom. The craft had a large cabin; it looked as though six dozen people could easily recreate themselves aboard on a day trip, and who could say how many the boat would sleep.

"This," he said, touched that the craft was named for him, "is a beauty."

"I'm glad you think so," Preston said. "It suffices for the occasional trip to the capital."

"I've never seen a design like this," Sebastian said. "It's radical. No sails?"

"Strictly speaking it isn't legal," said his father. "But since it's a custom build, privately owned, and not used for commercial purposes, it's not subject to the Transportation Commission's regulations and its construction and use are within the law."

"You got around those, huh?" Sebastian said approvingly.

"It pays to have expert legal counsel," Preston said. "Let's go aboard. Take a quick trip with me. I have some things to show you."

The two boarded the yacht, and in the opulent stateroom just aft of the bridge Sebastian found Gregg, the family's solicitor, waiting with an expectant look. The two greeted, and Gregg congratulated Sebastian on his new career as a military aviator.

Shortly they were underway west on the Morgan. Though motoring against the river's strong current, they were going *fast*, Sebastian noted: easily thirty knots. "What does this run on?" he asked his father over the drone of the engines. "I don't see a smokestack, so it's certainly not a steam engine."

"Methanol," came the answer.

"Methanol – you mean wood alcohol?" Sebastian asked, eyes wide. "As a vehicular fuel? I'll bet that definitely isn't legal."

"Nobody has asked yet," Preston said. "If they want to put the manacles on me, they know where to find me."

Sebastian was dumbstruck. Here he thought he was the technologist in the family, but after not having had a real conversation with his father for almost a year the old man showed up with a marvel of innovation on the day he lost his business. It was enough to unhinge him, but there wasn't much point in showing it.

"I am surprised," he told his father. "I have to admit that."

"We're just getting started," Preston said, pointing to a riverside warehouse just ahead as the pilot angled the yacht in its direction and throttled back on the engines. "That's the place."

"Sovereign Paper Works," read the large sign atop the roof. Sebastian knew that among the Cross family's investments were a large paper mill in Adalico, 300 miles north of the capital, and large tracts of timberland along the Allard River, which flowed north to the port of Winterstead.

"Are you buying me a card?" Sebastian joked to his father, who gave him a knowing look in response.

"Just keep an open mind," Preston told him.

They debarked, and Sebastian found himself greeted by an exceptionally cute female in her twenties when he entered the warehouse. She wore a name tag on the lapel of her blazer which identified her as Stacey, and he was keen to observe that her skirt came down only to her knees – giving him a magnificent view of a shapely pair of calves accentuated by a pair of three-inch heels she was wearing.

"Very modern," he complimented her. "I admire your style, Miss Stacey." She gave him a smile.

"Follow me, please, gentlemen," she said.

Sebastian mouthed "Wow!" to his father as they followed her into the warehouse, earning a nod from Preston and a chuckle from Gregg. The old man was a widower, as Sebastian's mother had passed away a decade earlier. He'd kept his own counsel as to his romantic life, though Sebastian had heard the odd bit of gossip about his father's various flirtations and distractions.

Stacey led them past a series of paper-cutting machines through which employees were feeding reams of various stocks for different uses: greeting cards, loose-leaf paper, even cardboard. Sebastian struggled to understand what he was doing here, until their guide brought them to an oversized freight elevator on the other side of the building.

"Going down, are we?" Sebastian deadpanned as Stacey held the door open for them.

"Mr. Sebastian, this is a professional operation," she admonished him.

"Yes, ma'am," he said. She shot him a flirty sideways glance.

The elevator descended for longer than Sebastian would expect, indicating they were deep below street level. Finally, Stacey opened the gate and the three men walked out onto what looked like a highly-advanced engineering laboratory.

"This is what we're here for," said Preston. "Thank you, Stacey," he told her as she returned to the elevator and ascended back to the ground floor.

Sebastian looked around, and what he saw made his heart sink. He'd been assured that Foreman Technologies, which had bought Airbound for a song, was the pioneer of the internal combustion engine. It was clear to him as he looked at the machines in this laboratory that he'd been lied to. In front of Sebastian was a motor attached to a twelve-foot boat propeller; its small size relative to the fan defied Sebastian's understanding. To his right was a vehicle he recognized as something like a steam wagon, but he saw no smokestack; instead there was a lifted hood in front of the vehicle's windshield, and underneath it was a motor.

Sebastian also saw a farm tractor to his left, of a far more advanced design than the Somerset tractor currently in more or less exclusive use around the country. And to his right he saw something he didn't recognize. It had a fuselage about fifteen feet long, and a pair of large propellers attached to what looked like metal wings; there were two stacked one atop the other. Fins above and to the side protruded from the back of the fuselage.

"What is this?" he asked.

"We'll get to that," Preston said. "But first let me say a few things you'll need to hear. And I should apologize that I'm saying them now, because it might have been more helpful had we had this conversation several weeks ago.

"I understand why you didn't come to me with your business problem," the old man continued. "I respect it. You're your own man, and you want to make your own way. And you're an honorable man who's willing to suffer in order to do what's right, which is how I raised you. And what I said earlier, about the arrangement you've made, I stand behind it. I respect that you've done it."

Gregg voiced his agreement.

"All right," said Sebastian, knowing he was on the verge of hearing a "but."

"But," his father continued, "I think things might– *might*–have worked out a little better had you come to me with your problem."

"Ugh," Sebastian said. "Are we really going to do this?"

"No," Preston said. "Please don't take what I am telling you in that way. This comes by way of information, not admonition, and what I offer you has value going forward beyond whatever regret it might bring to you."

Sebastian went quiet, allowing his father to continue. Just then a young man in a laboratory coat over a pair of knee boots approached the pair.

"A little later we're going to talk about last night's meeting," Gregg interjected, "because there are levels to what went on that you weren't privy to and couldn't really be. I think you'll understand after you've heard it all."

"I do love a good mystery," Sebastian said as he rolled his eyes. "You wise old men are making my spleen ache."

"Ahhh, Marcus," his father greeted the man. "Sebastian, meet Marcus Reeves, the best engineer in the world. Marcus, my son Sebastian."

"It's a wondrous pleasure, sir," Marcus said. "I am a great admirer of yours."

"I appreciate that," said Sebastian, unable to return the compliment to the man, whom he'd never heard of. "And I greatly appreciate this collection of machinery you have here. What is that contraption over there?"

"We shall get to that one," Marcus said, causing Preston and Gregg to chuckle and Sebastian to once again roll his eyes. "Consider this a nickel tour."

Marcus then led the pair to the boat propeller and its motor. "First, I want to show you this engine, because we are sending four of these by rail to Barley Point in the morning, along with a team of mechanics."

"Why is that?" Sebastian asked.

"To replace the trash Foreman is installing on the *Clyde* and the *Ann Marie*," Gregg answered. "Those engines will barely even get your airships down to Dunnan's Claim, if they even do, before they give out."

"Come again?" Sebastian responded. "Didn't you broker a deal for me to practically give away my company to those people? And now you're telling me their grand innovation is junk?"

174

Gregg put up his hands in a plea for patience.

Reeves then gave a quick explanation, which Sebastian could just about follow, of the design defects of the Foreman engines in comparison to the model which lay in front of them. The long and short of what he was telling Sebastian was that this engine was capable of generating considerably better speed for the airships than expected of the Foreman engines, and with far, far greater reliability.

"Wait," Sebastian said. "Run that number past me again? How fast?"

"One hundred twenty miles per hour projected from the horsepower and weight, based on Foreman's estimates of their own performance," Reeves said. "With an effective range of 1,000 miles."

"And what's it run on?"

"Methanol," said his father. "We do process wood in Adalico, after all."

"None of this is legal," Sebastian observed. "On the other hand, we're talking about airships, and the Transportation Commission doesn't regulate airships…"

With that, Reeves produced a thick file folder and passed it to Sebastian. "Here's some light reading for your locomotive trip."

Sebastian flipped quickly through the sheaf of papers he was given. "This is what, regulations?"

Gregg nodded. "What you will find is that the Transportation Commission is now assuming jurisdiction of the aviation industry, and what is in that file will be introduced at the Societam on Monday of next week. Essentially, it will codify the design specifications of the *Clyde* and the *Ann Marie* as the only legal designs for aviation vehicles. And while the Army is taking delivery of the airships, the intellectual property reflected in those specifications now belongs to Foreman Technologies."

"Meaning that Foreman is getting a monopoly on civilian aviation," Sebastian said, his heart sinking. "For 10.2 million decirans. I am an imbecile of legendary proportions."

"You aren't," said Preston. "You just got caught up in the same kind of thing every innovator in Ardenia has eventually been ensnared in for the last ten years."

Sebastian looked accusingly at Gregg, who gave him a sympathetic look. "You're going to understand all of it. Just listen and take a wide view."

"This tractor," said Reeves. "Superior in every way to the Somerset steam model, and illegal for commercial sale. Why?"

"You know why," Preston said.

"Somerset's chairman is Brenton Vines," Sebastian said. "Whose son is Mortimer Vines, of the Peace Party and the Belgarden delegation. You're telling me the design specifications for anything other than a Somerset tractor are illegal to manufacture for commercial sale, which is why they've got an effective monopoly on that industry."

His three interlocutors all nodded.

"So whose tractor is this?"

"It's a prototype," Preston said. "One of Marcus' designs. Built for Henry Dutton." Sebastian recognized Dutton as one of the Morgan River Valley landed elite; he had 15,000 acres of wheat and corn east of Greencastle.

"He can't even use it on his own land, I'll bet," Sebastian observed.

"No, he cannot," said Gregg. "Not if he wants to sell his harvest."

"But he's building a factory in Leria," Preston said, "and he's going to make them and sell them there. Before long the Lerians will have caught up to us in farm machinery and we won't be able to export grain to them anymore."

Sebastian whistled. "You know this how, Papa?"

"He's one of Dutton's investors," Gregg explained. "Lots of money to be made, and there's no restriction, yet, on technology export where the technology itself isn't legal here."

"How idiotic," said Sebastian, earning nods from all three. "This is more advanced tech than we allow in our market and it ends up in the hands of a trading partner a century behind us."

"And this lorry over here," Reeves said. "Internal combustion, can reach sixty miles per hour, which is twice the speed of either the Landale steam wagon or the Marvel steam lorry. Also illegal for commercial sale."

"Landale gave a million decirans to the Peace Party last year," Gregg said. "And Marvel is owned by the Barnaby family – which is Jonah Barnaby, who is the Director-General of the Peace Party."

He was starting to understand what they were telling him.

"Had you come to me before doing the deal you did yesterday," his father said, "I could have given you the capital to save Airbound, and furthermore, we could have refitted you with technology that would have solved your engineering problems."

Sebastian gave his father a stricken look.

"But I don't want you to regret that decision," his father said, "because the politicians had designs on you long before the *Justice* crashed. And they were going to set their hooks in you, because that's what they do."

"Did you ever isolate the cause of the *Justice* crash?" asked Reeves.

"We never did," said Sebastian.

"Don't be so sure it was an accident," Gregg said.

177

"Are you serious?" Sebastian asked him.

"Deadly," Gregg said, with a severe look. "And I mean that in every sense. You don't want to ask me any more about that issue, either."

Sebastian inhaled strenuously, then closed his eyes. "I feel like I'm going to be sick," he said.

"You need to know the kind of people we're dealing with here," Gregg said. "This was never about business. It's about power, and the more you were carving out a niche for yourself, the more you got yourself noticed."

"It sounds like becoming the patsy who coughed up my company for a song might have been the safe move," Sebastian said.

"No doubt about it," said Gregg. "That's why I pushed you so hard to get it done, and quickly. Fighting those people, especially with a war breaking out that Ardenia is totally unprepared for, would have been suicide."

"Let me make you feel better about this," his father said, offering the bright side to his son. "The real opportunity here isn't just commercial, and now that you're an Army man heading off to fight a war, the Peace Party crooks can't touch you. We have an opportunity for substantial reform now."

"Now, we can talk about this machine here," Reeves said. He explained that what had struck Sebastian's eye was called a biplane, and it was a flying machine capable of speeds in excess of 150 miles per hour.

"That's definitely not legal," his father chuckled.

"You designed this?" Sebastian asked Reeves.

"The engine, yes," the man answered. "The aeronautics and the assemblage aren't mine, though. That came from the Thorne workshop in Alvedorne."

"The Thornes are involved in your project?"

"They are," his father said. "And this machine here is one of ten. The other nine are on their way to an airfield just north of Trenory, where pilots are waiting to redeploy them to Barley Point as soon as you have a field available to take them."

Reeves then showed Sebastian something which wasn't readily apparent on first inspection, namely the barrels of four chain guns emplaced on the top wing of the biplane. "This is the most effective attack weapon in the world," he beamed. "Bear down on an enemy force with one of these and nothing in the open can survive."

"Check under the fuselage," his father suggested. Sebastian bent down and noticed a pair of notches. "Those are bomb ports," said Preston. "You can drop two hundred-pound shells on an enemy from those."

"Also," Reeves said, "We are shipping eight improved-model chain guns on the locomotive to Dunnansport, with a team of mechanics to install them on your two airships."

"Your designs?" Sebastian asked Reeves.

"No," the man replied. "These are the latest model from Trunxton, the Mark 11." Trunxton was the maker of chain guns for the Ardenian military until eight years earlier, when the company lost its contract.

"You don't want to go into battle with that standard-issue Dulsey gun," his father said. "That's nothing but refuse. The ammunition cartridges get bent as they're fed through the chain into the chamber, and then they jam and the gun is useless – and it stays inoperable until the chamber is unscrewed and taken apart."

The Dulsey Corporation, which now had the military's chain gun contracts, was owned by Riggs Dulsey, who sat on the Peace Party's National Fundraising Committee.

"This is some eye-opener," Sebastian said. "Makes me feel like a life of croquet and whisky naturals isn't so bad after all, compared to the filth of the commercial and political world."

179

"It doesn't have to be that way," his father said, as he started walking back to the elevator. "Come on."

...

The four rode the elevator back to the first floor, and then exited the warehouse to re-board the yacht. As he stood on the deck, Sebastian noticed what appeared to be a whale, or a large fish, approaching them under the water line. As it got closer, he could see that it was a watercraft rather than a monster from the deep, and what looked like a large turret began to poke out above the waterline. The craft pulled aside the *Sebastian,* and a hatch opened atop the turret, out of which popped a familiar face. Sebastian recognized Abraham Dees from the night before.

"Greetings," said the general, as he climbed from the submersible craft and clambered aboard the yacht. "Long time no see, Sebastian."

"I would not have expected you here," Cross told him. "You're a man of many parts, sir."

"I'm the Office of Special Warfare," Dees reminded him. "This cloak and dagger business is how I earn my living."

Preston and Gregg greeted Dees, and the four went inside to the yacht's stateroom where a table had been laid out for dinner. Reeves, who had been belowdecks, joined them.

As they sat, Gregg piped up. "Now, Sebastian, we will have our conversation about last night – and we will talk about the future."

"Did you talk to him about the *Justice?*" Dees asked Gregg.

"I only intimated."

"You didn't have anything to do with that, did you?" Sebastian asked Dees with a shocked expression on his face.

"Absolutely not," he said. "But we have evidence foul play was involved. Teletext message intercepts after the fact to indicate more knowledge of that explosion than anyone should have, by people with no reason to have such knowledge."

"By the Saints!" Sebastian hissed.

"When those were recovered," Preston said, "We decided to hold off from intervening in the problems you were having with Airbound. Had you come to me I would have helped, but it was important that you make your own decision on that issue."

"And equally important that we build a trap for the criminals who used your company to kill sixty-four of our countrymen to nourish their greed and lust for power," Gregg said.

At that point Sebastian decided the less he knew about the ruling cabal's designs on Airbound, the better. He had a job to do, after all, and going down the political rathole any further would only get in the way. And he told Gregg so.

"Maybe when this is all over you can fill me in on the details," he said. "I know enough to be dangerous already, right?"

"Essentially, yes," said Gregg. "There will be a dossier you can read if you want it."

"Good enough," Sebastian nodded.

"This is what you're going to do, Sebastian," Preston said. "You're going to go down there and you're going to throw away the equipment they give you. You refit those airships with this illegal hardware, and use and distribute the other things we're going to send down there, and you tear the enemy to pieces."

"And you're going to do it on my orders," said Dees. "I am your commanding officer, after all."

"And then, when this war is won by the industry and character of the Ardenian people in spite of our corrupt and incompetent ruling class," Preston continued, "the very people who stole your company out from under you, we will see real change in this city."

"You think you're going to beat the Peace Party in the elections next year?" Sebastian said, doubt in his voice. "With what? You're a Prosperitan, Papa. You hold how many seats in the Societam? Sixty-five out of 406? And the Territorialists aren't much better. They have what? Seventy? Where are the votes coming from?"

"The people, son. When the people see what the criminals in charge of the country have done, public opinion will turn."

"I would agree," said Sebastian, "but you'd have to find a way to fuse those two parties back into the Party of Enterprise."

"The Thornes are Territorialists," Gregg noted. "The Morgan River Valley barons are Prosperitans. Discussions are being had, very quietly."

"And not everybody who's in the Peace Party is an admirer of the Peace Party," said Dees.

"You'd be surprised how many detractors there are," Gregg said. "This kind of corruption rubs a lot of people the wrong way."

Preston and Gregg sent knowing looks Dees' way. Sebastian knew Dees was a Peace Party member; he'd given a speech at the party's convention four years earlier.

"That's interesting," he said. "But what about the land giveaway scam the Peace Party runs? How do you counter that?"

Full citizenship as an Ardenian, complete with the right to vote, depended on property ownership. That was something the nation's Constitution required as a safeguard against the public bankrupting the treasury by voting themselves money. Property ownership as a prerequisite for the franchise had been a staple of the Ardenian political order since Belgrave's revolution, but it had unraveled, thanks to a rather genius workaround the Peace Party had crafted.

Each year, the government that party controlled would transport tens of thousands of the nation's urban poor to an unsettled, or lightly-settled, rural area and have them pick out small plots of arable land they could claim as property owners as part of the Land Settlement Act passed a decade earlier, before bringing the newly-minted homesteaders back to their urban domiciles.

Technically, to qualify as a property owner, one had to make improvements to or live on the land in question, but several large Peace Party-affiliated agricultural concerns would immediately lease land granted to the poor under the Land Settlement Act. Those leases would confer a tidy little income to the underprivileged.

Those concerns would then farm the land, aided by infrastructure improvements in the south and west the Societam was funding like mad over the past decade under Peace Party control, and recoup the cost of the lease.

Or, and this is where Sebastian thought it got really diabolical, they would leave the land fallow and take a government price-supports subsidy which was passed by Parliament ten years earlier to keep Ardenia's farmers from outproducing the demand for their crops. The Delegates, moreover, passed a measure including the acceptance of the subsidy as a condition satisfactory to improving the land in question. In so doing Parliament conferred full citizenship upon the landowners, who'd obtained their land and the franchise from the government for free.

The effect of which was that the Peace Party was turning poor people who were not property owners and not entitled to the vote into voters and then paying them with taxpayer decirans to support the Peace Party.

"When this business breaks in the broadsheets, all the land in Ardenia won't save them," Preston said.

"This isn't theoretical, by the way," Gregg said. "These wheels are turning."

Sebastian was intrigued. Could a scandal like getting into a war with inoperable weapons and equipment from crony contractors be enough to shake those votes loose? Sebastian didn't know. What he did know was that he was angry enough to participate in this cockamamie plan, and, deliciously enough, he was registered as a Peace Party member. Therefore nobody would suspect him of anything other than trying to get the best materiel for the Special Air Force they'd put him in charge of, and what was more he'd have fellow Peace Party member Abraham Dees, the head of the Office of Special Warfare, running interference for him.

Sebastian found he had suddenly changed his attitude quite a bit about not antagonizing people who had transgressed against him. He was beginning to see the value in being a sonofabitch after all.

"Fine. I'm in," he said. "Let's make it happen. What do we do first?"

. . .

TWENTY FIVE

Sutton Hill – Noon (Second Day)

Will and Robert and the rest of the scouts had returned to the command line, and the Terhune contingent had now linked up with the smaller force making their way south from Battleford. The force had gathered on a landmark, a flat-top rise about 500 feet above sea level that had been the site of a great Dunnan's War battle.

"So this is Sutton Hill," said Rob. "What would Father think of me being here?"

"I imagine it would make him a little bit sad, son," said Latham. "I don't expect he would have wanted his children fighting on the same ground he bled for twenty-five years ago."

The Battle of Sutton Hill had been one of George Stuart's military highlights. Then a young lieutenant to the great general Henry Dunnan, Stuart led a detachment of scouts through this territory looking for an Udar *Var'asha* named Quawi and a war party they had intelligence was coming through the area. Instead, Stuart's mounted contingent found themselves faced with a lot more than just a war party, and by the time the thirty cavalrymen had retreated to this hilltop to dig in and mount a defense, some six hundred Udar warriors had surrounded them. For three days the Udar laid siege to the Ardenians, and for three days Stuart and his scouts held them off with marksmanship from atop that hill. By the time relief came, the Stuart contingent had lost a third of their number. They'd killed, however, more than two hundred Udar.

Sutton Hill had then retreated into obscurity. There had been talk a dozen years ago of building a fortress at the scene, as it commanded a good vantage to survey the area south to the coast and west to the northeast tip of Rogers Range, but no fort had been built.

But now the Ardenian cavalry was back on Sutton Hill.

Terhune's force now contained 432 men, with the Battleford group included. The colonel was concerned that number was hardly enough. He knew he was up against an *Anur* of Udar, at the least, and his concern that he was being lured into an ambush somewhere to the west was growing.

They were there to rescue prisoners taken by the Udar, though, and that meant any risk was justified. They would press on, in hopes that he could pin the enemy against the coastline and get some artillery support from *Adelaide*, or whatever other naval assets might be available.

Sutton Hill had a vantage of Watkins Gulf, about 25 miles away. If *Adelaide* was in position Terhune might be able to signal the ship and get some coordination going. The ship's twelve marines detached to his force had brought along a heliograph–a shuttered mirror capable of signaling in military code–for that very purpose. And while the troops were resting in the warm late-morning air, he gave orders to Lt. Wells, who commanded the marine detachment.

"Lieutenant Wells, let's see if your ship is in hailing range. Set up your signaler and try to flag down the *Adelaide*."

Things started happening quickly a few minutes later.

. . .

"Skipper, signal coming in," a young ensign called down from *Adelaide*'s observation tower "Starboard side."

"Call it out as you read it," Patrick ordered.

"Says they're atop Sutton Hill, sir," called the ensign as he made out the series of short and long flashes of light coming from the top of the hill as Wells' marines opened and closed the shuttered mirror of the heliograph. "No sign of the enemy's main party. They did encounter Udar scouts. They've linked up the Battleford, Dunnansport and Barley Point groups and have a full contingent, ready to head west."

Patrick had his own heliograph operator at the ready, and replied with his own message. "WARNING," it read. "STRONGSTEAD FALLEN. ENEMY USING RAPTORS AS WEAPONS. EXPECT DIVISION STRENGTH OR GREATER APPROACHING. RESCUE PRISONERS AND EVACUATE ASAP."

From the observation tower, the response: "They want to know if the naval assets are available for evacuation."

"Good question," muttered Patrick. He had *Yarmouth* approaching, and behind it *Castamere* and *Louise*. So far as he could tell none were within the twelve-mile hailing range he needed to coordinate something like an amphibious evacuation.

"WILL ADVISE ON NAVAL EVAC. HEADING WEST IN SEARCH OF ENEMY," Patrick had *Adelaide* signal Sutton Hill. "WILL ENGAGE WITH GUNS IF SEEN. HAIL WITH NEWS."

. . .

"None of that helps much," groused Terhune. "All right, we're going to move out along this ridge heading west. Forling, send the word along the line."

"Enemy riders six miles to the southwest!" called a lookout, scanning the expanse from the high vantage of the hilltop. "I make them a good hundred or so. They're heading to our north."

Terhune's assumption was that the riders were attempting to circle around to his rear from the west and smash his force from behind once he engaged some larger Udar contingent he might shortly come across. If he was wrong, though, and he detached a portion of his riders to block the Udar foray, he might be dividing his force in the face of that enemy. Without having a full understanding of the battle space, there was mortal risk in either decision.

"All right, this is what we're going to do."

. . .

187

TWENTY SIX

West of Sutton Hill – Afternoon (Second Day)

David Stuart wasn't exactly an experienced military commander, and he certainly wasn't well-equipped as a fighting man, with only a stub below the elbow on his left arm where a wrist and hand had been before he last met an Udar warrior. Nevertheless, as head of the Dunnansport militia he stood as the commander of the largest sub-group among the force gathered under Terhune, so when the Colonel ordered a foray to the west to meet the Udar riders spotted from Sutton Hill, and selected the militia group minus the *Adelaide* marines, plus the Battleford militia group to comprise it, that made David the senior officer available for command.

Particularly given the rather ad-hoc order of battle available in this crisis.

Stuart had with him Will Forling and his nephew Robert, who so far was the only of their number with an enemy kill. He also had ninety-four other militiamen of Dunnansport and fifty-three from Battleford, giving him a total force of 147 men to face down the Udar warriors. They galloped west, aiming to cut the enemy riders off, aligned in a straight line. David hoped that formation would allow him to turn and envelop the opposing force much like "crossing the T" in naval parlance.

And around noon on that balmy tenth-month day, the whistles rang out to signal that battle had been joined.

David was at the head of the line of militia; the Udar rode a wedge into the middle. Shots rang out to his east, and as his troops turned left to envelop the Udar, a hail of arrows rained in. The first volley of rifle shots had thinned the enemy's ranks considerably, but had barely dissuaded the Udar warriors.

In no time they were in close combat with the enemy, and the militiamen began to fall.

Including their commander. David was hit with an arrow to the thigh, and though he'd managed to land a pistol shot to the stomach of the bowman as he rode in, the Udar then unstowed his halberd and plunged it into David's ribs, which knocked him off his horse and took him out of the battle. His copper-mesh waistcoat might have been of some use against a *Gazol*, but a mighty thrust from a *Ba'kalo* was more than the armored garment was built for. David was now defenseless, on his back on the stony ridge with six inches of spear piercing his guts.

Before the Udar could finish him, David could see the man's head surrender much of its mass. In rode young Will, who had delivered a rifle shot through the Udar's temple as he thundered into the fray. Forling cocked and fired again, felling another Udar with a shot to the head. He then plugged a third Udar with a rifle shot to the chest, this one on foot as he had dismounted to engage a militiaman to David's right.

At that point, David lost consciousness.

...

"Uncle David, are you still with us?"

It was Robert. He was holding a canteen to his uncle's lips. David came to with excruciating pain in his right side and thigh, but he hadn't quite died yet.

"Barely," he croaked, and took a swig from the proffered canteen. "This needs to be whisky."

"He's not going to be able to ride." Will said. "We're going to have to rig up a stretcher for him."

"Is it over?" asked David. "Did we win?"

"We did," Robert replied. "Not without cost though. Thirty-four dead, twenty wounded, most not so bad they're out of action. But we wiped them out. All dead but one prisoner we're going to take back to Sutton Hill."

189

By the Saints, David thought. Some victory this was. More than a third of his force was now dead or injured, and now he was a liability if not yet a corpse. *My military career is finished one way or the other.*

Forling was busy with the others scrounging together a travois for David out of the wooden poles of the Udar halberds, and in short order had a means to convey him back to the main camp.

"Looks like we've found a use for these Udar after all," Robert quipped as the men looted the enemy corpses of weapons and equipment. After tightly bandaging his side and thigh, he was carefully lifted onto the travois, and as the other wounded were tended to and remounted as best they could, the party began slowly making its way back to the east.

Meanwhile, all hell had broken loose on Sutton Hill.

. . .

TWENTY SEVEN

The Mouth of the Cave – Afternoon (Second Day)

The pace had been considerable, far brisker than Sarah would have thought possible given the circumstances of the Udar raiding party and what it consisted of.

They had packed up last night's camp with impressive speed after making a human sacrifice out of a captive who had attempted to escape, and then the captives had their collars tied to long wooden poles, which were then attached by rope to saddles of horses riding in front and in back of their groups of ten. And in minutes, they were off.

Little concern was paid to the convenience of the captives, and Sarah saw several cut loose from their coffles as they failed to keep up with the march. Those unfortunate women were doused with what looked like crude oil, hogtied and then lit on fire as an example to the rest. Sarah counted a dozen such horrific episodes along the march.

But once every hour or so as they were marching southwest, their captors would come to each coffle and, one by one, remove each captive's gag and pour a swig of water from a leather canteen into her mouth. And the captors would also periodically pass through the coffles and deliver swigs of the intoxicating *marwai* liquid. There were no bathroom breaks, which for a second day didn't appear to be needed. Sarah started thinking there was maybe something about *marwai* that made the need to pee go away.

And Sarah noticed that very few of the Udar traveling along with the captives were men. Most of their warriors appeared to have ridden off in several directions as the march progressed, perhaps scouting the path forward or guarding against pursuers.

Dare I even dream about pursuers? Sarah thought. *Should I even hope that?*

She knew she should. Though she hadn't read the book written by Georgia Broadham of her time as a captive of the Udar, Sarah did know of her story. In Mrs. Broadham's case it took six months, but she did get rescued. And that, Sarah determined, would be her fate.

Somebody will come and take me home, she thought. *It might take years, but it will happen. I'm going to keep my head about me and do what it takes to stay alive, and then I will get to go home to my family.*

Or what's left of it.

But as the sun began to make its descent toward the peaks of the Rogers Range, which had drawn progressively closer as the march continued throughout the day, Sarah found it more and more difficult to maintain that faith. It really wasn't rescue that drove her forward, she thought. It was not wanting to be burned alive out here.

The women escorting the prisoners didn't just have the threat of immolation as a motivational tool. They each brandished three-foot long quirts made of rawhide with handles of bone, and they were not sparing with their use. Marching last in her coffle, Sarah felt the sting on her backside a dozen times as an exhortation to speed her pace.

At long last, the mountains were within shouting range, as the ground rose to a jagged, diagonal set of cliffs. They had also come to the coast, as to her left Sarah could see the broad expanse of Watkins Gulf. The shoreline cut a path in front of them in close proximity to the cliffside.

This was going to be their campsite for the night. Sarah knew that, because tents were in place at that site even before the captors began making camp with their own supplies and equipment.

It wasn't just their group here. There were more Udar than the 200 or so women that she'd seen escorting them during the day. But the vast majority of the people already at the camp when they arrived were also women.

So where were the men? she thought. *If they were all out defending the camp, and the Ardenians did come to save them, a major battle was inevitable.*

One by one the coffles were marched into place in a holding area in the middle of the tent village, and then the captors indicated by use of the quirt that the prisoners should kneel. The wooden poles were removed, and Sarah and her compatriots were left in the sand under guard.

She was one day closer to Uris Udar, and one day closer to slavery.

The women came around again distributing swigs of *marwai*. Sarah couldn't really tell, but she was beginning to think they were getting a bit more frequent with the dosage of the drug. The effect it was having on her was strange. She wasn't getting as high with each swig, but the effect was starting to become continuous, and it affected her thoughts.

Namely, she really missed her conversations with Charlotte. She was hoping she'd get to have another one. She had also been thinking about the kiss Charlotte had given her the night before and how sweet she'd been. Most of all, Sarah felt really guilty about having told Charlotte off the way she had that morning. That had clearly made Charlotte angry–*really angry*– and Sarah regretted treating her so shabbily. Charlotte really was her friend, the only one she had in the camp, and she'd abused and rejected that friendship.

If Charlotte would talk to her again, she was thinking, she would stop being so bitchy to her and she'd be more agreeable. Whatever Charlotte wanted her to do, she'd do.

And then Sarah stopped herself. *What in the world are you thinking?* she screamed internally. *That's absolutely crazy.* Sarah realized that was the *marwai* thinking for her, and the resulting internal dialogue was beginning to be very dangerous.

This is how they get us to agree to be javeen, she thought. *And it's awfully effective.*

These people weren't as stupid as they appeared. They were diabolical, and when it came to making slaves out of Ardenian girls they knew what they were doing.

Sarah noticed something as she surveyed the busy scene in front of her. There was a slit in the cliffside to her right, on a rise about thirty feet up, with a path leading down into the camp. It wasn't gigantic, but it certainly seemed big enough to walk through. And it didn't look like it was there naturally. In fact, it had all the appearance of having been either blasted or dug out of the mountain.

She wondered where that cave led. She had a pretty good idea that it went west into the mountains, and came out somewhere very unfriendly on the other side.

. . .

TWENTY EIGHT

Sutton Hill – Afternoon (Second Day)

Latham wasn't a bad shot, and he'd killed a man in combat before. After what he'd seen along the way south of Barley Point, he had no qualms about killing again. Nevertheless, as he lined up his shot at the Udar rider coming up Sutton Hill from the south, he hesitated.

It was fear, he thought. *Just fear. Everybody feels it in battle. Nothing to be ashamed of, you just have to fight through it. Pull the trigger and kill this guy.*

He did, and scored a hit center mass. But the man didn't fall off his horse. He kept coming, at a high speed – closing from seventy-five yards to fifty, then forty…

Latham shot him again. This time the bullet hit higher, splitting the man's lower jaw and knocking him back off his horse.

He reloaded his rifle and searched for another target. Finding one, he pulled the trigger and missed an Udar riding a bit to his left. As he aimed again, he saw the man come off his horse from another Ardenian bullet. Latham scanned for another potential victim.

Finding one coming up to his right, he dropped the man with a bullet to the right shoulder. *You won't be much use with your sword now*, he thought. *Might as well go home.*

Little chance of that. The force of Udars attacking up Sutton Hill from the south numbered close to 300, all on horseback, and they were the very definition of reckless abandon. There was no nuance or guile in the frontal assault the enemy was attempting against the Terhune contingent, diminished as it was by the Colonel's choice to send 147 men west to counter the riders they'd seen attempting a flanking maneuver. Terhune had been correct to split his force, though that was risky. They were perhaps now outnumbered here against this party of savages, but not by an enormous measure; when David Stuart's force left camp, they'd still had 285 men.

The Ardenians held the all-important high ground on Sutton Hill, which, as Latham and the rest of the Terhune contingent poured fire on the advancing Udar, was worth double or triple their number. Just as it had been in Dunnan's War.

The enemy was losing warriors at a ghastly pace, but not enough to dissuade their charge. Arrows flew overhead in flocks, as Latham and the rest of the Ardenians took cover with saddles and other equipment set in front as shields at the edge of the rise. A few arrows here and there lodged among the horses, which were collected in the middle of Sutton Hill.

As Latham fired again, missing wide of a gigantic Udar galloping directly for him, to his right he could see one of the warriors spear an Ardenian with a halberd. He took better aim and drilled the huge man through the heart with a rifle shot. The Udar who'd crested the hill and killed one of Latham's colleagues was unhorsed by a pistol shot from Terhune; the colonel fired another bullet in him as he landed on his back from the fall.

However, the Udar were getting closer to the top of the hill. There were still at least half of them in the battle. If they managed to turn this into a hand-to-hand fight, there was no guarantee of Ardenian victory and even less of managing to save the survivors of the previous day's raids on Dunnan's Claim.

Just then, Latham could see a line of riders to his right cutting across the hillside behind the Udar. It was, he deduced, most of Stuart's detachment from Dunnansport and Battleford. Latham estimated ninety or so riders, led by the Forling boy. He appeared to be an expert shot, scoring kills time after time with his rifle while at a gallop, and leading the Ardenians to a flanking maneuver which all but trapped the enemy on that hillside. Several of the Udar turned to face the cavalrymen pumping bullets into the rear of their ranks, and the charge up the hill stalled.

The defenders of Sutton Hill then poured on their rifle fire, and the battle quickly turned Ardenia's way. It was over in just a few minutes from there, the last shot fired knocking an Udar off his horse as he attempted to flee to the southeast. Only two or three dozen of the enemy managed a successful retreat.

Not a rout. Almost an annihilation.

Forling rode up the hill to a chorus of "Huzzah!" from the defenders. His comrades followed. To the west, another contingent of riders approached much more slowly.

"We've engaged the enemy to the west," Forling reported as he dismounted in Terhune's presence, "and closed and destroyed him. Took some casualties, though. Thirty-four dead and twenty wounded. That'll be the wounded coming up now."

"Where's your commander?" asked Terhune.

"He's one of the wounded, sir."

Damned poor fortune, thought Latham. *The Stuarts can hardly catch a break this week.*

As the camp's three doctors tended to the wounded, Stuart's travois mounted the hill. Latham helped carry his stretcher, untied from the horse drawing it, to the hilltop. The aging one-armed man looked white as a sheet.

"A capital victory," he croaked in Terhune's direction. "You have my congratulations, colonel."

"Too expensive if we lose you, commander," the colonel said. "Don't you stop fighting."

"I've had it," Stuart said. And to Robert, who had been with him for the ride back from the battle to the west, he shot a fervent look. "Listen to me, boy," he said, feebly.

"Yes, Uncle?"

197

"Tell your aunt, tell Rebecca..." he trailed off, then summoned his strength again. "You tell her I love her. You tell her I'll be waiting for her in the afterlife. And tell your cousins Josey and Peter, tell them their father's going to miss them."

David gasped in pain.

"Robert," he wheezed. "get Sarah. You go get Sarah."

"You think they have her, Uncle?"

"Go get Sarah. Bring her home safe. Ethan and Hannah too. You're the head of the family now. Don't let them down."

"I will, Uncle. I will. Stay with me. We can't lose you. Fight for us!"

"Gone to see my brother," he whispered. "See your dad and mom. Give 'em your love."

And with that he was no more.

. . .

TWENTY NINE

Watkins Gulf – Evening (Second Day)

There was good news and bad news on the communications front where *Adelaide* was concerned.

On the good side, *Yarmouth* had finally come within signaling range. The sidewheeler was fast gaining on *Adelaide's* position as the frigate came west, and the two ships were able to trade news of the ongoing efforts to place military assets on the scene. Because of that development, Patrick had *Adelaide* increase its speed heading west to eighteen knots toward Strongstead.

On the negative side, they'd lost contact with the troops on Sutton Hill, and Patrick was concerned they wouldn't be able to re-establish it as they moved west. Because of the topography of the Watkins Gulf coastline this far west of Barley Point, line of sight to Sutton Hill was going to be chancy. Patrick assumed the Terhune camp would be moving quickly to close with the enemy. That ought to bring them closer to his position, but it also might put them behind one of the smaller hills which came nearer to the coastline.

They'd been signaling with the mirror heliograph in the afternoon, and now that dusk was arriving, they were doing so by signal lantern. Nothing in the way of a response so far.

And then there was the lack of news from *Castamere* and *Louise*. The other two frigates were said to be on the way. *Yarmouth* had relayed an estimate from the Admiralty of *Castamere's* arrival by midnight tonight, with *Louise* to follow by dawn or earlier. On his previous timetable, those arrivals would have been acceptable to Patrick, but given the revelations offered earlier in the day by his Udar prisoner Edyene, who'd said the warriors rampaging through Dunnan's Claim two days earlier were only the lead element of a gigantic invasion force massing to the west and south, he didn't know if his support frigates would arrive in time to make a difference.

But finally, as the sun dipped into the horizon, a blinking light was seen on the ridgeline to the ship's starboard.

"Signal comin' in!" came the call from *Adelaide's* observation tower.

"They say they engaged a war party on Sutton Hill and had nearly 300 kills." *Adelaide*'s crew broke into cheers. "Movin' westward in search of the enemy's base camp. Will locate tonight and close with them in the morning. They're going to signal us on the hour with latest developments."

Patrick had *Adelaide* send a message in return. "YARMOUTH APPROACHING FROM EAST FOR EVAC. CASTAMERE, LOUISE ARRIVE BY DAWN. WILL CONTINUE SEARCH FOR ENEMY CAMP BY SEA AND MAINTAIN CONTACT."

Broadham appeared on the bridge.

"You've made your interrogations of all nine of our guests?" Patrick queried.

"All nine, sir," said Broadham. "Only one truly productive."

The commander gave a wry smile. *Yeah, I kinda like her too*, he thought.

"That said, I did manage to get confirmation of most elements of her story by bits and pieces of what the others would tell me. We're in a major war, sir."

"Yes we are, young ensign," Patrick replied. "Yes, we are."

"What about our old chum Ago'an?" Patrick inquired.

"He did seem impressed that I knew who he was," Broadham said. "And I passed along the fact he was up on a murder charge and subject to hanging."

"And?" asked the commander.

"He spat on me," Broadham said.

"That shit-eating sonofabitch," Patrick said, with mild indignance.

"All right, Broadham. I want your best call here. You've interrogated the others. Do you believe any of them cough us up information of strategic or tactical value in the event they see their commander swinging?"

"I want to say yes, sir," Broadham answered.

"But you're not saying yes, are you?"

"No, sir. I am not. I wish I did believe it."

"I appreciate the candor, Ensign," Patrick said.

Shit, he thought.

Of course, bringing Ago'an to Dunnansport and letting the Marines hang him in front of the public wouldn't be a terrible idea. If nothing else it would do a little bit of good for morale after the trauma those people were going through. He guessed he could wait a couple of days for this savage to get what was coming to him.

A few moments later, another call came from the observation tower. "Campfires, commander! Could be the enemy. They're west of the Terhune camp."

Patrick used his field glasses and surveyed the coastline to the northwest and spotted what the tower had called. It was clearly a camp. It looked as though there was a large fire in the middle with other fires scattered around it.

"There you bastards are," he snarled. "All ahead full, heading three-one-five."

The *Adelaide* increased its speed to the full twenty-two knots, rounding a bend in the coastline, making its way to the site of the fires on the beach a few miles ahead.

. . .

THIRTY

The Mouth of the Cave – Evening (Second Day)

After a short time kneeling on the sand with her fellow captives, Sarah found herself fetched by the Udar women again. And again she was brought to Rapan'na's tent.

"I am pleased you completed your journey," said Charlotte, who sat in a side-saddle position on the cushion laid out in the middle of the tent. Sarah was forced onto her knees before the *javeen*. Her gag was removed.

"I'm still breathing," she smiled, not entirely sure if it was proper to do so. "What happens now?"

Charlotte motioned to the guards, who untied Sarah's arms from their painful folded position behind her back. "First, let us give you some nourishment." She waved in two other women, who bore a platter laden with berries, a bowl of the porridge Sarah had eaten the previous night and, this time, a chicken which had been freshly roasted.

Sarah ate, as did Charlotte. Neither spoke for a few minutes. Sarah had questions, but was apprehensive about the answers, and she figured she had all the time in the world at this point. Charlotte was similarly in no hurry.

And Charlotte handed her a goblet half-filled with *marwai*. Sarah took it, and under Charlotte's watchful eye, sipped from it. Her head began to spin a little again.

Finally, the older woman spoke.

"Tonight is an important point in your life, Sarah. Tonight you will take a step toward your new existence as a *javeen*. We will celebrate that step in due time."

Sarah protested, delicately. She didn't want to upset Charlotte again "I still haven't made any such decision," she stammered. "I wasn't kidding when I said I'd rather be killed."

Charlotte eyed her carefully, and then smiled. "You lie," she chuckled. "You are here. One dozen are not. If you truly wished to die rather than embrace your future you would have perished in the fields to the east today."

Sarah had no response. She felt the inevitability of whatever was coming fall upon her.

"And so tonight you will take the intermediate step, as will your fellow novitiates."

"Meaning?" Sarah asked.

"First you will be prepared," said Charlotte. She turned to the guards. *"Le'aylora. Mizonreen. Sa'avori,"* she said.

The women collected Sarah gently and helped her to her feet. Her shift, which by now was little more than a rag, was taken off her, leaving her naked in the warm air. One guard pointed to the sandals on her feet. *"Oonet,"* she said.

"Take off your shoes," explained Charlotte.

Sarah shot her a worried look, then untied the sandals at her ankles.

She was then led out of the tent by a chain leash attached to her collar. From there it was down to the beach, where the guards walked her into Watkins Gulf with another woman following just behind. She carried a large sponge, which she used to roughly scrub Sarah down in the saltwater.

Not the best bath I've ever had, she thought to herself as she attempted to cover herself with her hands.

The bath mercifully did not last long, and Sarah was marched close to the large bonfire in the middle of the camp. A tall woman awaited her with a pair of shears.

"Ssssou'ru!" chanted the women of the camp.

The guards forced Sarah down to her knees as the tall woman approached her. They held her still by the shoulders and chin as the shears went to work, shortly reducing her below-the-shoulder-length locks to nothing. Sarah's head was shorn close, to match that of the Udar women.

"You are almost prepared," said Charlotte, as she approached Sarah from behind.

Another of the women arrived, a bowl containing some sort of gray paste in her arms.

Sarah was picked up by the guards and made to stand as two of the women proceeded to smear the sticky substance, which smelled like blackberries, tar, and sadness, all over her body: on her shoulders, back, breasts, stomach, arms, legs and nether regions. It was a highly unpleasant experience, and Sarah couldn't hold back tears at her debasement.

Especially as she noticed her audience. Though her view was obscured by the large bonfire in front of her, Sarah could see that many of her fellow captives had been made to watch her ordeal, and the looks on the faces she could see were of dull panic and resigned horror.

"They will be prepared as well," Charlotte said, as she gave Sarah another sip of *marwai*. "It is the way of the *Anur*."

Guards then came for the Ardenian captives in their groups of ten, and over the next hour the whole of the captives had been stripped, washed, shorn and covered in the gray paste.

"Now what?" Sarah, slightly recovered from her emotional spell, asked Charlotte. She was happy that her friend was still talking to her, and she had resolved again not to be enraged and bitchy.

"We wait for Rapan'na and the rest of the *Anur*, and you all begin your novitiation."

Sarah guessed that would be all right, as her head continued to spin pleasantly. And though she was naked as the evening got cooler, she felt comfortably warm.

. . .

THIRTY ONE

The Ridge – Night (Second Day)

Will and Robert had ridden ahead of the Terhune force as scouts once again, and once again they found themselves encountering the enemy ahead of the main battle to come.

This time, fortunately, they weren't being shot at, which Robert regarded as progress as he and Will regarded the campfires from a ridgeline 400 yards to the north of the Udar campsite. Will had dispatched Paul Tyler, a young militiaman from Dunnansport, whose day job was as a clerk in Uncle David's cotton storehouse, to ride at speed back to the command line to report the location of the Udar camp.

Their position was well hidden, with the bulk of their ten-man scouting party twenty yards behind. If the enemy spotted them, Will surmised, they would have the ability to get away quickly.

"By the Saints, they've taken a lot of captives," whispered Robert. "Look at all of them, Will!"

"I see it," Will said softly. "Know what else I see?"

"No men," Rob answered.

"That's right. You don't think we wiped out their riders, do you?"

"I wouldn't bet on it," Rob said. "Nothing's worked out that well on this trip."

"True that," Will groused.

The two watched as some sort of ritual was taking place. At several spots throughout the camp, near the multiple fires laid on the sandy beach between Watkins Gulf and the cliffside where Will and Rob were observing, the Udar women were holding up captives and cutting their hair, then smearing them with a gray substance. The rest of the captives, heavily guarded by women with spears and whips handy, were made to watch. Then the guards took more captives in groups to the water, returning them to the firesides to repeat the ritual.

Will remarked that nobody was resisting. "Seems strange," he observed. "Wonder what they do to get that kind of compliance."

"Sarah is down there," Rob seethed. "I can feel it. Uncle David was right."

"I think he was, too," Will said. "But we are not going to lose our cool and do something stupid. We're going down there with the whole force."

"I know," Rob said. "But they're going to pay for doing this shit, whatever it is."

"Psssst!" came a voice from the main scout party to the rear.

Will and Rob scampered back from the ridgeside, rejoining the rest of the scouts.

"We've gotta go," said Louis Turnbull, a farmboy from just west of Dunnansport, who'd been with Will and Rob from the beginning. "Riders to the southwest approaching the camp. We can't be seen apart from the main force."

"Agreed," said Will as he mounted his horse. "Come on, Rob. Let's go call in the cavalry."

Rob said nothing as he quickly stepped into a stirrup and threw his right leg over the saddle. He slapped his horse's hind-quarter and the mare took off at a trot for the command line. The rest of the scouts followed hard behind him.

. . .

THIRTY TWO

The Mouth of the Cave – Night (Second Day)

Sarah thought it was quite peculiar, and even more educational, that when the riders approached the camp, the reaction was less than enthusiastic among the waiting women.

She was one of some 370-odd kneeling captives, all naked, their heads shaven and covered in foul-smelling gray paste, waiting for some further stage of whatever ritual the *Anur* was initiating them into. Sarah silently cursed that the prisoners hadn't taken action against the women when all the warriors had left the camp.

That was unrealistic, she knew. They'd just been on an all-day march at spear- and whip-point, with very little food and water, and though they'd all been freed from their painful arm bondage, the captives were each exhausted. Resistance in this case was suicide. After watching more than a dozen of their number executed in the flames for crimes as slight as failing to keep up with the march, moreover, they all knew the enemy would show no mercy for noncompliance.

Of course, there was the *marwai*, too. Sarah wondered when that would be passed around again.

In any event, things appeared to be going as planned for their captors.

But then the riders approached the camp, and what initially were whoops of celebration from the women of the *Anur* quickly went silent and even turned to quiet murmurs and sobs.

Something was wrong, and Sarah figured out quickly what that was.

There were too few of them.

207

Sarah only counted about thirty of the riders. They had more than 300 in the camp the night before. Something had happened to the rest.

Charlotte was standing nearby as she knelt near the large bonfire.

"Where are the rest of them?" Sarah asked.

"Keep quiet," Charlotte said.

She did. Charlotte walked toward the approaching horsemen.

Seconds later, the headman, Rapan'na, descended from his horse in front of her. Charlotte kneeled and bowed her head, and Rapan'na put his hands on her temples.

Sarah heard her ask him a question, and he grunted in response as he led her to his tent. Similar exchanges were had throughout the camp as riders dismounted and the women led their horses to the makeshift rope stable on the camp's west side. It was clear they'd lost a battle.

Ardenia was coming, Sarah now knew. *There was hope after all.*

Just then Sarah heard an unmistakable sound of civilization. There was a large steam engine chugging away in close proximity, and she could see a bright light flashing rapidly from just off the coast.

. . .

THIRTY THREE

The Ridge – Midnight (Second Day)

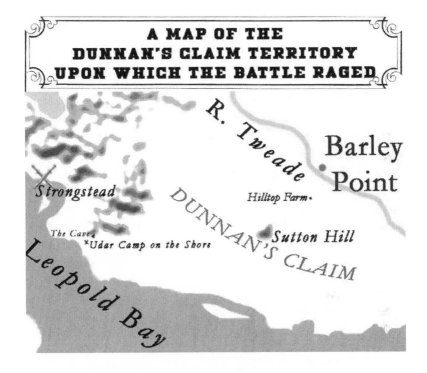

A MAP OF THE DUNNAN'S CLAIM TERRITORY UPON WHICH THE BATTLE RAGED

R. Tweade

Barley Point

Strongstead

Hilltop Farm

DUNNAN'S CLAIM

The Cave
*Udar Camp on the Shore

Sutton Hill

Leopold Bay

"We're camping here tonight," Terhune insisted. "But we're riding hard before dawn and we'll take the enemy unprepared."

"Colonel," Will interjected. "Right now we may have a 10-to-1 advantage on them, and we can be there in less than half an hour. Do we not want to do this immediately?"

"Considerations, my boy," said Terhune. "First, we know the enemy has reinforcements on the way in numbers that would wipe us out. We don't know when they'll arrive, but we do know if we go down there and take those Udars, now we've got to rescue those survivors and get them back across the Tweade.

"Our best hope to do that successfully is to get them on boats and then get the hell out of here. We've been signaling with *Adelaide,* and they'll have three other ships here by dawn. That's our best option."

Will shrugged, acquiescing. "There's something about the captives," he reported. "We saw zero signs of resistance."

He and Rob recounted the ritual to which the Udar were subjecting their prisoners.

"They're drugged," Terhune explained. "Udar uses a hallucinogen laced into some sort of hooch they make from belladonna berries. It's amazingly powerful stuff and it'll turn anybody into a wet noodle."

Terhune noted the rage on Rob's face.

"That's why trying to get them out of here on foot isn't realistic, Stuart," he said. "We need the *Yarmouth* or we'll be sitting ducks in the event of a counterattack."

Rob said nothing, but Terhune could see he understood.

"And something else. Those reinforcements might be here by dawn. Or they might be getting there now. I don't want to be feeling my way through the dark and happen upon 10,000 of those bastards with only tired troops who can't shoot straight."

The colonel had made up his mind, and after a day of what felt like nonstop battle, few in the camp were prepared to argue with his logic. The Ardenians quickly set up the camp, eschewing their fires save the one inside the signal lantern the Marines were using to coordinate with *Adelaide.*

The plan was laid. The Ardenians were camping about three miles from the Udar tent village – less than fifteen minutes' ride away at a gallop. They would depart for battle in time to arrive just at dawn, and on their arrival *Adelaide* and its sister ships would bombard the outskirts of the village, remaining careful to keep the shells away from the holding area in the middle of the Udar camp. With such a shock attack and with so few–it was hoped–Udar warriors available for the defense of the camp, the enemy might well decide to abandon the captives and flee, or perhaps there would be a way to negotiate the release of the captives without any further violence.

Adelaide was putting ashore its twenty-two remaining Marines in four lifeboats as dawn approached, along with a translator from the ship to assist in any parlay which might be had. In addition, the sidewheel steamer *Yarmouth*, which had arrived shortly after sundown, would advance to the beach by dawn; its retractable paddlewheel and relatively light draft, plus its foldable ramp, would allow it to serve as a landing craft. The frigates *Castamere* and *Louise*, which were advancing to the battle space at top speed and would arrive overnight, would cover the beach to the west of the camp in an effort to seal it off from the Udar reinforcements coming from Strongstead.

But if the enemy was bringing raptors, there wasn't a lot the Terhune contingent could do. They were as good as dead if the giant birds came on the scene.

Lookouts were posted, horses were watered and the men bundled inside their blankets for a short four-hour respite. Few could sleep, their mission nearly at hand.

Will and Rob, in particular.

"What are you going to do after this, Will? Back to Aldingham to finish your third year?" Rob asked.

"I can't see that now," Will said. "We're at war. From here I imagine it's back to Barley Point, and I'll take whatever commission Col. Terhune offers. I'm going to guess we're going to have the scrap of our lives along the Tweade if those bastards have the strength they're saying. The whole country's going to have to show up for this fight.

"What's your plan, Rob?"

"I don't have one," came the response. "Get my brother and my sisters together, I imagine, and bring them all to Uncle David's place in Dunnansport. Be with Aunt Rebecca and the kids for a while, and do what I can to protect them. If that means getting them out to safer ground I'll do that. You know I'm no good at this Army shit."

"You got the first mission kill in this whole war," Will responded. "That should count for something."

"Yeah, it counts for me losing my mind," said Rob. "I wanted to torture that savage to death. I'll have to live with that forever."

"Look, you," said Will, his voice gaining some real inflection for the first time since Dunnansport. "Don't do that to yourself. Now isn't the *time* for humanity. You saw what those shit-eaters did on their way to your doorstep. You know what *their* morals are. You can't beat yourself up for getting your hands dirty on this little adventure. Drop that baggage right now; it will weigh you down and break your back."

"The only way to do that is to get out of this fight," Rob said. "Cutting that Udar sonofabitch up…it wasn't traumatic, man. I *enjoyed* it. How am I going to live with that?"

"I'll tell you how," retorted Will. "You accept it. *Of course* you enjoyed it. Bastard got what he deserved. He'd done the same to friends and neighbors…hell, family of ours. For all I know he was at Grayvern and did my mother in. I'm glad you sliced him up. My only concern was we were going to run out of time out there."

"I don't want to accept it," Rob said. "I think it'll drive me mad. And the family needs more from me than to be some crazed killer."

"Understood," said Will. "But the *country* needs exactly that. Crazed killers are all the other guys know how to make, and they're coming for us."

Rob grunted. "I'm getting a little sleep. Good talk, Will."

"Suit yourself, little man."

...

213

THIRTY FOUR

The Mouth of the Cave – Midnight (Second Day)

The Udar could also tell there was a ship nearby on the water, but didn't appear overly concerned. They weren't dousing the campfires, there was no particular effort made to move to higher ground, and the mood among the *Anur* was unchanged.

Nevertheless, this was clearly a more somber camp than it had been the previous night. Sarah could tell the Udar were shaken by their reduced number of warriors, and, as a result, the guards were more than a little surly in treating the captives. The guards had returned to the captors and proceeded to bind their arms in the all-too-familiar painful folded position behind their backs. That was a change, as following the unfinished ritual they'd been left unbound other than having their collars strung together with ropes. They'd been fed a mouthful of gruel and swigs of water, but no *marwai*, then the guards admonished them with prodding from spears and quirts to be still.

Sarah noticed that the gray goo she'd had covering her body was stiffening and becoming exceptionally uncomfortable as it dried. It wasn't just sticky anymore. She felt as though her body hair was being plucked out of its follicles as the paste had its way.

But whatever the climax of tonight's ritual was supposed to be, clearly it wouldn't be happening now. The Udar were largely ignoring their prisoners at this point. Sarah wondered–*dreaded*–that whatever was planned after their debasement earlier in the evening might have involved the presence of the warriors of the *Anur* who didn't make it back to the camp.

Sex, she guessed. *We were probably all getting raped.*

214

Then again, Charlotte had said the aim was to make them all *javeen*. She figured that meant they'd be sold all over Uris Udar, since it sounded like an *Anur* only had a handful or less *javeen* in service at any particular time. Charlotte had also said being a *javeen* was a choice, although not much of one. Either consenting to being a whore for the tribe or being set on fire was an unacceptabe lose-lose proposition. But that didn't make it straight-up rape, did it?

Then again, the more *marwai* she drank the more agreeable she was to whatever they'd planned for her. So would it be rape if the *marwai* said yes for you?

She had lots of opinions on that topic, for sure, but as she worked it out in her head she didn't think what was coming was rape, or even *marwai*-rape. It was surely something unpleasant, though.

We need the cavalry in here, she thought. *Faster, please.*

That also got her thinking. Who was coming? There was obviously an Ardenian force out there, and close by. And she knew there was at least one warship floating just off the coast, probably with its guns trained directly on them. In the morning this was surely to be a dangerous place, with either an exceptionally awful outcome, or maybe the one she'd obstinately dared to hope for.

Sarah figured the force pursuing the Udar and so badly thinning their ranks earlier that day, in all likelihood, had come from the army base at Barley Point. It would have been Col. Terhune's men, which would be a source of Sarah's confidence. Father had known the Colonel well and called him a capable man; he had said Robert would do well serving under Terhune for his five-year Army service following graduation at the academy at Aldingham.

Then she had another thought. *I'll bet there's militia from Dunnansport too.* And if that was the case, it could well have been Uncle David out in those hills somewhere, since he was the commander of the town's militia force. That made her smile. Her uncle was, next to her father, the kindest man she knew. If Uncle David came to rescue her in the morning, she thought, that would be just fine by her.

But wait. What if Robert were there? He was coming back from Aldingham by train this week, she thought, and was to arrive at Dunnansport a couple of days ago. He could well have joined up with the expedition. Was Robert really out there battling Udar warriors?

She didn't like that idea much. Her brother hadn't had a good time of it at the academy. He was barely bigger than Sarah. In fact, though she was a year younger, she was actually taller than her brother. Imagining him trading sword or dagger blows with some Udar raider filled her with panic.

No, he wouldn't survive that, she thought. *Father, Mother, Matthew, Tabitha – and Robert, too?*

It was too much.

And then there was William Forling, who she reckoned would have been traveling with Robert. That was at least something. William, for all his clumsiness, was at least a giant of a man and certainly physical enough to hold his own with the Udar. Maybe if William was there with him, Robert might be safe.

At least, she hoped so.

We'll find out tomorrow, she mused.

. . .

THIRTY FIVE

Along The Coast – Dawn (Third Day)

The ride began at a trot, as the cavalrymen made their way, first south over the patchy grass of the coastal plain, then west along the beach toward the campfires not far from their location. The riders were quiet, wearing steely, murderous glances. Even the horses picked up on the mood.

Behind them, the first streaks of sunlight began to appear in the eastern sky, almost as fingers of a hand stretching out to grab the enemy and wring the life out of him.

At least that's how Latham thought of it.

He looked around at the 200 riders advancing in a wedge along the sandy shore toward the enemy camp. With him were a number of men who had distinguished themselves during the expedition – Wells, the Marine lieutenant from the *Adelaide* who'd supervised the signal communication with his ship and fought with a lion's heart at Sutton Hill, Sgt. Michael Pearson of the Barley Point garrison who shrugged off an arrow to his collarbone to continue the battle on the hill, the Forling boy who was the true hero of the battle, and Robert Stuart who was the first of the expeditionary force to kill one of the enemy.

He was proud to serve with these men. Shortly they'd have their moment of truth. They'd either accomplish their mission or die valiantly in the effort.

It was anything but the fate he expected forty-eight hours earlier, but though every cell in his out-of-shape, overweight and too-old body screamed in agony at the nonstop riding, lack of sleep, and uncustomary physical exertion of the last two days, Latham decided that he was satisfied regardless of how things turned out.

I've done my duty, he thought, *and I'll keep doing it. If that means I'm a cavalryman instead of an architect, so be it.*

He was fighting for his country, and there'd been nothing more noble in his life than that.

A small contingent of the Terhune force was to their north, riding along the ridgeline into the lee of the Rogers Range, and would descend south to the camp from the rolling cliffside to its northwest. They'd flank the Udar while Latham's wedge, commanded as it was by young Forling–he thought Will was an excellent choice–was making the frontal attack.

Just before they began their pre-dawn march, *Adelaide* signaled that the four ships were all in place and *Yarmouth* would steam to the beach at dawn along with the frigate's lifeboats containing its twenty-two Marines. Though the sea looked glassy in the dawn gloom, Latham was worried that *Adelaide*'s 100-pound guns would be less than accurate in shelling the outskirts of the tent village and cause too much collateral damage for the success of the mission.

Just ahead, he saw Forling raise his sword and stand in his stirrups.

"It's time, men," he called, flinching to spur his horse into a full gallop. "*CHARGE!*"

The men of the Forling contingent let out war whoops and followed closely on.

They covered the 3,000 yards to the camp in less than five minutes, but as the cavalrymen drew closer, it was clear that the enemy was ready for them. Standing in front of a large bonfire on the eastern edge of the camp were more than 300 Udar, mostly women, Latham noticed. In front of each of them, with necks outstretched and arms bound, were the Ardenian female captives, all naked and covered in what appeared to be mud.

Each captive had an *Izwei* dagger pressed to her neck by an Udar.

Forling held his hand up, and the charge petered out to a slow, careful approach to the camp.

And as they entered, a woman naked in the mild morning air stepped forward.

"I will translate," she announced.

Forling dismounted.

"You're a prisoner?" he asked. "Or are you one of them?"

"I am Shori'zel," she responded. "Formerly my name was Charlotte Naughton, wife of Col. John Naughton of the Strongstead citadel garrison."

"We heard about Strongstead," said Forling.

"I have a message from the *Var'asha*," Charlotte told him. "Brave Rapan'na, Cleanser of Profaner Lands, Master of Horse and Avenger of *Gana'fali*, declares *Kawes'kin* and challenges you to honor your humanity in single combat."

"I don't know what any of that shit is," Forling responded.

"You will choose a champion to fight Rapan'na with the dagger," she informed him. "If your champion bests him, you may have your captives returned to you. If you do not, you will leave your weapons and horses and depart from this place."

"Or else what?"

"Refusing *Kawes'kin* is the ultimate dishonor," Charlotte said. "Such a grave insult would be disastrous."

Just then an Udar warrior dragged one of the captives forward. The Ardenians trained their guns on him intently as tension escalated.

"That's far enough," barked Forling.

The warrior then dragged his *Izwei* across her throat. She collapsed in a heap, blood spattering the sand.

219

With his pistol, Rob shot the man in the heart. He crumpled and fell atop his victim.

"The requirements of *Kawes 'kin* have been satisfied," Charlotte announced. "You must choose your champion, or we will all die here this morning."

It was at that point when *Yarmouth* and the four lifeboats from *Adelaide* made their way to the beach, though very slowly as the events at the camp were clearly at a delicate stage.

Broadham disembarked from one of the lifeboats and hustled, half-swimming, half-wading, to the shore astride the Ardenian cavalry. "Who's in command?" he asked.

Forling gave a wiggle of his raised wrist. "You're the translator?"

"Ensign Joseph Broadham, sir, of the *ANS Adelaide*."

"Will Forling, Lieutenant, Ardenian Cavalry," came the response. "Damn glad to meet you."

"What's the situation?" Broadham asked.

"Kawas-keen. I think they want me to fight their head guy over the hostages."

"Right," said Broadham. "This is the heart and soul of who they are. If you do this, it's a fight to the death. And their champion is going to be really, really good."

"I'm better," Forling responded. "It's either do that or they start cutting throats and we end up in a bloodbath."

The rest of the Terhune contingent slowly rode up, with the Colonel jumping off his horse and approaching the discussion. "What in the red hell is this?" he spluttered.

"The Udar want to fight this with single combat," Latham said. "Forling against their guy, whose name is Rapan-na. If Will wins, they give up the hostages. If the Udar wins, we lay down our weapons, leave the horses and get on the boat without the hostages."

"Absolutely not," said Terhune.

"Who is Rapan-na?" Forling asked loudly. "I don't see him."

Just then a hulking Udar, standing almost six feet tall and easily twenty stone, his massive torso barely contained by a leather vest and rippling arms bare save for a series of iron rings lining his left arm from his wrist to just below his elbow, his head covered by a helmet wired together with cascading bits of bone topped by the enormous skull of a raptor, stepped forward. His *Izwei* was pressed to the throat of an Ardenian captive he dragged with him to the front of the line.

"Sarah!" called Rob. She gave him a desperate glance, but then she cast a look at Will and her eyes grew perceptively larger from Rob's vantage. It was clear Sarah no longer saw the clumsy oaf of his youth. This was a warrior and a man; the kind of man she could see herself sharing a life with.

"Let her go," Will said through gritted teeth, holding his composure as he pointed to Rapan'na. "You let her go, now."

"Vivatz," the man shouted at him. *"Adoa cassuna kefuzui! Kawes'kin!"*

"He said…" began Broadham…

"I know what he fucking said," Will cut him off.

Terhune then spoke. "We have already killed most of your warriors," he said, as Charlotte translated aloud. "We are not here to kill you. We wish to free our people and return them home. Those who want to survive this day may lay down their weapons and leave. We will not pursue you. Let them go and we will let you go."

None moved. Rapan'na continued pressing his *Izwei* to Sarah's throat below her collar. *"Kawes'kin!"* he hissed.

"Colonel, they've orchestrated this thing to get just this result," said Latham. "It might be the only way to save the hostages."

"Refusing the single combat challenge is seen as the worst insult imaginable, Colonel," added Broadham. "Their reaction to a rebuff won't be a good one."

"They will kill all of the women if you refuse," Charlotte interjected from across the de-facto neutral ground between the Ardenian contingent and the Udar camp.

Terhune pointed at her. "Who are you? Don't I know you?"

"She was Col. Naughton's wife, Colonel," said Latham. "At Strongstead. It seems she's one of them now."

The Colonel shot Latham a pained look, then stared disconcertedly at Charlotte, at Rapan'na and Sarah under his knife and across the camp at the Udar holding knives to the terrified hostages.

Terhune threw up his hands and turned to Forling. "It's either the bloodbath or it's your show, Will. I'll leave it up to you. So you know, though, I'm not giving up my weapon and neither are any members of my command."

"Don't you worry, Colonel. I'm going to kill him," Forling said, staring at Sarah. Her eyes grew wider still.

Will then got himself ready for a fight. He began by pulling off his gauntlets and, with the gloves held in his teeth, stripping off his coat. He turned toward Charlotte and threw the outergarment to her. "Give that to Sarah, for mercy's sake," he growled.

Will then replaced the gloves on his hands and drew his cavalry fighting knife from its sheath along his belt.

Broadham approached Will and confided softly, "So you'll know, those rings on his left arm? You get one of those for each time you kill somebody in single combat. He's done this a few times before. But those have likely all been against daggers like the one he's got, so you can maybe take advantage."

Forling nodded and placed a hand on Broadham's shoulder. He then pointed the knife at the Udar and waved it lazily in his direction.

"You ready, you animal?" he shouted at the Udar. "You want some? Come get it."

...

THIRTY SIX

Kawes'kin – Morning (Third Day)

Unlike the Udar *Izwei*, the Ardenian cavalry fighting knife isn't dotted with prominent barbs along its shaft. But the knife, manufactured exclusively by the Pearson Standard Co. of Greencastle, is similar to the *Izwei* in that it is also a wide, double-bladed knife designed for slashing an enemy rather than simply stabbing at him. The Pearson Standard C-1 fighting knife, known by its users simply as the C-1, is a steel instrument with a serrated edge along the top blade and a straight edge on the bottom, with the tip of its nine-inch blade–three inches longer than the *Izwei*–curving slightly to the top. It's a fourteen-inch monster of a dagger, and very deadly in the hands of a man who knows how to use it.

Will was such a man, having become a student of knife-fighting as a means of transforming himself from a gangly, clumsy oaf of a boy to a trained killing machine at the defense academy at Aldingham. Close-combat training became an obsession of Will's when, during his first week at the academy, he'd been plucked out of a class by an instructor for a demonstration of knife-fighting techniques and been badly embarrassed in repeated fashion. That was a critical-mass moment for Will, whose youth had been spent as an overgrown, poorly-coordinated, though powerfully wiry child with undeveloped athletic skill. He sought out the instructor, a Major James Tennant, who had not just been a veteran of Dunnan's War but had also posted four enemy kills in the very close-combat situation Will was about to undertake today.

Tennant had taken Forling under his wing, and in virtually every free moment in that first year at the academy the major mentored Will in the use of the C-1 in single combat situations. Knife fighting unlocked a level of hand-eye coordination and body control the young cadet didn't know he had, and within months the resulting athleticism translated to boxing, horsemanship and even rugby. In a short time, Forling's 6-foot-4 frame was an asset rather than an impediment, especially as he began filling out that frame, and shortly following his physical transformation, Will shed his stumbling, graceless interpersonal immaturity, becoming a confident young man and an indomitable cavalry officer respected, and even feared a little, by his peers.

A year and a half later, Forling had forgotten none of those lessons. He would put them, and his C-1, to the test at this moment.

The Udar had doffed his headgear and released Sarah from his grasp. He stepped forward, away from the assembled captors and hostages. Sarah wasn't free to step toward Ardenian lines, but Charlotte did drape Forling's coat around her naked body.

Rapan'na began circling around Will, his face contorted into a series of furious and menacing expressions, his tongue intermittently displaying in full.

Forling stood still in a fighting stance, eyeing the man with a steely gaze. "I came here to fight, not make faces," he said calmly.

The Udar then rushed at him, his right hand raised and the blade of his *Izwei* pointed downward in a stabbing position.

Will crossed his raised arms in a blocking position, right hand forward, catching the wrist holding the *Izwei* in the resulting X. Unlike Rapan'na, Will held his C-1 in a forward position, the effect of which was that when he disengaged from the block, he ripped the Udar's knife wrist with the serrated edge of his C-1.

He'd drawn first blood. The Udar howled with rage.

. . .

"What the red hell is that?" said Patrick from the bridge of the *Adelaide* 1,000 yards from the shore, as close as

225

the ship's draft would allow without running it aground. He was one of four of the ship's officers observing the events on the beach through field glasses.

"Single combat," said Rawer, who stood next to him. "Same as that savage in the brig challenged you with."

Patrick deduced the rest. The cavalry had probably gutted the Udar force at Sutton's Hill the previous day, and in a pitched battle the enemy would have little chance of survival. With those hostages, though, the Udar would still have had the leverage to shape this encounter as they wanted.

And if their headman's attitude was anything like that of the beast Ago'an his crew had hauled out of the drink the previous afternoon, the Udar probably expected no Ardenians would be a match for their champion. So they'd have a chance at salvaging their foray.

It was more than that, though, he thought. This was also a way to slow the action down and fix the Ardenians in a disadvantaged position.

"Just look at this," he told Rawer. "The whole force, almost 400 men, standing around on a beach watching a knife fight. Sitting ducks, they are."

"I imagine they figure this is the only way they're getting those hostages out," Rawer observed.

"I don't disagree," said Patrick. "But Udar has something else up his sleeve. Why'd they stay here last night instead of rushing away down the beach to meet the reinforcements? Why *here*? And now this spectacle with the knives," he groaned. "Wasting time."

"You think they're circling around from the mountains?" asked Rawer.

"Can't say. Just feels like something else is going on that we're not seeing."

"Commander, signal comin' in from the *Louise*!" the observation tower called down. "They say they've sighted an enemy column coming up the beach. Division strength at least, cavalry and infantry."

Louise had pulled into position slightly before dawn, locating herself three miles north of the Udar camp along the coast, on the other side of a small cape jutting west into Leopold Bay, just ten miles south of Strongstead. If they were spotting the enemy, that meant the Udar were advancing from the citadel, and the Ardenians would have maybe an hour to complete the evacuation before being overrun.

"*Castamere* confirms!" called the tower. The other frigate was parked just off the coast slightly to the east of *Louise* at the opposite end of the small cape; the two ships were perhaps a mile apart.

"And there it is," Patrick said. He ordered a message sent via the signal lamp to both ships: OPEN FIRE.

Loud, rumbling booms issued forth in the distance as *Castamere* and *Louise* let loose barrages from their 100-pounder guns.

"There's more of them somewhere," Patrick said. He knew Udar attacked from the back whenever they could.

He panned the scene as the two champions circled each other–left, right, and up...

"There. You see that? One o'clock from the knife fight, about thirty feet up the cliffside."

"I see a path," Rawer said. "And it leads to...what is that?"

"It's the mouth of a cave," Patrick answered.

"Looks more like a doorway," Rawer observed. "That looks like it's been cut or blasted open, don't you think?"

"Decidedly straight walls and an arc shape at the ceiling," the commander agreed.

He put down his field glasses for a moment, his head in a nod. Then he raised them again and looked at the peculiar feature of the rock face.

Through the glasses, Patrick made out the figure of a man in the garb of an Udar warrior emerging from the cave mouth. He was shortly joined by another, and another, until the entire ledge adjoining the cave was full of Udar. Less than 300 yards down the rocky path from that ledge was the beach–and the Ardenians.

"Sonofabitch," Patrick lamented. "I knew it."

"All right," he snarled. "Here's what I want. Give me a firing solution for that rock face just above our little doorway. Continuous fire, please."

Rawer relayed the order to the ship's weapons officer, and *Adelaide*'s three 100-pounder pivot guns opened up with a series of thunderous blasts.

. . .

THIRTY SEVEN

The Beach – Morning (Third Day)

After Will's opening score on Rapan'na, the Udar then withdrew into mostly defensive movements, continuing to circle the young cavalryman and restraining himself to a few feints, but no more lunges.

Forling decided it was time to take the initiative. He noticed that his opponent was bleeding freely from the slash on his right wrist, and questioned whether Rapan'na's grip on his *Izwei* was strong enough to resist being disarmed.

So he advanced on the Udar, his blade in a forward position in his right hand at chest level. Will feinted at a knife-punch to the heart, bringing Rapan'na's left hand up in a blocking motion to his inside, and instead he ripped down at the Udar's wrist, opening a gash on the inside of his forearm. Rapan'na counterattacked, stabbing at Will's throat with his right hand. That was exactly what Will anticipated, sweeping across with his left arm and blocking the Udar's thrust.

Not quite enough, though, as the tip of the *Izwei* grazed Will's left cheek as he turned his head away from the attack. A one-inch gash opened under his eye.

Will wasn't through with the exchange. Having brought his C-1 down for the ripping motion on Rapan'na's blocking arm, he swung his body back to his left and caught the Udar in the abdomen just above his navel with the tip of his knife, and then stepped away.

Two cuts for one. He wouldn't be as pretty, but he was closer to getting out of this fight alive.

Just then Will could hear thunder up the beach from his location, and then three loud cracks in succession from very close by, followed by the whistling of shells flying overhead.

229

The ground shook as those munitions pounded the rock face of the cliffside to his right.

Rapan'na suddenly appeared rattled, and clutched at the cut on his abdomen. "*Zohi!*" he barked at Will. "*Sisgohad'da, mizuon. Quee bin'an.*"

"There's more where that came from, you sonofabitch," Will replied, wiping the cut on his cheek and noticing the blood was flowing a bit more freely than he was comfortable with.

Little else was audible after that as *Adelaide's* guns unleashed a maelstrom on the cliffside.

...

The first volley of fire from *Adelaide's* 100-pounder guns didn't quite land on the rock face above the cliff mouth. One shell landed below and pulverized the ledge some fifty Udar were standing on, sending the men into the air and tumbling down the cliff in a free fall.

They were out of this fight before they were in it.

Another shell directly hit the rock to the left of the cave, but didn't do any structural damage Patrick could see. The third hit below the ledge, sending a hail of dirt and rock flying out in the direction of the Udar camp.

"Adjust fire," came the call from Captain Horace Frey, the ship's weapons officer, relaying coordinates to the battery of pivot guns. Seconds later, the guns blasted out a new round of shells.

This time the rock face above the cave crumpled with the force of the three blasts hitting it. Large boulders tumbled down to what was the ledge at the cave's mouth and rolled to the beach in a mini-avalanche. Smaller ones fell, it appeared, into the cave's floor.

Patrick could see Udar pouring to the cave mouth, desperately attempting to clamber down the uneven cliffside where the path had been.

"Fire for effect!" called Frey. Another volley blasted out of the 100-pounders.

This time the cliffside just seemed to give way completely, and after the rumbling that followed, there was no evidence of a cave at all – just a large pile of stones filling a crevice in the rock.

...

In the human abdominal arena, on the exterior of the peritoneal cavity running through the rectus abdominus muscles from the ribs to the pelvis, is a blood vessel called the superior epigastric artery. The epigastric artery carries oxygenated blood from the heart to the anterior abdominal wall.

A lot of blood, as it turns out.

And when Will cut Rapan'na in the abdomen just before the cannon fire interrupted their bout of single combat, the tip of his C-1 severed the Udar's superior epigastric artery.

A laceration to that particular blood vessel isn't immediately fatal, but it's far more serious than it appears. That became clear in this case, as blood continued seeping steadily from Rapan'na's abdomen as he continued circling Will, cursing at him with utmost vituperation.

But Rapan'na's fighting demeanor slowly became weaker and weaker, and after the cliff face exploded in a hail of flying stones, Will knew it was time to finish the Udar. He feinted to the right, noting his opponent's loss of coordination in clumsily reacting to the feint, and lunged toward his knife hand. Will extended his left hand to block Rapan'na's counterthrust, knocking the Udar's right hand upward and loosening his grip on the *Izwei*. With his own right hand, Will plunged his C-1 into Rapan'na's right shoulder.

He then ripped the C-1 out of the man's body while planting a boot into his chest. Rapan'na fell to his back with a gurgle, then frantically rolled to his right in an attempt to get up. He crouched on his side, reaching for the *Izwei,* which had fallen just away from his hand.

231

But Will kicked the knife away.

"You're finished," he said.

Rapan'na silently rolled onto his stomach, attempting to push himself to his feet. His strength was fading.

"I said you're finished," Will said, as he brought his C-1 down on the man's upper spine, driving him into the sand.

The Udar lay lifeless, his eyes filled with dull terror.

. . .

THIRTY EIGHT

The Beach – Morning (Third Day)

When Rapan'na hit the sand, and the reverberation of *Adelaide*'s cannonade began to ebb from the camp with only the lingering thunder from up the beach providing the roar of battle, the morale of the Udar subsided as quickly as the sound of the ship's guns.

"Now hand over those hostages," Terhune ordered to the woman standing next to Sarah. "And I mean right now."

Charlotte, stricken, nodded. Sarah ran past the body of Rapan'na into the arms of her brother. The remainder of the Ardenian captives followed suit into the mass of the Ardenian cavalry, who were busily shedding jackets, unfurling bedrolls and coughing up whatever items they could to cover the captives' state of undress.

What happened next had been discussed, but not rehearsed. *Adelaide's* Marines set up a chain, a receiving line, of sorts, to usher the captives onto the ramp that *Yarmouth's* crew had unfolded into the shallow water of Watkins Gulf next to the shore, and two by two the women quickly filed up the ramp to the sidewheeler's deck. The cavalrymen assisted, some carrying captives too weakened or dazed by their ordeal to climb the ramp, and shortly a relatively smooth evacuation was underway.

"Come with us," Will said to Charlotte. "It's time to go home. You've had an awful time of it. Nobody should have to go through what they've put you through."

"No," she said, her eyes welling with tears. "It's too late."

"It's not," he said. "The boat's here. We can get you out right now."

"You don't understand," she said. "My three daughters are in Uris Udar. They are only safe because I made a promise. If I leave with you, I've betrayed them and they will suffer for my actions. One does not renege on a promise to the Udar."

"So what are you going to do?" asked Sarah, who had stayed behind. "Go with the rest of your camp?"

Charlotte shook her head. "I can't do that either."

"Why not?" asked Latham.

"Rapan'na never appointed a successor as *Var'asha*," she explained. "So this *Anur* has no leader, and without a leader there can be no *javeen*. It is the law."

"I don't understand," said Sarah. "So you're not a *javeen*. So what?"

"I am not Udar," she said, as a pair of warriors quietly came behind her. "If I am not *javeen*, I am *azmeri*."

The others gave quizzical looks.

"No," said Sarah, who understood what she was saying. "No, no, no. That can't happen. You don't have to…"

"Shhh," Charlotte said, softly. She embraced Sarah lovingly, gasping with tears as she did so.

And then to Robert. "You look so much like Matthew," she said, a weeping smile across her face as she put her hand to his cheek. "He was a wonderful young man. Take care of your sister."

The noise of shells exploding got progressively louder to the west as the two Udar warriors approached Charlotte. She turned and nodded at them both, and then the three ambled away toward the large blaze still very much alight in the center of the camp.

Latham caught Will as he staggered a bit, his left hand pressed to the gash on his cheek. "It's time to get you out of here," he said.

The Ardenian group left on the beach was beginning to thin considerably. Nearly all of the captives had already been loaded onto *Yarmouth*; now it was the cavalrymen loading their horses onto its deck.

"Let's go home," said Terhune. "Come on now. That's an order. I'm still the one giving orders around here, dammit."

As she neared the bonfire, they could see Charlotte lifting a roll of necklaces off her shoulders and over her head and handing them to one of the women, while another buckled a collar around her neck. Two ropes were threaded through rings in the collar, to her right and left. And the Udar warriors escorting her then pulled those ropes taut, standing ten feet apart from her in each direction. Slowly, they walked her toward the fire.

"No bloody way," Rob said.

"It's the way of their world," Broadham replied. "This is what we've been up against for as long as we've had a country."

The sound of the guns increased again, and beyond the camp up the beach they could see Udar horsemen approaching rapidly, as they attempted to outrun the shells from *Castamere* and *Louise*.

Nothing else needed to be said, as that beach was about to become an inferno of violence. The cavalrymen had managed to escort the last of the captives and horses onto *Yarmouth*, which was now tightly packed. Not all of the Ardenians would fit aboard.

"There's enough room in the lifeboats for the rest of us," Broadham said. "We've got to move if we don't want to end up in that fire."

The remainder of the party, including Latham, Terhune, Rob, Will, Sarah, and the Marines, pushed the four rowboats off the beach and clambered aboard.

As they rowed away, they could see Charlotte, her head held high, calmly walking into the fire as the Udar warriors held the ropes taut against her collar.

Just then, the rain clouds which had been gathering since before dawn began letting loose their wares, and a warm rain pelted the evacuation.

In the second boat, Sarah buried her head in Rob's chest and wept. He enveloped her in the most complete embrace he could manage as his own composure melted away. The two Stuart children silently disintegrated into mourning as the four boats made their way for *Adelaide* and safety.

As he rowed in the first boat, Will fixed his gaze on Sarah and Robert. The latter happened to look up at that moment, saw his friend amid the downpour, a bloody bandage wrapped around his head to cover the gash under his left eye. Will had a vacant, spent look in his eyes.

It was then Robert recognized that as shattering as the experience had been for him, he might have come through it better than Will had.

. . .

THIRTY NINE

Cross wasn't unfamiliar with all-nighters, but for most of his life the circumstances of his skipping nocturnal respite involved intoxicating liquors and pleasures of the flesh. This time he'd almost pulled another.

The previous night's activities had no such recreational component to them, though if Cross were to be honest with himself, the great game he was joining was as much a source of entertainment as any debauchery he could find in the Elkstrand on a Saturday.

The five conspirators, Sebastian, his father, Gregg, Dees and Reeves, stayed aboard the yacht until after midnight, going over a plan to turn the Special Air Force into a showpiece for Ardenian technology buried by bureaucracy and corruption over the past ten years. The fresh outbreak of war with the Udar two days earlier had provided them with a perfect opportunity to do just that. With a desperate disadvantage in manpower against what was rumored to be an Udar invasion force numbering in the millions approaching the Tweade, firepower to serve as a force multiplier was Ardenia's only hope to avoid being overrun, and that prospect meant no one in his right mind would refuse hardware donated to the cause when it was brought to the battlefield.

The Special Air Force was going to be the conduit for that hardware.

Reeves informed Sebastian that in ten days he'd be able to take delivery of the *Wainwright*, an airship built on the basic design of the *Clyde* and *Ann Marie* but with some key improvements, most notably in an increased top travel speed of 145 miles per hour and a significant improvement in cargo capacity due to a much larger cabin and use of hydrogen, rather than hot air, as a lifting gas. Reeves would be bringing the *Wainwright* down to Barley Point himself, and it would be loaded with armaments: Trunxton chain guns, Thurman rifles, mortar tubes, crates of a new invention called a hand grenade, land mines and much more. Being close to the battlefront, Sebastian would then be in a position to distribute the material to commanders in the field who needed it most, outside of the highly-politicized and bureaucratized Army central command.

In the meantime, the *Clyde* and *Ann Marie* would be covering and haranguing the enemy's advance with the Trunxton guns they'd soon have mounted to their cabins. The biplanes would be patrolling Ardenia's southern skies in search of the flock of blood raptors which had apparently been on the scene at Strongstead per messages Dees had received.

Dees also informed Sebastian that his ticket on the morning's commercial locomotive was canceled. He was instead riding on a train chartered by the Office of Special Warfare along with his new boss, plus a security force of 300 ex-Army infantry and cavalry warriors privately hired and equipped with advanced weapons the enemy hadn't yet seen.

"To make sure you don't catch a *Gazol* in your sleep," the General said.

The meeting broke up, with Gregg shaking Sebastian's hand and wishing him well, and Reeves reminding him he'd be seeing him soon in Barley Point. His father gave him an embrace.

"I'm proud of you, son" he said. "Stay safe down there, do what General Dees says and your future is secure."

"Thank you, Papa," Sebastian responded. "I love you."

Sebastian then followed Dees aboard his submersible, which headed back downriver for a few miles and left the Morgan for the Shelton River, a smaller tributary which joined the Morgan from the south just east of the Capitol District. Following the Shelton for two miles to the south, the craft then docked just across a thoroughfare from Belgrave Station.

"You'll get to see some interesting toys now," Dees said, leading Sebastian through the mostly deserted train station. It was three of the clock; no commercial trains would be leaving for another three hours and arrivals were only dribbling in.

After several minutes of hustling through the station away from its central hub the two came upon a train parked at Track Eighteen, an out-of-the-way berth clearly not favored by the commercial locomotive lines. Sebastian marveled at the engine, a sleek design without a smokestack, that Dees told him was powered by methanol and an electric battery. That was something he hadn't known was possible. Dees further said the locomotive was capable of traveling in excess of 100 miles per hour on tracks which could support such a speed.

They walked along the tracks surveying the cars attached to the engine. There were four regular passenger cars, along with two first-class cars, that Dees said would accommodate the security force and engineers making the trip south.

Then came the flatcars, which contained a few other toys Sebastian hadn't seen. For example, Dees was sending down twelve lorries like the one he'd seen in the basement of the warehouse, but these had chain gun emplacements mounted aft of their beds to offer superior firepower as well as high-speed troop and equipment transport. Sebastian also saw six artillery pieces which appeared to be land-based versions of the navy's 100-pounder pivot guns, but of a lighter weight. These were four-inch breech-loaded guns with nine-foot barrels that could be either horse-drawn or attached to the lorries Dees was sending to Barley Point.

"Effective range of fire of just under seven miles," the general said.

On another flatcar was a pair of four-foot calcium lanterns, which Dees said were excellent for use as searchlights to illuminate the enemy from a distance, especially from the air.

Finally, after a dozen boxcars loaded with ammunition and supplies, they came across a truly unexpected surprise on a flatcar. It was a motor sedan, a four-seat roadster with a convertible canvas cover.

"For speed and comfort," Dees said. "You'll have fun driving that contraption."

"I can imagine," said Cross. He'd had a motor sedan of his own until a couple of months ago, that he'd had to sell amid Airbound's financial exigencies, but it had been nothing as sexy as this.

The two walked back toward the front of the train, and as they climbed aboard the first-class cars Dees pointed out Cross' berth.

"Get some sleep, will you?" he said. "You look like hell."

Entering, Cross noted he'd been provided with several Army uniforms in the wardrobe closet, and a case sat on the overhead bunk with a tag bearing the sign "Light Reading," assumedly for the day-long trip to Dunnansport. It was after four of the clock, and the autumn sunrise was less than two hours away.

He climbed in the bunk without even undressing, and was asleep almost as his head hit the pillow. Cross didn't even stir when the train left the station.

...

FORTY

Watkins Gulf – Noon (Third Day)

Aboard the sidewheeler, the *Yarmouth's* crew had laid out a spread of barley bread, chicken broth and hot tea for the rescuees, along with converting its cavernous saloon into Ardenia's largest dressing room. There, the rescuees picked through clothing items donated from the crews of *Adelaide, Castamere* and *Louise* to satisfy the requirements of the modern civilization they were happy to rejoin after two days in primitive captivity. That activity led to a swap meet of sorts, as the newly-clothed rescuees were then returning the items borrowed from the rescuers on the beach in what began to resemble a quite convivial, and greatly relieved, social gathering aboardship. *Yarmouth's* folding ramp was locked back in its stowed position and the steamboat's side-mounted paddlewheels began churning quickly in reverse, backing it away from the coast to the safety awaiting to the east.

As *Yarmouth* pulled away from the beach, *Adelaide's* four lifeboats were being rowed in a similar direction. The Marines made quick time of closing the 1,000 yards through the increasing rain to the mother ship and, as *Yarmouth* executed a tight spin by reversing the direction of its paddles so as to point its stern forward, the lifeboats drew, one by one, to the side of *Adelaide's* hull. The ship's crew quickly attached lines to each boat as their occupants climbed rope ladders onto its deck, Sarah and Will getting help from the Marines in charge of their embarkation.

On deck, Terhune gave a salute to Patrick, and a handshake. "Flawlessly done, Commander," he said. "And in particular, thanks for that late save on the cliffside. We might have been cut to pieces if you hadn't solved that problem for us."

"It was a close shave today," Patrick said. "Everyone did their duty. You, young man," he said, turning to Will, "put on one hell of a spectator sport on that beach."

"This is my Lieutenant, Will Forling," Terhune said. "He's one hell of a cavalry officer."

Patrick extended a hand to Will, who'd saluted him. "Outstanding, son."

"Thank you, sir," said Will. He reached for the commander's hand to shake it, and noticeably wobbled on his feet.

"Let's get this young man some medical attention," Patrick said, as Will attempted to wave him off. He summoned a pair of crew members to escort Forling to *Adelaide's* sick bay.

Sarah went with them as they hustled Will belowdecks.

...

The lifeboats secured, *Adelaide* took up a position flanking *Yarmouth's* right as the two ships made their way east to Cotter's Point, where they'd follow the coast north to Dunnansport. In less than a day they'd be on dry land on the opposite side of the Tweade, though nobody really thought that meant safety.

In his sea-cabin after personally supervising the billeting of his passengers in the staterooms, the commander set to work composing two documents. The first would be a concise message to be circulated via the teletext wires as soon as *Adelaide* docked at Dunnansport, and the second, a longer report to be delivered to the Admiralty at Port William, Port Excelsior and Principia and every other military destination in Ardenia shortly thereafter. Patrick knew Terhune would be doing the same thing.

...

Will's stay in the ship's sick bay wasn't a long one. After the ship's surgeon gave him seven stitches on the gash below his left eye, she replaced his bandage with a new one treated with carbolic acid to guard against infection. The surgeon also prescribed a gallon of hot tea for what she suggested was dehydration at the head of his faint condition, and he was brought to a stateroom to clean up and rest for the journey back to Dunnansport.

Before Will found a bed to sleep in for the first time in four days, though, there was a bit of friction.

Sarah had accompanied Will to the sick bay, and she attempted to make herself useful as a spare nurse while his wound was dressed. Will was having none of that. He was crashing quickly from the adrenaline of the fight at the beach and the grief of his loss was finally beginning to hit him after more than a day of feeling little other than numbness as the battle raged. What Will did not need was for Sarah, who'd thought of him as a clumsy oaf since she was little, to see the show of weakness that he knew was coming as his energy and spirit left him.

So he chased her off.

"Sarah," he said, as the doctor began working on him.

"Yes, Will?" she responded.

"Get out."

"Are you serious?"

"Yes. Leave me alone, will you?"

Shocked and furious, she did just that, storming out of the sick bay and running into Rob outside of the door.

"What happened?" he asked. "Is he all right?"

"Evidently!" she seethed, tears in her eyes. "He threw me out of there."

Rob chuckled.

"What?" she demanded. "You think that's funny?"

"A little," he said, and then had the first good laugh he could remember.

After a few seconds, so did Sarah.

Rob advised her to go easy on Will, who had fought very hard not to break down after learning of the death of his parents during the expedition of the past three days. She didn't know, though she certainly expected, that he'd lost his loved ones as well.

This is hard on all of us, she thought. But she wasn't about to leave Will alone. Not anymore.

At that point she remembered she was wearing Will's coat and nothing else, and decided it was long past time to rejoin the ranks of civilization. Soon she was in the shower of her stateroom scrubbing herself with the potassium-based "saltwater soap" *Adelaide* carried. The gray paste she'd been covered with the previous night had dried and become painful on her skin, and it came off only grudgingly in the hot alkaline water pumping through the ship's plumbing system. Finally, she judged that she was passably clean, though it felt like she'd scraped away half her skin cells in the process, not to mention every hair south of her neck to go with them.

Sarah could clearly feel herself coming down from the high of the *marwai* the Udar had made her drink, and it wasn't like an alcohol hangover. She just felt bone-tired, even after an invigorating shower. After forty-eight hours in a drug-induced haze where she could feel her judgement slipping away from her, Sarah was just grateful the rescue came when it did.

She'd had a couple of quick minutes on the lifeboat to talk to the Navy translator, Joe Broadham, and he'd asked her about the effects of the *marwai,* noticing that her lips had darkened and assuming that came from taking it. She'd quickly told him of the experience, and he'd answered that his mother had gone through the same thing.

"You're Georgia Broadham's son," she realized.

"I am. And if I can help you in any way, just say so."

Which he'd already done. A naval uniform was laid out on the bed for her, with a note from Broadham that said "No need returning this one; it's a gift and maybe a collector's item someday." She figured that would suit her just fine, and after fashioning a scarf to cover the stubble atop her head she made her way to the ship's mess. There she found most of the rest of the *Adelaide's* passengers around a table.

The men stood at attention as she approached. Rob gave her a tight brotherly hug.

"Gentlemen," she greeted them. They returned the greeting.

Rob then tried to make some formal introductions, which weren't needed. She'd met the colonel through her father at the Barley Point Ball the previous year, and she'd met Latham on his previous trip to Hilltop Farm a few weeks earlier. Latham told the story of finding Ethan and Hannah, giving Sarah the good news that she'd meet up with them in Dunnansport, and Rob delivered the bad news about Uncle David, which made Sarah cry all over again. And Latham and Terhune also expressed their regrets about her brother Matthew at Strongstead.

It was an awful lot to take, and she made her excuses, saying she'd like to be alone for a little while if that was all right. Of course, was the unanimous response.

But Sarah had no desire to be alone.

She knocked on the door of Will's stateroom, and entered without permission. It turned out that Will was a side-sleeper, something she hadn't known about him.

"Go away," he croaked, his back turned to the door as he lay in the stateroom's small bed.

"I already did that," she said, approaching the bunk and sitting aside Will.

"Sarah," she heard him protest faintly, "leave me alone."

"No, Will, I'm not going to do that," she scolded him. "You're more alone than you've ever been in your life. So am I, and so is Robert. Now's not the time for us to be alone."

He didn't move. She pulled on his shoulder, trying to get him to roll toward her. He resisted.

"I want to see it," she said, leaning over him and gently pulling at the bandage.

"Are you crazy?" he snapped, quietly. "Let it be."

"Oh, come on. It's my scar, after all."

"Yours? How is it yours?"

"Because you got it saving me," she said sweetly.

Will turned his head, ever so slightly, and squinted at her with his left eye. "I got it fulfilling my mission," he mumbled.

"Which was saving me," she asserted.

"Which was saving 367 people," he responded matter-of-factly.

"Well, but none of them are more grateful than I am," she said. "If you want, I'll show you how much."

Another look from Will's left eye.

"There is something you can do," he said.

"Oh? What is that?"

"Let me sleeeeeeep," he croaked.

Sarah was taken aback, and gave a little frustrated grunt. But after a short pause, she cheerily responded, "Sure!"

And then kicked off her shoes and spooned up behind Will on the bed, throwing her arm over him and laying down for a nice, long nap. She needed it just as much as he did, after all.

...

In his sea-cabin, Patrick had finished his message for the wires, calling in an ensign to hustle it to the teletext as soon as they made Dunnansport. It said…

"367 FEMALE CAPTIVES RESCUED, EVACUATED FROM BEACH SOUTHEAST OF STRONGSTEAD. CITADEL FELL TO THE ENEMY 31 DAYS PRIOR, SENT FALSE TELETEXT MESSAGES MASKING UDAR CONQUEST. ENEMY CAPABLE OF WEAPONIZING RAPTORS, USED TO WIPE OUT STRONGSTEAD, NONE SEEN DURING DUNNAN'S CLAIM CAMPAIGN. ALL FORTS, CITIES SHOULD BE ON ALERT FOR AIR ATTACK.

"ENEMY ADVANCING TO DUNNAN'S CLAIM, AT MINIMUM DIVISION STRENGTH AND LIKELY LARGER FORCE, ALONG COAST, POSSIBLE RAT-LINES IN MOUNTAIN CAVES ALONG ROGERS RANGE. ADVISE FULL MOBILIZATION TO DEFEND EAST BANK OF TWEADE AND NAVAL BLOCKADE OF WATKINS GULF FROM COASTLINE SOUTH.

"UDAR PRISONERS TAKEN, INCLUDING ONE AGO'AN, BROTHER OF UDAR KING, AND EDYENE, DAUGHTER OF CAPTIVE ANN LUDLOW OF MAIDENSTEAD, WHO HAS COOPERATED AND PROVIDED MUCH INTEL. EDYENE WISHES TO DEFECT, AM SUBMITTING POSITIVE REPORT TO DUNNANSPORT JUDGE ADVOCATE. AGO'AN ACCUSED OF MURDERING ANN LUDLOW, REQUEST TRIAL UNDER MARTIAL CODE."

He'd have a lot more detail in the longer report he was writing, that he was bound and determined to finish before *Adelaide* made port.

"Commander," Rawer said, "*Castamere* and *Louise* have pulled alongside."

"I'll be right there," he said as the First Mate ascended to the bridge.

The four ships then sailed abreast, into the downpour with *Yarmouth* hugging closest to the shore as the convoy rounded Cotter's Point and headed north.

. . .

FORTY ONE

It wasn't quite dawn yet, but outside the window of Will's stateroom aboard the *Adelaide* there were lights visible. Those were from the city of Dunnansport, which the ship was approaching from the south along with the three others in its convoy, and they were just bright enough to wake Will from a deep, necessary slumber.

He smiled, for the first time in a while, when he felt an arm draped over his side. That was Sarah, who had refused to leave him alone when he demanded it.

So that's how it is with this one now, he thought. *Well, she always has run hot and cold.*

He reached over with his right hand and gently pulled on the pinky finger of the hand hanging over his shoulder. He heard her give a little squeal. So he pulled again, just a little harder.

"I let you sleep, you know," she said.

"You did. Thank you."

"I'm going to have to tell everybody I slept with you."

"Funny. You'd better not. You'll get us in trouble."

"Well, it's true. We did sleep together."

"That's right. You took advantage of me. What a loose woman you are."

"A loose woman?" she gasped, feigning offense. "Why, Will Forling! You're going to have to be a lot nicer to me than that from now on."

"Why is that?"

She sprang up into a sitting position and roughly rocked him onto his back.

"OK, joke's over," she said. "I want to be serious with you."

"Sarah," Will began…

"No. I have something to say."

"Before you do that," he retorted, "*I* have something to say. Because I have a pretty good idea where this is going, and it's not going to work."

"What?" she gasped.

"Think about it, Sarah," he said. "You've been right about me all your life. I'm the goofy kid next door and you always knew you were out of my league. Well, that's a lot more true than it's ever been."

"It is certainly *not*," protested Sarah.

"Yes it is. Who am I now? I've got no parents and no relatives, other than a half-dozen brothers who all now live 500 miles away or more, and I barely even know any of them because the youngest one is ten years older than me. I have no money and no prospect of getting any in the near future. I couldn't even buy you a ring, and I can't pay tuition to finish school at the Academy. Which is the least of my concerns, because as soon as this ship docks I'm going right back to Barley Point to fight in a war that we might not even win. I am the last guy you should give your heart to right now."

"Oh, that is just completely *wrong*," she reprimanded him. "Everything you just said are reasons for you to marry me right this very minute."

"How can you possibly figure that?" he asked, sitting up.

"You say you don't have any family? Well, that's not true – you have family all over Ardenia and they are going to be there for you, Will. Your brothers are great people and you know it.

"And even if what you were saying was true, which it's not, you should marry me and then you'll be surrounded by people who love you and have known you all our lives. So that's not a problem."

"That's not what I'm saying, Sarah."

"Shut up," she fussed. "I'm talking. And no money? Please. The Stuarts have money we don't even know about. You marry me and you're *immediately* rich. And by the way, we now have more than one family business without people to run it, so not only would you have a job, you'd have a great one."

"I have no idea how to run a storehouse or broker commodities or any of that," he said.

"So? You'll learn," she said. "You're not stupid, Will.

"And as for the war, you chased down an entire *Anur* and took out their headman in a knife fight to save me from the worst nightmare there is. You have no idea how close I was to being gone forever. Do you think I don't have faith you'll make it back from the war? You're an even bigger hero than my father, and I didn't think that was possible."

"There are millions of them out there," he said. "You don't know what you're saying."

"I'm saying I'm willing to bet on you, you big goat!" she said. "Will, I've never been out of your league. I was a stupid, silly girl who never realized I had the man of my dreams right next door. And now that I finally woke up and you're right here there is no way in the world I'm going to let you go."

Silence ensued for a few moments.

251

"Damn, Sarah," he said. "That was pretty good stuff just now."

"You think so?" she wiped away a tear.

"Yeah, I do," he said.

"Ssssooooo…" she ran her hand over his chest, "what do you think?"

"I think we need to have a talk with Rob, and I think we'd also better have a talk with your aunt," he said. "We need to make some wise decisions right now, not rash ones."

"I'll take that for now," she said, getting off the bed and heading for his door, shoes in hand. "Ship's about to dock. Get up, Forling."

…

FORTY TWO

Dunnansport – Morning (Fourth Day)

Cross had been to this up-and-coming little burg a few weeks ago, having taken the *Clyde* on a public-relations tour stop after the *Justice's* crash, but he hadn't seen its train station before.

It's nice, he thought. *Looks like it's brand new.*

There was a platform which reeked of freshly-cut wood, and a station house which looked newly completed, or not quite so, as even in the pre-dawn hours Cross could hear hammering from the wall furthest from the tracks. The train station gave off the impression of being the center of a crash construction program in Dunnansport, which had swelled to multiple times its normal size as resources and manpower began pouring into the city in advance of its expected defense against the Udar.

Cross, who two days earlier would have laughed at the idea of himself as a military man, was now an integral part of that defense.

He'd noticed just before the locomotive reached the station that workers were laying more tracks to the west of the city, which he'd read in his briefing book was a rush-job on finishing a rail line to Barley Point, and then from there northwest to Battleford and on to Trenory to the north along the Tweade. The Army was being dragooned into that construction effort, and the two infantry divisions already in place had devoted half their number, a total of 9,000 men, to completing the Dunnansport-to-Barley Point leg of that line. The crash construction program meant that in a week the line would likely be finished after ten years of inaction that had greatly frustrated the locals. In another week, it was likely to be through to Battleford.

Which assumed Ardenia had that much time, Cross groused to himself.

As the train stopped and Cross and three of the other officers of the new Special Air Force took coffee with General Dees in his private car, a young lieutenant climbed aboard and found them for a briefing.

"Speak, Lieutenant Mason," Dees said.

"Yes, General. Here's what I've found out. The mission was successful, and just downriver at the port the naval convoy is docking, or will be in the next few minutes. A regiment of cavalry from Barley Point under Colonel Terhune, supplemented by militia from Dunnansport and Battleford along with a few Marines, went almost all the way to Rogers Range and tracked down the Udar raiders, wiping them out in a battle on Sutton Hill and then entering their camp.

"You won't believe this, sir, but they secured the release of 367 hostages by putting up one of their number, a Lieutenant Will Forling, against the Udar headman in a knife fight, and Forling won."

"Bloody good show!" Dees exclaimed.

Cross had to agree. "I want to meet that guy," he said.

"They evac'ed the force and the hostages by sea," the lieutenant said, "but despite some shelling of the coastline by the frigates in the convoy, the enemy was advancing at full speed up the coast. In a couple of days they could well be at the Tweade – either here, Barley Point or Battleford or, given their numbers, at all three. Barley Point so far is the weak point in the defense of the river; we don't have reinforcements there."

"We are the reinforcements," Cross said. Dees agreed.

"Two more things, sir," Lt. Mason added.

"First, I'm sure you've heard that somehow the enemy has managed to train and deploy raptors as military assets. We have no intel yet as to where they will surface next."

"That's what SAF is for," Cross said. "And that equipment we're carrying. All of it."

"We can handle the raptors," Dees agreed. "How many of them can Udar have?"

"And finally," Mason concluded, "it wasn't known that Strongstead had fallen for practically an entire month because they'd been signaling via teletext that all was well. Dunnansport wired them a message yesterday saying they knew those messages were lies, and got a response."

"What was it?" Dees asked.

"The respondent identified himself as a Lt. Daniel Thorne of Alvedorne, teletext operator at Strongstead, and said he was responding under duress with the lives of six other officers from the citadel forfeit to his cooperation."

"Thorne of Alvedorne," Dees said, recognizing the name of the nation's wealthiest family. "That isn't good. Who are the other six?"

"Naval ensign Frederick Hale of Newmarket, Marine Lt. Victor Smith of Aldingham, Army Lt. Luke Abrams of Cheatham, Army Lt. Tobias Evans of Belgarden, Army Lt. Peter Curtis of Trenory…and Army Captain Matthew Stuart of Barley Point."

. . .

FORTY THREE

Dunnansport – Morning (Fourth Day)

The wharf at the small city of, now, close to 15,000 was already a hive of activity when the ships reached the docks near the mouth of the Tweade just after dawn, proving that the grapevine was still a more effective rapid disseminator of information than even the teletext. Everybody in town knew about the Udar invasion to come, and everybody knew about the rescue along the coast of Watkins Gulf.

So when the *Yarmouth* docked at the Dunnansport wharf, a large crowd had gathered to cheer and welcome the rescuees and the cavalrymen, militia, and others who played a part in the rescue. An aid station had been set up near the wharf with hot food, lavatories and clothing for the survivors, while in a field nearby, a tent city was being constructed to house the thousands of volunteers streaming into the city via the nonstop locomotives and steamships beginning to pour in via land and sea. One of the Stuart warehouses had been cleared out and temporarily refitted as a hospital and recovery center for the captives, whose lives had been destroyed in the Udar raids and who would need help finding the strength to begin anew.

Ardenia was frantically mobilizing for war, with Dunnansport a major hub in that mobilization.

The main Army forces were being filtered to the west, as the defense of Trenory and its 200,000 residents were considered the top priority. Reinforcements were being established as well at Battleford along the Tweade, as the Fourteenth Infantry Division had passed through from its base at Carteret to the north the day before, disembarking from locomotive cars and immediately marching up the river road on the east bank. Horse-drawn artillery and steam wagons carrying armaments and supplies dotted the column. The Fourteenth had detached a large number of their soldiers to assist in the rushed program building out the rail line, and those soldiers had stayed behind to help lay track along the river road west of Dunnansport. Impressively they'd laid an incredible eleven miles of the seventy-mile distance on the first day. In a mere week, the line, which locals had groused for years should already have been finished, would be complete.

Thus when Latham, Rob, Sarah and Will ambled down the gangplank into the city from *Adelaide*, they instantly saw that the plucky little city of Dunnansport wasn't so little anymore.

"Not the same place it was three days ago," Will said.

"You've got that right," said Latham, as he dodged a rushing Marine.

"Let's collect our horses and go see Aunt Rebecca," Rob said.

He held his sister's hand and gave her a smile. She returned it, and straightened the beret on her head. That was another gift from Broadham, who had donated his headgear to the cause of her sartorial reinforcement after remarking that nobody had ever looked better in a navy uniform.

Sarah had told Will about the origins of her outfit, and she could tell he had a bit of the jealous type in him.

"You look ridiculous in that hat," Will said.

"You just can't handle that I'm wearing another man's clothes," she needled him back.

"Nah," he said, looking at the leather coat he'd draped over his arm. "You had mine on first."

Which was a good point. She hadn't realized Will had so much skill in snappy repartee; he certainly didn't have it before he went off to school.

And that brought her a sharp pang of sadness, because it struck her that Will had sent her dozens of letters over the past two and a half years and she'd read only a few of them. They were all back at Hilltop Farm, and they were now almost assuredly ashes.

Will had seen the look on her face. "What's wrong?" he asked.

"Your letters. I think I've lost them all. Will, I didn't even read a lot of them. I'm such a shrew. I'm so sorry."

"Oh, those?" he chuckled. "Don't worry about those. I embarrassed myself with most of those letters and it's better you didn't read them."

"I really doubt that."

"Look, it's not a problem. Besides, I'll write you new ones. And this time I bet you actually will read them."

She'd kissed him hard then. "You bet right, Forling. And from now on whenever we're apart I'm going to be writing you all the time."

Terhune had debarked from *Adelaide* first, as he was now the commander of the newly-formed Lower Tweade Military District, and that meant he might be the busiest man in the region. He said he needed to get a handle on the logistics of the resupply of his garrison at Barley Point and arrange transport for his soldiers back to the base, and then he himself would be off to the smaller city up the river. Terhune gave Will one day's leave in Dunnansport to "do what you gotta go," and then directed him back to Barley Point. Forling was getting a promotion and an appointment as the Executive Officer of the Barley Point command.

Latham also was given permission to stay behind a day in Dunnansport, because Terhune told him he was putting him in command of Barley Point's engineer corps and he'd need to round up men and materials for several projects the two had discussed on the way in. "Start with that damn railroad," he'd said, "and see if you can't help those people get it done any faster."

As for Rob, Terhune told him not to even think about trying to join back up with his command. "Your family needs you, son," he said. "Consider this an indefinite leave. If you want, you can play with your militia friends in Dunnansport, but you're the man of that house now and you should act accordingly."

All of which meant that the quintet of passengers on the *Adelaide* were going their separate ways. All agreed to one last meeting before splitting up, though, that being at the Stuart mansion in Tweade's Landing where Rob and Sarah would be taking up residence.

Latham still wasn't sure what he was going to do about Ethan and Hannah, who he felt were his responsibility to deliver to the Stuarts. Perhaps he'd bring Jefferson, the manservant David brought with him on the expedition–Jefferson had made it out alive largely by keeping his head down, as best as Latham could tell, though that wasn't a negative judgment on the man's combat abilities–up to Barley Point, and then Jefferson could transport the children home. He'd have to find out if that would be necessary.

Rob had suggested to Sarah that when the contents of the Hilltop Farm strongbox showed up, they would have some decisions to make and a strategy to put together. Sarah responded that she thought Will ought to be part of that discussion, and Rob immediately knew why, giving her a big hug and yelling, "Congratulations, sis!"

"Don't say congratulations!" she scolded. "It's bad luck. You're supposed to say 'Best wishes' about an engagement."

"Oh," Rob said. "I didn't know that."

Nearly an hour later, the four had fought their way through the crowds and chaos and made their way to the Stuarts' Tweade Landing mansion. It was up to Rob to deliver the news of his death to his aunt. They'd buried David atop Sutton Hill after the battle, he told her, before riding west to rescue Sarah.

Rebecca was a wreck. She clung tightly to her niece and nephew. She gave her sympathies to Will for the loss of his parents and told him he was welcome at the house any time he wanted. And she cried, nonstop.

The burden of Rebecca's grief would have lots of bearers, however. As the morning continued, a steady stream of well-wishers made their way to the Tweade Landing mansion to pay their respects, in a makeshift wake, to one of the city's commercial giants, and David's fellow militiamen who survived the battle on the ridge west of Sutton Hill sought out Aunt Rebecca to tell her of her husband's bravery.

"I never thought of him as a military hero," she sobbed. "Even in death the old coot can still surprise me."

Rebecca said they'd soon have as complete a family reunion as was still possible. Their cousins Josey and Peter were due in later in the week; Josey was married to a banker in Port William, while Peter was a lawyer in Principia. But civilian travel into Dunnansport was rapidly becoming a challenge with all the traffic coming into the city.

Also arriving to pay his respects to David's widow was Col. Terhune. "You don't know me, ma'am," he said, "but I had the pleasure of commanding the expeditionary force out there in the last few days. And let me say that your husband is a hero. He gave his life for his country, and without him we couldn't have brought 367 of our friends, relatives, and neighbors out of the clutches of the enemy."

With that he presented her with an Ardenian flag, and the thanks of a grateful nation.

And just before lunchtime, there was another party of guests at the door, this one headed by Mistress Helen Irving of Barley Point, who had brought Ethan and Hannah the seventy miles downriver on the small river steamer *Blackbird*. They'd left early that morning and arrived with two men carrying a large trunk, which Helen said contained all of the papers Latham had rescued from Hilltop Farm, "plus a few things we thought the children might need." Helen had put the word out among the ladies of Barley Point and taken up a collection of toys, books and clothes that might replace, in some small way, what the children had lost at Hilltop Farm.

Rebecca was moved, again, to tears. "That is just the most decent thing," she said. "Mistress Irving, you are truly a saint and our newest, truest friend."

Latham smiled at Helen, and she smiled back. She kissed the children, who were being smothered by their aunt and older siblings. They then joined Latham on a pair of wicker chairs on the back veranda of the house.

"It seems you're a war hero, H.V.," she said.

"Hardly," he responded. "And call me Henry."

"Henry Latham – like the famous actor? Were you related?"

"I was. In fact, he was my father. It's a long story."

"I'd like to hear it sometime."

"I'll tell it sometime," he said. "So, you're headed home?"

"On the next boat back to Barley Point. My work here is done."

"You were amazing, Helen. Simply amazing."

"Henry, what's your plan?"

"Well, it appears I'm headed for Barley Point as well. I'm now the head of the engineering corps for the Lower Tweade Military District. I'll be leaving to make my way up there tomorrow."

"That sounds important."

"Desperate is probably a better description. But it's how I can best help the cause right now, so I'm happy to take it on."

"Well, do you have a place to stay in Barley Point?" she asked.

"I haven't even got that far. I had a room at the inn by the customs house, but with all the people coming into town, I don't know if I've still got that. And I don't know that the barracks at the military base has a spare bed, either."

"Then it's settled," she said. "There's a guest bedroom at the house that just opened up, and it's all yours."

"I'd like that, Helen. I really would."

...

FORTY FOUR

Tweade Landing – Evening (Fourth Day)

In the afternoon, two more parties of guests made their way to the Stuart house in Tweade Landing.

Will answered the door to find a pair of Army officers, a general and a major, on the front stoop. He stiffened and saluted. "General, Major. Lieutenant William Forling, sirs," he said.

"So you're the one," Dees responded, returning the salute. "Well, you're a damn celebrity for certain in this man's war. My name is Abraham Dees, and this greenhorn sonofabitch who has forgot to salute you back is Major Sebastian Cross."

"Sorry, Lieutenant," Cross said, saluting. "You'll forgive me. I'm new."

"Are you Sebastian Cross the aviator, sir?" Forling said, surprised. "It's a real honor."

"The honor's mine, son. We heard about your exploits west of here. Outstanding."

"Please come in, sirs," Will invited. He introduced the two to Rebecca, Rob, Sarah, Latham and Helen, who hadn't quite left for her return trip to Barley Point yet.

Rebecca fussed over her latest guests, insisting on serving them a late lunch from the colossal spread laid out in the dining room, thanks to donations from that morning's many well-wishers. Having been hard at work with preparations since their arrival in the morning, Dees and Cross accepted.

Rob, Will and Latham sat in with the general and the major as they ate, while the women adjourned to the kitchen.

Dees said he'd been directed to the house by Col. Terhune, who he had met at the train station as the latter had rode over to inspect the equipment being brought in on the locomotive from the Special Warfare Office and the two trains which followed it in quick succession. He said he had some surprise news for Will.

"Colonel Terhune, who by the way is now Lieutenant General Terhune," Dees said, "has put you in for not just one but two battlefield promotions. You aren't Lieutenant Forling anymore. You're now Major Forling. You became a captain on Sutton Hill and you got your current rank on that beach. Congratulations, son."

"Wow," Will said. "I don't know what to say."

"You don't have to *say* a thing," Dees said. "You have to keep doing what you're doing. Great work, son."

"The Colonel also told us you're going to be his XO at Barley Point," Cross said. "That will make us great pals, because I'm going to be quite the conduit for you to get some weapons and equipment you all have not had."

"That's good news," said Latham. "It's bare bones there now."

"And you're going to be a big part of the club too, Latham," said Dees. "Lieutenant General Terhune says you're running his engineering corps."

"That's my understanding, sir."

"Well," Cross said, "then you're going to have to build me an air base. As close to the enemy as you can get. I'll give you, oh, let's say three days or so."

Latham's eyes went wide. "I'd be more qualified to do that if I knew what an airbase looks like."

"Don't worry," Cross said. "I can walk you through that."

The two engaged in a spirited one-on-one conversation about the nature of that beast, while Dees then pulled Rob aside.

"I have something to tell you, son, that's very delicate. It's about your brother Matthew."

"I already know, sir. I was told he died when Strongstead fell."

"Actually," Dees said, "it turns out that wasn't true." He related the story of the last transmission from the citadel's captive signal officer. Rob was shocked and relieved, and so were Sarah and Rebecca when he told them, but not overly so. They knew Matthew was still a prisoner of war held by an enemy whose practice was not to keep prisoners.

Just then there was another party of guests at the door. This time it was Rebecca opening it and greeting Commander Patrick Baker of the Ardenian Navy and his girlfriend Alice Wade, who lived just a couple of blocks away.

"Oh, Patrick," she said, giving him a kiss on the cheek. "So good of you to come. And thank you so much for bringing dear Sarah home safe."

"Just wish I could have done more, ma'am."

"And Alice! Thank you for coming as well. Is this young Joseph you have with you?"

"It's nice to see you, Miss Rebecca," Alice's son said as his mother beamed.

"Oh, he's adorable! Come in, come in."

Introductions were made, and shortly, Patrick was absorbed in the conversation Dees, Cross and Latham were having. He had met Cross a few weeks before when he'd taken the *Clyde* on its public relations tour, and the aviator remembered. "It didn't strike me at the time that you were a rescuer of damsels in distress, Patrick," Cross said. "I guess I underestimated your vast capabilities for heroism!"

"Says the man who's a major in his first day of the service," came the response. "If ever there was somebody who knows how to be a hero it'd have to be you."

Patrick related that he'd fished ten Udar out of Watkins Gulf and he was awaiting orders for what to do with them as they remained aboard *Adelaide* under guard.

"We're going to have a trial for the headman in the morning," he said, "and, I imagine, a public hanging the next day."

"The folks will come from all over to see that," said Rob, who had joined the conversation. "Probably good for morale given what's ahead."

"We might make better use of this Ago'an than that," Dees said. "I may have to have a talk with your commodore." He told Patrick of the news about the officers held at Strongstead.

"What happens to the woman?" Cross asked. "What's her name again?"

"Ed-yen-nay," Patrick said, sounding it out. "I gave a letter to the judge advocate this morning suggesting she be given asylum as a defector. It'll be his call, but her mother was an Ardenian from Maidenstead who'd been taken captive. Legally I think she's probably entitled to immigrate, which is what she says she wants."

"What's she going to do?" Cross pressed.

Patrick shrugged.

"Reason I ask is we could use a translator," Cross explained. "And since we're going to be scouting the enemy from the air it might be useful to have somebody along who's traveled with them."

"That's a hell of an idea, Cross," said Dees. "If that girl is willing to cooperate, we'll take her."

"I'm all for it," said Patrick. "And she seems willing to help. Her Civil Tongue isn't the most fluent, but I imagine that would improve pretty fast."

Dees quickly scribbled down a message, then ambled out to the front yard of the house where two corporals were standing watch. "Run this over to the judge advocate at the Naval Munitions Building," he told one of them. The man took off at a dead sprint.

When Dees returned, Cross was telling Baker of the plan to deploy the airships over the battlefield in Dunnan's Claim. Patrick thought that was a brilliant idea, and swore he'd had it himself.

"That's just the start of it," said Cross. "We've got more tricks up our sleeve as we go."

"What are *Adelaide's* orders?" Dees asked Patrick. "Or are you at liberty to say?"

"They haven't come through," Patrick said, "though I expect we should have something tonight. I imagine we'll either be ordered up the Tweade to lend some artillery to the fight, or else it's back out to Watkins Gulf to kill pirates. We'll be busy either way."

In the study, Rob, Rebecca, Sarah and Will opened Latham's case and splayed its contents out onto Uncle David's desk. There were files and documents everywhere, hundreds of them. One had a key attached to a tag glued to the top left corner.

"It's a vault at the First Bank of Dunnansport," Rob said.

"That would be the gold," Rebecca noted.

The other three looked at her.

"What gold?" Sarah asked.

267

"I think it was 498 bars," she said, meaning just short of two million decirans of value. Gold bars in Ardenia had a standard weight of 400 ounces.

"Whoa," Will blurted.

They found stock certificates indicating that George Stuart was the majority owner of the First Bank of Dunnansport and the Riverside Bank of Barley Point, which wasn't particularly good news. Those two banks were heavily leveraged with mortgages on farmland in Dunnan's Claim, virtually all of the manor houses and outbuildings of which had been ruined and their occupants displaced or killed.

"It's worse than that," mentioned Cross, who had made his way to the study to check on Aunt Rebecca and had been brought into the conversation. "Udar hit right at harvest-time, which for them was a brilliant move. They do the maximum amount of economic damage, because you can't bring in the crops now that the whole area is a war zone, and they get to live off the land while they're invading.

"But that means nobody can sell the harvest to pay their mortgage. Those two banks are insolvent as we speak."

"What do we do?" Rob said.

"Let me put you in touch with some people," Cross said. "You're cousins with Peter Stuart, right? He's a solicitor in Principia. He does mergers and acquisitions. My brother's in stock brokerage at the Havener exchange. I bet there's a deal to be made, because in the long term all that land collateralizing those mortgages will be worth holding. It won't be a bad investment to recapitalize those banks so long as we win this war."

"Good thing Hilltop Farm doesn't have a mortgage anymore," Rob mused. "But we don't have anybody to bring in the harvest, and it isn't safe to try, so who can say when that place will have any value again."

"Actually," said Latham, who had wandered in along with Dees, Patrick, Helen and Alice, "I had an idea about

268

Hilltop Farm that Sebastian and General Dees will agree with me on."

The conversations continued, and by sundown Aunt Rebecca insisted that all the guests, save for Patrick and Alice with little Joseph, spend the night so they could get an early start with a good breakfast in the morning. Because Dees had sent the engineers and security men along with the SAF's officers in the lorries with the other gear to Barley Point as an advance party and he was heading back to Principia the next morning, the general agreed. Cross and Latham had continued their conversation about the structural and engineering needs of a nascent air force and were nowhere near at a stopping point, so they both agreed. Since Helen had missed her boat back to her own empty house, she joined everyone else in taking Rebecca up on her offer.

After dinner, Will and Sarah finally had another moment alone after a whole day of obligations.

"Leaving in the morning, huh?" she pouted.

"Duty calls, you know," said Will. He'd pirated a bottle of Uncle David's whisky and a couple of glasses from the study. "Care to join me in some self-medication?"

Sarah, who had been indulged by her father to enjoy an occasional sip after her sixteenth birthday and whose pharmacological horizons had been recently broadened beyond her comfort level, nodded in assent. She'd gone quiet.

"You look like you're lost in thought," said Will. "Or found in it."

"I'm just wondering where we are on that subject we discussed this morning."

"Ahh, that," he said, sipping from his glass. "Well, it turns out that I did have a short conversation with your brother…"

She raised an eyebrow at him.

"…and he seems all right with the idea."

"Interesting," she said. "Because I had a similar conversation with my aunt."

"She likes me," Will said.

"But you're leaving in the morning."

She took a sip from her glass, and made an agonized face.

Will laughed. "It's an acquired taste. We all acquired it at the academy."

"I doubt I'll acquire it at finishing school," Sarah said. "Never mind, I'm not going to finishing school."

"You're a finished product to me, Sarah," Will said. "I wouldn't change anything about you. Except for that hat. The hat is terrible."

She punched him in the shoulder. He laughed, and downed a swig of Beacon Point's finest.

"By the way, I have something for you," he said, producing a thick package wrapped in paper.

"When would you have had time to get me a gift?" she said, eyeing him suspiciously.

"Just open it, silly," he said.

She did, and out popped nearly 100 envelopes containing the letters he'd written her.

"How?" she gasped.

"It seems your folks kept them in the strongbox," Will told her. "Rob found them when he looked through the stuff Mr. Latham brought, and he put them all aside. He figured it was better if I gave them to you. Smart kid, your brother."

She kissed him deeply. "I don't have any excuse now, do I?"

"Nope," he said. "Now you've got to read them. The later ones are better than the earlier ones."

In the sitting room, Latham and Helen were having their first long conversation of their very brief relationship, though Latham felt they'd known each other forever. He told her the sordid story of his father, and how his mother had vanished with the admiral amid the broadsheet circus, and then the story of his divorce with Astrid. She told him she'd heard it differently from her Port William acquaintances, though she didn't find that version credible.

And then she told him her own story. Her parents had both died of influenza in Stannifer, a city along the Tweade north of Trenory, when she was twelve and her brother a decade older. Irving had re-upped with the Marines for a second term, having no other viable or desired profession, and so her brother had dragged her to Barley Point where he'd risen to head of the customs office. Irving sold their house in Stannifer, leaving a substantial inheritance that he'd given completely to Helen. Her brother had built her the Barley Point house and helped raise her, and she'd been reasonably happy, but in a small town full of farmers and Army men she'd never met anybody she liked and didn't think she ever would.

What was more, Irving had been a very overprotective brother, shielding most potential suitors away. Other than the two years she'd spent at nursing school in Port William, where she'd learned many things but mostly that she didn't want to be a nurse, Helen hadn't had much of an opportunity to present herself to society.

Latham told her that she might have to change her residence, because Barley Point was dangerously likely to become the battlefront in the next few days. He said he would make arrangements with Cross to get her safely behind the lines at the first sign of trouble.

"No," she said. "I'm staying. I can help dress wounds and I can be useful. And no Udar is ripping me out of my home without a fight."

Latham thought that was a spirit he could get behind.

. . .

271

That left Rob, Dees and Cross to share a final drink and a conversation about his service to the Special Air Force before retiring.

"I feel like I'm doing something wrong," Rob said to the two men. "But on the other hand, it's really the only right choice I can make just now. The country needs it, and I've got to do my part."

"I think you're making the right choice, son," Dees said. "It's the smart call for your future, and I can tell you that the Office of Special Warfare will be deeply in your debt. That's something we'll reward you for."

"Plus," Cross said, "this will give you and me an opportunity to do a lot of great work together. I see a long-term relationship that'll be great for both of us."

"You're right, of course," Rob said. "Both of you. It's just such a big commitment. And not something I expected. But yeah, we're going to do this."

...

FORTY FIVE

Dunnansport – Morning (Fifth Day)

There were four people departing for Barley Point, a number perfect to fit in the convertible automobile Cross had fished off the Special Warfare train the previous day. The roadster was packed and ready for the 70-mile journey up the dirt track to Barley Point, and it was time to say goodbye in the front yard of the Stuart mansion in Tweade Landing.

"OK, lovebirds," Cross teased from the driver's seat. "Let's wrap this up. Sarah, I promise I'll have your beau back to you in one piece soon."

She stuck her tongue out at him, and smiled. Then she looked at Will, sporting a fresh bandage courtesy of Helen, who remarked she was getting back into practice as a nurse as her own contribution to the war effort.

"She did a good job. You look dashing," Sarah told him.

"I don't want to go," he said. "I swear I'll be back."

"I know you will," she said, holding Broadham's beret on her head against a sudden gust of wind.

"That thing does *not* go with your dress," Will noticed, as Sarah's blue naval beret certainly looked out of place with the borrowed formal frock Rebecca's closet had yielded to her the previous night for today's goodbyes. Her aunt had suggested a more ladylike chapeau for the sendoff as she fussed over Sarah's appearance, but Sarah would have nothing of that.

"And here you are, the fashion critic," she said, knowing he was still playing the jealous fiancé. Broadham had an appointment to drop in for lunch, as she'd agreed to let him interview her for his report to the Admiralty on the Udar raids.

273

"That's Major Fashion Critic to you," Will responded.

She kissed him. Hard.

"Take care of yourself, Forling," she said. "Don't get killed. And keep those letters coming."

"I'll try," he said. "Stay safe, and I'll come and see you as soon as I can."

She kissed him again, and then he was gone.

. . .

FORTY SIX

Barley Point (Afternoon, Sixth Day)

The ride in the motor sedan from Dunnansport was a productive one from Cross's perspective, as it turned out he had a passenger in Helen Irving who boasted a complete command of the town of Barley Point. Most importantly for Cross's purposes, that meant she knew what houses of quality were available in the small town.

Helen particularly clued him in to the availability of a stately two-story abode, which had not yet gone on the market, only a block off Main Street. The house was by far, she assured him, the most suitable property in town. Its owner was an aging friend of hers who had been considering moving to Port William to be with her children, and with the outbreak of war so close to Barley Point, she was the very definition of "motivated seller." After dropping Helen and Latham off at her house, Cross pulled up at the prospect residence with Will, who said he wouldn't miss this potential transaction for the world.

Within twenty minutes Cross had bought his first piece of property in the South. He thought he probably overpaid, having written a check for 40,000 decirans for a four-bedroom house not yet wired for electricity, but this was a small town, the pickings were slim, and Cross had more money than time. The house was spacious and well-built, and he couldn't think of a more advantageous location. His new residence was five minutes from the army base by sedan, only three blocks from the ferry, and five blocks from the site of what would be the rail station. Perhaps more importantly, until he could secure himself a bit of staff for the residence, he was only one block from the inn.

The house would also come largely furnished, as Mrs. Jordan, the fabulously cordial matron who agreed to part with her home for the cause of the motherland (and Cross' price), was not so fond of the hardware as to demand it make the move with her. Cross promised her the use of one of the Special Air Force's lorries to transport her valuables and intimates to Dunnansport; from there they would join her on the train to Port William. In no time, she had produced three volunteers to pack up her belongings, and by nightfall was ready for departure, but not before insisting on offering Cross and Will a meal and a room for the evening since neither had secured a billet in the overcrowded town. Both greatly preferred Mrs. Jordan's lodgings to a cot at the army base, which was all that would be available in town that night.

At nine of the clock the next morning, Cross's lorry arrived to load Mrs. Jordan and her property for the two-hour journey to Dunnansport. She had never been a passenger in a motor vehicle before and considered the seventy-mile ride the pinnacle of her life's excitement. Cross simply saw it as a utilitarian approach to getting a problem of headquarters and executive lodging solved quickly and without much cost, as the lorries were busy bringing material in from the Dunnansport train station and were otherwise empty on the return trip.

It turned out that when the lorry returned from Dunnansport, though, it contained an unexpected cargo. General Dees marched through the front door unannounced as Cross moved furniture around, attempting to construct an office out of what had been a parlor.

"I like what you've done with the place," Dees said.

"It isn't exactly elegant," was Cross's response. "I don't suppose you fancy taking up tenancy here?"

"I do not," Dees said. "though I may be prevailing upon you from time to time. Good work securing a place for us to operate from in town, though. I want our exploits to be largely unseen by the army, despite my admiration for Messrs. Terhune and Forling."

"Forling I can't help with," Cross replied. "He's billeted in one of the guest rooms. Too late to stop that."

Dees pitched in to craft something workable for an office out of the tables and chairs left in the house from Mrs. Jordan's departure, and while Cross recognized the place would fall far short of his Elkstrand digs, he could at least stand it. A man from the Barley Point Electric Works was coming that afternoon to begin a rush-job installing electrical wiring, and a steam generator was due to be dropped off shortly, at its designated location in the side yard.

"Let's talk," Dees said as the furniture moving came to a conclusion. "I want to clue you in on what's going to happen in the next few days, because it's all very fluid and you're going to need to be ready."

"I was at the base and saw the airships come in early this morning," Cross said. "Those Foreman engines aren't the smoothest-running contraptions I've seen."

"Not indeed," said Dees. "Your engineers know what to do, I assume."

"Two days," Cross affirmed, "and we should be ready for battle with the new equipment."

"Good, because in four days we will likely be in a tempest for the history books."

"You tell me this after I just bought a house on the front lines?"

"That was your choice, young Sebastian," Dees said. "You could have had a wonderfully inexpensive cot at the base."

"Where are the Udars coming?" Cross asked. "I take it you have intelligence."

"I have some. We think the main action will be west of here. We think it will be Battleford, Trenory or Azuria bearing the brunt of the assault."

"I shouldn't ask, but how exactly do you come by such knowledge?"

277

"Painfully," the general said. "The risk our people are taking among the Udar is at a level you can't even fathom. When they're caught, they're burned alive on the spot, and they're caught at an alarming rate. Your air power will make a revolutionary difference in the speed of transmitting intelligence and saving the lives of our operatives when their cover gets blown."

"Makes me happy we can help," Cross said, "but your tidings aren't the sunniest."

"I don't deal in good news this week," Dees said. "That's why I'm still down here despite having planned yesterday to head back to the capital. And you need to know some unpleasant truths."

Cross plopped down on his new desk chair, which had formerly served as a parlor chaise.

"That doesn't sound like fun," he said.

"The enemy's numbers are more than we can withstand," Dees said. "Holding along the length of the Tweade is probably impossible. At least for now this is a salvage operation more than anything else. We're going to have to save what we can until we can reverse the tide."

"Don't we have three divisions setting up fortifications at Trenory?" Cross asked, puzzled. "Don't we have the Fourteenth Infantry garrisoning Battleford? That would seem like the makings of a stout defense."

"The Fourteenth is useless, Sebastian. General Oliver is a political appointment who can't lead a bowel movement, and his men have never smelled blood before. We're trying to resupply them with better armaments and equipment, but Oliver has so far rejected the Office of Special Warfare's help. It's a lost cause.

"As for Trenory, I've seen General Rosedale's plan of defense, and it's completely unsuitable. The enemy will go right around his positions and storm the town."

278

"I can't believe it," said Cross, stricken. "A city that large? It can't be that bad."

"Trenory isn't even the worst of it," said Dees. "As of now there is no defense of note for Azuria. Other than three steam frigates currently en route from Port Adler to the north and two brigantines due back from tours of the Sunset Sea in the next two weeks, the city is open for the taking. We don't even have five hundred men in defense as yet. I've been advocating for an evacuation, but the Societam and President Greene don't want to touch off a panic. As if that is somehow worse than letting the enemy enslave and slaughter 75,000 people."

"Sounds bleak," Cross said. "We're not that much better here. Maybe 1,000 available to fight, 1,500 at the most."

"Barley Point must hold," Dees said, steel in his eyes. "We can't lose this town or Dunnansport. We can retake what's west of here, but we can't lose the Lower Tweade. Whatever it takes – *whatever it takes* – we will hold this area."

Dees then hit Cross with a surprise. "I'm bringing you some Udar tomorrow. You're going to take them for a ride in your balloons."

"That's an unusual request."

"You're going to drop these people off behind Udar lines and let them link up with their troops."

"And why on earth would we do that?"

Dees gave him a look indicating to Sebastian that he probably didn't want to know.

"Let's focus on the job at hand and not so much the reasons why at this point, shall we?" he said.

Dees indicated on a map he'd produced where he wanted the eight Udar to be deposited.

"What about the headman? What was his name? Ago'an or something?"

"He's going back to Strongstead," Dees answered. "We're going to exchange him for our people the Udar are holding there."

"Bit of a poor trade for us, no?"

"We have our reasons for making it."

"You're operating on a level I have neither the information nor the cloak-and-dagger skill to match," Cross said, grimacing. "I'm in far over my head right now."

"Don't you go to pieces on me, Cross," said Dees, admonishing him. "This thing is going to get infinitely worse before it gets better. You've got to be prepared for adversity and atrocities you haven't even read about in books, and you had better be ready to do things you never, ever considered doing. And you had also better be prepared not to question the morality of anything we'll need to do to survive what's coming."

Sebastian blanched. "Just seeing the grief of the Stuarts gave me an inkling of how bad this is."

"What you saw with those good people is what just about every family from Azuria to Dunnansport faces in the next few weeks," Dees said. "We don't have the troops to stop them. They could easily be 1,000 miles toward Principia before we could effectively counterattack. That's how poorly prepared we are."

It was then that Sebastian felt a great deal of gratitude to Rebecca Stuart, the magnificent widow of David Stuart who had supplied him with a parting gift of two bottles of the deceased hero's reserve of Beacon Point whisky. He retrieved a fifth from the kitchen with a pair of glasses, offering one to his guest. Dees eagerly accepted and Cross poured a pair of indecently substantial drinks.

"On to a different subject," Dees said, "and perhaps a happier one."

"If this is about my love life," Cross answered, "leave it."

Dees smiled at the joke. "One of the reasons you are so well-suited for this job isn't just that you know aviation and almost no one else does. It's that you have money and connections and you can do some things off the books that others can't."

"That sounds like it spills the bounds of ethics," said Cross.

"Not at all," Dees said. "There is in fact no code of ethics for the Office of Special Warfare, and as such, all is fair game. And what I will suggest that you do is limited only by the time you have available to do it, which means I strongly suggest you employ someone to act as your agent."

"Agent for what?"

"I think you should go into business down here."

Cross wasn't opposed to that idea, as from what he'd seen of Dunnansport and Barley Point so far there were immense opportunities for growth if the Udar could be fought off. "What kind of business are you specifically thinking of, General?"

"Real estate and banking would be a start," Dees said. "You need to buy up those two banks here and in Dunnansport. The ones Stuart is sitting on that are insolvent. Do that and you'll be in a position to drive the entire economy in these parts. And I would snap up all the land you can from here to the mouth of the river."

"How do you know about Rob's holdings?" asked Cross.

"Let's just assume I know everything," Dees said. "It's quicker that way. I didn't get where I am by being uninformed."

"All right. To what end?"

"You need to save the economy of this area," Dees said. "If it goes and everybody goes broke, they'll just pack up and leave. Then, besides the fact we have no civilian infrastructure backing the military effort, it's a rolling economic collapse. Barley Point and Dunnansport take Port William down, which destroys Aldingham, Sapphire Bay and Newmarket, and the contagion spreads. This war is already going to cause a major bank panic and recession, and the worse it gets the more trouble we're going to have fielding an army that can withstand twenty million fanatics riding at us."

"Did you just say twenty million?" Cross gulped down half his glass.

"At least," Dees said as he quaffed his own beverage.

"By the Saints!" Cross said. "We can't mobilize that."

"We don't have to. We can win with firepower and technology. In a year we will counterattack with weapons you haven't even dreamed of. But our active army is less than 400,000 men. We're outnumbered fifty to one at present and the invasion is coming within a few days."

Down the hatch went the rest of Cross' whisky. He reached for the bottle. "Top you off?" he asked Dees.

"Sure," said the general.

"I feel like investing in land and finance in a climate like this is more suicide than duty or opportunity," Cross said.

"I understand," Dees responded, "but you've got good people down here. And when we hold, *and we will hold*, this is going to be the area Ardenia looks to for a new political order. There is a delegate from Port William; his name is Roth...."

"I know him. Good guy. Territorialist, right?"

"Yes. He's bold. Very sharp. Has a future. He needs a base of support. We need you to make sure that base isn't bankrupt. Takes a lot of money to finance a revolution."

...

FORTY SEVEN

Principia (Morning, Seventh Day)

"TERROR IN DUNNAN'S CLAIM," read the above-the-fold headline just under the masthead of the opposition-leaning Principia *Herald*. "SAVAGE MARAUDERS WREAK HAVOC AT ESTATE OF FAMED DUNNAN'S WAR HERO."

The story carried the byline of Nathaniel Prince, the *Herald's* national correspondent.

DUNNANSPORT – The fresh outbreak of war with the savage Udar nation began in earnest not with the capture of the citadel at Strongstead one month earlier, but on the sixth day of this month when raiders under the command of a headman named Rapan'na surged into the rich, but poorly-defended, estates of Dunnan's Claim south of the Tweade.

One such estate was Hilltop Farm, owned and operated by the Stuart family of Dunnan's War fame. George Stuart, hero of the Battle of Sutton Hill, was killed in a raid by Udar marauders led by Rapan'na as he attempted to save his wife and children from rape and murder. Stuart was decapitated, but not before he had killed seven of the invaders. His wife and daughters killed five more before succumbing to superior numbers. Sarah Stuart, the eldest daughter, was taken captive. Her mother Judith Stuart, a Thurman of Trenory, and sister Tabitha were slaughtered. Two younger siblings survived the attack by hiding in the cellar of the manor-house and were later rescued.

Sarah's older brothers Matthew and Robert were not at the scene of the attack. Matthew, the eldest of the Stuart children, was a member of the Strongstead garrison and, as reports indicate, was captured when it fell. Robert returned from the Aldingham Defense Academy, where he was a first-year cadet, and joined the hastily-organized force to defeat the enemy and rescue the captives.

The loss of George Stuart, who was rumored to be the Territorialist Party candidate for Governor-General of Trenory Province in next year's elections, and alternatively the likely holder of the Presidium of the new Dunnan's Claim County to be formed following the next Census, was a grievous blow to the nation and a thorough rebuke to failed Peace Party leadership. In recent letters written to the Societam on behalf of other Dunnan's Claim landholders, but not read into the legislative record despite demands from the Territorialist delegation, Stuart had decried the poor provisioning and insufficient manpower of the cavalry force tasked to protect the nation's southern frontier. His warning that Peace Party policy of demilitarization was creating an unsafe border area, a warning echoed by Delegates from both Territorialist and Prosperitan camps in recent months during parliamentary debate, proved prescient.

"My father risked his life for his country as a young soldier," said Sarah Stuart, who granted this reporter a long-ranging interview from the home of her aunt Rebecca Stuart in Dunnansport, where she is recuperating from her capture and ordeal at the hands of the savages, "and then he gave it as a middle-aged landholder. It shouldn't have been this way."

The Stuarts also lost George's brother David, a cotton merchant of significant means who had lost an arm in Dunnan's War but nevertheless joined the responding force and was killed in battle. Robert Stuart will assume management of the family's vast holdings.

Sarah Stuart provided detailed description of the Udar raiders, led by Rapan'na. Army sources indicate Rapan'na was in charge of the invading force at Strongstead and had taken as a slave Charlotte Naughton, the wife of Col. John Naughton, who commanded the doomed garrison. Sarah Stuart made contact with Mrs. Naughton while in captivity and reported the widow had, amid grief and abuse, broken under the strain. She said Mrs. Naughton was deeply disturbed by the lack of resources available to the Strongstead garrison, which she believed was the cause of its fall.

The Udar held the Naughtons' three daughters in captivity at their capital, Qor Udar. Mrs. Naughton was killed by the savages during the battle to free the captives.

Sarah's story of captivity, typical of the 367 women rescued from the clutches of the Udar by the responding cavalry and militia force, included debasement and depredation. Bound and transported to an Udar camp, she was drugged and prepared for the savages' slave-rituals, and she feared for her soul.

"Had the cavalry not come I would have been lost," she said. "We were all helpless and devastated in our grief."

More than 2,000 settlers perished in the Udar raids on Dunnan's Claim, which covered estates as far west as Stonehouse Farm to the southwest of Battleford, and east to Landsdowne Farm near the Watkins Gulf coast. Some 255 Udar corpses were found at the scenes of the attacks, however, an indication that the settlers fought hard in a losing cause against the marauders.

"The atrocities of last week cannot go unaccounted for," said Louis Roth, Territorialist Delegate from Port William. "The Peace Party bears responsibility for its neglect of our national security in the face of so savage and determined an enemy. George Stuart's death is upon their heads."

Roth called for the resignation of President Catherine Greene in the wake of the Udar attacks. He was joined by all members of both Territorialist and Prosperitan parties in the Societam, and fourteen Peace Party delegates, including Frances Laine of Dunnansport, have echoed the call as well.

Sarah Stuart told this reporter she would like to be counted among those calling for Greene's removal. "My father had been outspoken in warning that our defenses against the enemy were too thin," she said, "and he was ignored. He had taken to preparing us children to defend ourselves on the farm for fear it would be needed. He was right. We shall miss him terribly and our family, who have given so much to our nation, have paid an awful price for the politics at the capital."

Robert Stuart declined to be interviewed for this story, citing his grief over the loss of his parents, uncle and sister. He would have comment at a future time, he said. Also refusing to be interviewed was Rebecca Stuart, who is similarly grief-stricken over the loss of her husband. Mrs. Stuart was nevertheless a gracious hostess of this reporter.

Amid the political and human carnage of the Dunnan's Claim disaster, though, comes a story of hope and romance. Maj. Will Forling, who helped to lead the rescue of the captives, including a dramatic victory in single combat over the headman Rapan'na that freed the women, was recently engaged to be wed to Sarah Stuart. A date for the nuptials has not been set, as Maj. Forling is serving in the defense of the frontier from the garrison at Barley Point and is therein occupied until further notice.

"He's my hero," Sarah said of her betrothed. "If it weren't for him, I would be a slave to the savages and I would never see my country and family again."

...

FORTY EIGHT

Hilltop Farm – Morning (Eighth Day)

The heavily-armed force numbered around 400 men. Some had been veterans of Terhune's force from the previous week, others being new arrivals as the privately-contracted security force for the Special Air Force, and another hundred had been plucked from the hasty volunteer training being conducted at the Army base at Barley Point. They had made their way from Barley Point south to the deserted heart of Dunnan's Claim carefully, for the leading edge of the Udar invasion force was expected within days. That fueled the urgency of their mission; namely to establish an operating base south of the Tweade so that the Ardenians could bleed the invaders, if not stop them, before the battle came all the way to the river.

So far there were only reports of minor skirmishes to the west, particularly in The Throat south of the line of fortresses the Army was constructing with sudden increasing urgency. Directly in the path of the enemy, if he was advancing up The Throat, would be Trenory, which had swelled to nearly double in size thanks to the evacuations of the farms south of the city and the arrival of the Nineteenth Infantry Division, based in Alvedorne to the north, the Eighth Cavalry Division, from Aldingham in the east, and the Twenty-Fourth Infantry, coming down from Oakham upriver along the Tweade. The firepower at Trenory, it was thought, would make that city the hardest target in the world.

Meanwhile, the Fourteenth Infantry from Carteret and the Sixth Cavalry, based in Greyhill, had made their way to Battleford to the west, and the newly-formed Twenty-Sixth Infantry was now garrisoning Dunnansport at the mouth of the Tweade with the help of a sizable naval armada now plying the coastline of Watkins Gulf. At Barley Point and the areas around it, though, reinforcements were scarce so far. That meant the newly-promoted Lt. General Terhune, who learned of his ascension when he'd made his way back to Barley Point four days before, knew he had to place his sparse assets as strategically as possible.

There was talk of refitting Terhune's regiment, which had begun training volunteers at a maddening pace over the past few days as they streamed in from the countryside, swelling to 750 cavalrymen and an additional 200 support troops, into a full-fledged division which would be the Eleventh Cavalry. But that commission had not come through yet. Terhune knew, moreover, that most of his horsemen would be green as grass when the fight came.

At least he'd dropped his complaints about the poor provisioning of his force. Those were no longer valid.

While manpower, and experienced manpower at that, was at a premium, Terhune's regiment was bristling with high-end weaponry, thanks to the nonstop deliveries of small arms, artillery, rockets and grenades Cross had organized from down the river in Dunnansport. The lorries were plying the river road continuously, and a steady flow of river traffic was stopping in Barley Point to deliver food, fuel, ammo and other material. That supply line was days away from expanding, furthermore, as the locomotive line from Dunnansport was now just fifteen miles from Barley Point. A warehouse next to the ferry landing had been cleared out to be repurposed as a train station, and land along the batture was being cleared and prepared for the rail line to come straight into the town.

If Barley Point withstood the Udar invasion to come, it likely had a promising commercial future.

In another development, the town's bank, which three days earlier looked certain to fail, had received a bailout from a consortium of Morgan River Valley investors who had bought up its Dunnan's Claim mortgage portfolio at a slight discount. The Riverside Bank had survived an initial run made on it by panicked depositors and was still standing. A similar situation had played out at the First Bank of Dunnansport, though two banks in Battleford up the river had not been saved.

The resources coming into Barley Point were a source of hope. But marshaling those resources was the key to survival. Everyone knew it.

That was one reason Terhune had sent Latham to build that forward operating base south of the river. "We're at the point where we're well-provisioned and armed-up enough that if they come we can put a real dent in 'em," Terhune said. "And we can't maximize that by shootin' at 'em across a river. I'd rather shoot at 'em down a hill."

In discussions of high ground on which the base could be built, Sutton Hill was seen as a bit too far afield and definitely too close to the enemy's slow advance. Not to mention the Barley Point road didn't extend that far.

Which is why Latham was here with Major Forling, Major Cross and the 400 troops. It had been agreed back in Dunnansport three days earlier that Hilltop Farm ought to be the site for the new Fort Stuart, and the peacetime plans Latham had made for the property only needed some minor tweaks and additions to recast it as a fortress. Rob Stuart, who was now the agent for the family, had signed over the Hilltop Farm land to the Office of Special Warfare on a ninety-nine-year lease that made the Stuarts a decent penny, and now the military was in possession of the best property in Dunnan's Claim on which to build a fortress.

Accordingly, today's mission was to secure Hilltop Farm for the construction brigade which was on its way in with a menagerie of mechanical wonders and all the materials they could scrounge for Latham's crash building program to create Fort Stuart. The stronghold would first consist of a wooden palisade square with chain gun emplacements on the south facing of the ridge Hilltop Farm sat on, almost precisely on the spot George Stuart breathed his last. Then Latham planned the further construction of a stone presidio where the manor house had stood just a few days earlier. Clearing the property and salvaging stone for the new construction was first up on the agenda for today.

That afternoon they expected to have a pair of special guests. The *Clyde* and the *Ann-Marie* were on their way down from a temporary airfield north of Barley Point where the SAF's engineers had changed out the Foreman engines, which had performed about as well as Cross' father and Reeves had predicted, and the Dulsey guns they'd been sent down from Belgarden with. The SAF's engineers had taken a couple of days to rebuild the ships' burners and propeller rigs and were finally satisfied with the outcome. This afternoon they'd go into service scouting the enemy in the southern end of Dunnan's Claim, west to Strongstead and on into The Throat before returning home to Barley Point. The Udar were up to something, they all knew. There was no point in stretching too far with cavalry scouts to find that out; not when the airships could safely and effectively perform the reconnaissance mission while inflicting significant damage to the enemy's lead elements along the way.

The biplanes were still north of Trenory, because an adequate runway for them wasn't ready at Barley Point. But Latham expected that could be fixed, and Fort Stuart was a great candidate for that as well. There was a good flat space on a ridge running east of the old manor house which would suffice for a couple of runways. He was working, with Cross' help, on getting concrete down to the site to quickly lay down pavement.

Latham and Cross were still quibbling over exactly what the air base would look like, the latter advocating something considerably more grandiose than Latham thought practicable with a battle in the offing. Cross was thinking an aerodrome with a steel tower; Latham suggested a log tower and a tent collection surrounded by pickets and foxholes.

He's fresh out of the corporate world, Latham realized. *He'll learn.*

"All clear," Major Forling said as he entered the command tent where Latham had set up operations. "We've set up a bivouac, we're putting picket lines in place and the men are standing their posts. What have you got?"

"I've got a pair of airships coming in three hours to deal death to the enemy and report back his position," Cross said. "I trust that's satisfactory. Oh, also – our new translator will be on the *Ann Marie* when the ship gets here. You've not met Eddie Ludlow, have you?"

"I have not," Will said. "What do you think of her?"

"Impressive," Cross said. "She's an extremely bright kid. Can't speak the Civil Tongue worth spit yet, though she can make herself reasonably understood. But she's a fountain of knowledge about the Udar, which you'll see. And she looks pretty good in an SAF uniform, too."

"Eddie?" Will asked.

"She said she didn't want to be called Edyene. She said that was too Udar. So we decided she's an Eddie."

"Cute," said Latham.

"I like her already," Forling said. "Hank, how are you set up?" They were all calling him Hank now, seeing as though Helen was the only one he'd let call him Henry.

"I've got a dozen lorries coming up that road in one hour with lumber and metal braces for palisades," Latham said, looking at the plans laid out on the table, "I've got fifty men with a crane, a half-dozen teams of horses drawing wagons full of tools and other materials and I've got these," he thumped his knuckles on the blueprints laid out on the table, "which are the best you can hope for in the piss-poor time allotted for this project. We will work day and night to get this fortress stood up for you, sir. And then I'll be building this air base of ours once Major Cross realizes we don't need the National Temple as a base from which to fight this war. Your job is to make sure we don't get killed before I can make all of it happen."

"We'll do what we can, Captain," Will said.

The three exited the tent and surveyed the scene, as Forling's company had turned the ruined farm into a hive of activity in the space of a morning. They were doing their best to establish a defensive position in an impossibly short period, and none of them had slept much in the past week. Will's left cheek still bore the train-track marks of the seven stitches the Udar's knife had necessitated on the beach four days earlier, and Latham noticed he appeared to have aged well beyond his nineteen years.

Can't imagine he's impressed with my youthful looks either, he thought.

It struck Latham that this was quite a strong defensive position. If he could just buy forty-eight hours they'd have the palisade constructed and then Fort Stuart would be up and running.

"Beautiful day," Forling said, looking east to a sparkling autumn sun.

"Sure is," Latham agreed, staring to the south.

Cross, who was looking to the west, squinted, then pulled out his field glasses. Raising them, he searched out the unusual shape in the sky he'd glanced at with his naked eyes mere seconds before.

And in the lenses of those field glasses, as he adjusted the magnification, he saw that he wasn't looking at one shape at all – but hundreds, maybe thousands, moving off to the northwest.

"Gentlemen," he said, "we have ourselves a war."

. . .

EPILOGUE

He was unaccustomed to living in a cage, and yet for most of the last week Ago'an had spent virtually every minute in one.

He'd been hauled aboard the Profaner ship six days ago following his one mistake of the Great Holy War to date. That had been his risking himself to make a trip to the front by boat rather than on horseback, which he thought would save time. But for those six days following his error the enemy had kept him bound and caged exclusively when he wasn't questioned by the unmanly men of the Profaner navy.

Their cowardice, and his disgust with them, was complete. Ago'an had, after all, made his demand for *Kawes'kin*, and had the enemy any honor that demand would have resulted in his killing their commander and earning the right to be deposited with his people ashore to continue his mission back to the sacred shore of Gana'fali from the front.

Instead, he was caged like an animal, and the questioner, a childlike little man who called himself Broaddum, informed him that things had not gone according to his plan. That came after Broaddum insulted Ago'an by announcing his mother had been a prisoner of the Udar somewhat like Ago'an was a prisoner of the Profaners now.

His deputy Rapan'na, who had disobeyed Ago'an's orders and attacked the Profaner force pursuing him and his prizes, had died after squandering his company at a place the Profaners called Sutton Hill. Rapan'na had lost his nearly 400 future *javeen* after his rash and ill-advised attack on the enemy's fortified position, diverging from the plan, which was to retreat and reel in the Profaners until the Udar force could emerge from the tunnel behind them and smash them along the beach.

293

And worse, Rapan'na had then lost to a Profaner in single combat. Broaddum claimed to have seen it personally.

Rapan'na had performed brilliantly in the battle to reclaim Gana'fali from the Profaners. His men had tunneled under their fortress and slaughtered nearly all of the enemy's soldiers not made meals of by the *Vitau'hi*. But his success had then gone directly to his head.

It was the woman, Ago'an knew. Rapan'na insisted on having her, because she was shapely and because she had belonged to the Profaner commander. He should have taken one or two of the commander's daughters as *javeen*, and burned the woman in the sanctified fire to celebrate the victory for Ur'akeen, but his pride and lust got the best of him. Ago'an had at least procured the three daughters as spoils for his brother the *sahal'et*, conceding the woman to Rapan'na in exchange.

Rapan'na was so infatuated that he told the woman he would spare the girls in exchange for her agreement. She had said no, and then quickly changed her tune after she saw Ago'an cut her son's throat. Ago'an acted to spare Rapan'na the loss of face from being rebuked by a Profaner woman in front of his troops. For that he received no gratitude from his deputy.

Then to prove his might to her, Rapan'na sent his warriors to attack the Profaner pursuers on that hill and lost virtually his entire force. Only one more day of retreat down the coast and they would have surrounded the Profaners and slaughtered them to a man.

Had that happened, there would have been nothing between the army of Ur'akeen and the Profaner cities along the Big River.

Ago'an had given Rapan'na his orders and then reboarded his sloop for the journey back to Gana'fali, and then he'd been taken. For six days he'd been kept like an animal, fed little and subjected to intermittent bouts of interrogation by Broaddum and the other effeminate Profaners.

But now he was being led from his cage once again, two enemy pistols at his head. He was being brought to a room with bright lights, and chained to a chair. Broaddum was there along with an old man Ago'an had not seen before.

The old man spoke, in the gibberish Profaner tongue. Broaddum translated.

"His name is General Dees," Broaddum said, "and he is in charge of all the forces deploying to destroy your army here in the south."

Ago'an snorted. "Tell him I will kill him in single combat, if he dares to fight. If he does not, he is no man and lies with goats and dogs for his pleasure."

Broaddum did not translate, and instead looked blankly at Ago'an.

"You tell him, boy," Ago'an said.

The old man asked Broaddum a question, and Broaddum answered it. The old man then stood and approached Ago'an.

Ago'an noticed, as the old man came toward him calmly, that he was much more substantial than he had appeared sitting in the dark. He was tall, much taller than Ago'an, and despite being twenty years or so older, he had maintained an athletic, muscular physique. This man looked as though he could hold his own in a fight.

And he proved it, landing a hard punch to Ago'an's left temple which toppled his chair and sent him crashing to the floor.

Two Profaner soldiers hurriedly stood the chair back up, and then the old man delivered another blow. This time Ago'an's nose exploded with the force of the uppercut. In all his years in combat he had never experienced so much pain.

"He would like to know if he has your attention," Broaddum said, as the old man glowered at him, ready to strike again.

Ago'an nodded, gasping for breath.

"What is the disposition of the Udar force?"

He smiled, blood pouring down from his abused nostrils.

"This is a poor question," he told Broaddum. "Our force is everywhere. Everywhere. When it comes it will overwhelm your womanish defenses."

"Where will the first attack come?"

Ago'an shook his head. "No. I will not tell you."

The old man then unsheathed his knife, a fearsome instrument longer and sharper even than a well-made Udar *Izwei*. Standing behind Ago'an, he traced a thin line across the Udar's chest with the tip of that knife, opening the skin from his left armpit to his right. The old man looked down on him and spoke to him in the gibberish Profaner tongue.

"He says he knows what material the Udar use to make their clothing," Broaddum translated. "He knows that it is human skin. He says perhaps he will make clothing from your skin, and you may watch him do it."

Ago'an looked at Broaddum, who looked back at him blankly. He looked up at the old man, who smiled as he brought the knife, dripping as it was with his blood, down to his chest for a second time. The tip met his wound just a bit above his sternum.

"Trenory," he said, quickly. "The place you call Trenory. And the port you call Azuria."

Ago'an knew he had just committed a great dishonor. But by now, he rationalized, it would be too late for the enemy to stop the invasion to come. He was not prepared to be skinned alive, and this man menacing him looked serious enough to carry out his threat.

"The Ardenian officers at Strongstead that you kept as prisoners while maintaining your ruse that the citadel had not fallen," Broaddum said, "are they still alive?"

296

"Yes," Ago'an answered, "though they have no further value now that you know Gana'fali has been retaken. They will be brought to Qor Udar and sacrificed on the steps of the Great Ziggurat of Ur'akeen."

"They will not," Broaddum said. "They will be traded to Ardenia."

"Traded?" Ago'an snorted. "For what?"

"For you."

"You would trade me for six children of no account?" Ago'an laughed. "Fools, you are. By all means, let us make this trade."

Broaddum looked at the old man and nodded. He pushed paper and a pen-brush at Ago'an. Ago'an's right arm was freed.

"Sign this note ordering the exchange," Broaddum said. Ago'an saw that it was written in Udar rune.

He signed the paper, and his hands were bound again. Broaddum and the old man departed, and then his captors dragged him into another room.

Waiting for him there were two men wearing heavy hoods and gloves with glasses over their eyes. He was bound to a chair and his captors left the room. After re-setting his nose and packing it with gauze, the two men produced cloths they dabbed in a green mixture from a bowl and proceeded to clean the wound on his chest, setting it newly afire in pain.

He was then tightly bandaged. One of the men knocked on the door of the room and his captors, now similarly wearing hoods and gloves with glasses over their eyes, arrived to bring him back to his cage.

Broaddum was there, with the old man and the captain of the ship he'd been hauled aboard when taken six days before. Bay-ker, Ago'an remembered he was called.

"We are taking you back aboard the *Adelaide*," Broaddum said. "Your people have signaled over the teletext that they will accept the exchange. We depart at once for Strongstead."

"I shall return here soon enough," Ago'an said, "at the head of one million men to crush your defenses as I did at Gana'fali."

"Of course you will," mocked the old man, in perfect Udar. "Of course you will."

THE END

ACKNOWLEDGEMENTS

I'll preface this with an author's note, which is to say I spent a very long time contemplating the transition between a would-be author of fiction and the actual thing (though perhaps that is too pretentious; I leave it to the reader to judge whether the transition is complete). When I finally did sit down to write *Animus*, it was with the encouragement of a few friends who share my feeling that too few of us who believe in values and principles tending to the traditional actually participate in the generation of cultural and artistic content. I spent twenty years thinking that I'd write a novel at some point, and when I did sit down to do it I managed to crank out the first draft of this book – 165 pages' worth – in only eight days. I'm still trying to contain my regret in not venturing forth as an author sooner.

Among those who helped push me over the edge into this path I'd like to single out two; Chris Treadaway and Eric Skrmetta, who were most persuasive in encouraging me to light the fuse on this project. Chris and Eric also read early drafts of *Animus* and offered valuable insights, for which I also must thank them.

They weren't alone. Thanks go out also to Ron and Susan McKay, my parents, who read each draft and helped guide the story along by pointing our plot holes and good ideas, Millard Mule and Claire McCrary for their encouragement and input, Mark Mainous for contributing technical expertise on matters medical, and Kurt Schlichter for his inspiration and advice. And to Hugh Howey, whose author blog was invaluable as I began this process.

Thanks also to Carol Butler for assistance in providing edits for grammar, punctuation, sentence structure and readability. This book went from a daydream to a finished product in just more than three months largely because I was able to focus on the plot and story with the knowledge she would help to clean up the messes made along the way. And to

Kevin Gallagher, whose voiceover for the audiobook version of *Animus* is a masterpiece.

Thanks, of course, to David Caruso and Kortney Cleveland for their work on graphic design. David took the description of the C-1 cavalry fighting knife in the book and turned it into that monster you see on the cover, and in so doing might have created a miniature marketing sensation. If you're interested in owning one, check out our website at http://talesofardenia.com and watch for updates.

And finally, thanks to all the others that have helped me along the way to make it possible for me to write this book, and to those who deserve it I deeply apologize for having omitted a specific mention of your name.

Scott McKay

September 17, 2019

APPENDIX

GLOSSARY, PRONUNCIATION

GUIDE AND CHARACTERS

Places and things

Udar

Afan'di (Uh-FAWN-dee) - a home camp of the Udar

Aniwa'di (AHN-ee-WAD-dee) - an hallucinogenic cactus which grows in Uris Udar; used to make the intoxicating marwai liquor

Anur (Uh-NOOR) - a mobile military camp; the basic unit of Udar society

Avoy (Uh-VOY) - An Udar exclamation meaning "Now!"

Azmeri (Uhz-MERRY) - a sacrifice to the Udar god Ur'akeen

Ba'kalo (Buh-KAH-low) – An Udar halberd

Enafan'di (In-a-FAWN-dee) - an Udar religious law holding that no Udar warrior should ever die a peaceful death outside his Afan'di, or home camp.

Gana'fali (GANN-a-FAHL-ee) - a shoreline on the Leopold Bay coast on which the Ardenian fortress of Strongstead was built. The Udar consider the shore a sacred place.

Gazol (Ga-ZOLL) – An Udar curved sword; like a cutlass, but with a skinnier blade

Gibor (Gee-BORR) - a berry similar to belladonna, though less toxic; which grows in Uris Udar; used to make the intoxicating marwai liquor

Izwei (IZZway) – An Udar fighting knife, consisting of a two-sided blade with thick barbs on each side

Javeen (Jah-VEEN) - an Ardenian woman held as a concubine by an Udar Anur

Kawes'kin (COW-us-KEEN) - an Udar tradition in which battles and disputes are decided through single combat

Lepon'hin (Luh-pun-HEEN) - the Udar name for The Throat, the isthmus dividing the two lands

Marwai (MARR-wye) - an intoxicating Udar liquor made from gibor berries similar to belladonna and aniwa'di, a hallucinogenic cactus; its effects include making its user quite docile

Qur Udar (KOOR-OO-DAR) - the capital city of Uris Udar

Rochat (Ro-KOTT) - An Udar command meaning "Submit!"

Sa'halet (Suh-HALL-it) - the title given to the Udar king; also the high priest of the Udar religion, who communicates with the god Ur'akeen through dreams and visions

Ur'akeen (Oo-rah-KEEN) - The Udar god

Var'asha (Varr-ASH-uh) - an Udar headman of an Anur tribe

Vitau'hi (Vee-TAU-hye) - the dreaded Blood Raptor, a giant predatory bird thought to be extinct which kills its victims in an especially gruesome way

Ardenia and others

Bergod (Berr-GOAD) - a port in the nation of Thosia.

Cavol (Kuh-VOLL) - a nation across the Great Sea; the home of the infamous Mottled Men

Divinate (Duh-VINE-et) **Academy**- the most prestigious religious school in Ardenia Deciran - the unit of Ardenian currency, based on the value of 1/10th of an ounce of gold

Faith Supernal - the national religion in Ardenia

Lord of All - the deity worshipped in Ardenia according to the Faith Supernal

Peace Party - the dominant political party in Ardenia, holding the large majority of Delegate seats in the Parliament

Prosperitans - one of two opposition parties in Ardenia. When the former majority party the Party of Enterprise split apart, Prosperitans and Terrorialists became competing opposition factions to the Peace Party.

Resinan (Rez-ZINN-un) - principal city of Leria

Societam (So-SY-et-um) - The legislative seat of Ardenia, akin to the U.S. Capitol. The Ardenian parliament, composed of delegates, meets at the Societam.

Strongstead - a massive Ardenian fortress located on the coast of Leopold Bay, on a shoreline the Udar call Gana'fali. Thought impregnable.

Sunrise Temple - one of Principia's most prominent institutions dedicated to worship of the Lord of All and provision of social aid; located in the mostly-poor Ackerton District on the east side of the capital city.

Territorialists - one of two opposition parties in Ardenia. When the former majority party the Party of Enterprise split apart, Prosperitans and Terrorialists became competing opposition factions to the Peace Party.

The Throat - a mountainous isthmus dividing the northern and southern portions of the Great Continent. Closing The Throat to the Udar is a national-security imperative the Ardenians have, according to critics, paid insufficient attention to.

Trenory (TRENN-or-ry) - The largest city in southwest Ardenia

Waldiver (WALL-div-ver) - a prominent finishing school for girls in Trenory

People

Ago'an (AH-go-AWN) - an Udar military commander, brother of the Udar king and in charge of the Udar invasion of Ardenia

Baker, Patrick - a naval commander and captain of the Ardenian naval ship Adelaide

Broadham, Joseph - translator on the Ardenian naval ship Adelaide, and son of famous Ardenian author Georgia Broadham

Cross, Preston - father of Sebastian Cross; the head of a super-rich Morgan River Valley family

Cross, Sebastian - a famous aviator who circumnavigated the planet in an airship; CEO of the Airbound Corporation, an airship line

Dees, Abraham - an Ardenian general, the head of the Army-Navy Office of Special Warfare

Edyene (Edd-YENN-ay) - an Udar female captured at sea by the Ardenian vessel Adelaide; she asked for and was granted permission to defect

Forling, William - the youngest son of John and Lillian Forling of Grayvern Farm in the Dunnan's Claim territory; a cadet at the Aldingham military academy

Gray, Ralph - a powerful Delegate of the Ardenian Parliament from Belgarden

Gregg, Madison - the Cross family solicitor and a powerful lobbyist at the Ardenian capitol

Gregory, Winston - a prominent Peace Party political boss from Belgarden

Gresham, Winford - an aviation engineer and Sebastian Cross' business partner in the Airbound Corporation airship line

Harms, Horace - a powerful Delegate to the Ardenian Parliament from the city of Belgarden

Irving, Boyd - an Ardenian Marine captain in charge of customs at the river port of Barley Point

Irving, Helen - sister of Boyd Irving and a resident of Barley Point

Latham, H.V. - an architect from Port William engaged to design an upgrade to Hilltop Farm

Naughton, Charlotte - wife of John Naughton, the commander of Ardenian forces at Strongstead; when captured by the Udar, her name was changed to Shori'zel

Pleasance, Oliver - a politically-connected executive with Foreman Technologies of Belgarden

Rapan'na (RAH-PANN-NA) - commander of the Udar raid into Dunnan's Claim

Rawer, Jack - First Mate on the Ardenian naval ship Adelaide

Reeves, Marcus - an engineer in Principia on the forefront of military technology, working for Preston Cross

Stuart, David - brother of George Stuart; a wealthy businessman in Dunnansport and the head of the town's militia

Stuart, Ethan - the youngest of George and Judith Stuart's children

Stuart, George - a famous hero of Dunnan's War and the head of the wealthy Stuart family of Hilltop Farm in Dunnan's Claim

Stuart, Hannah - the youngest daughter of George and Judith Stuart

Stuart, Judith - wife of George Stuart

Stuart, Matthew - the oldest son of George and Judith Stuart; an officer at the Ardenian fortress of Strongstead

Stuart, Rebecca - wife of David Stuart

Stuart, Robert - the second-oldest child of George and Judith Stuart; a cadet at the Aldingham military academy

Stuart, Sarah - the oldest daughter and third-oldest child of George and Judith Stuart

Stuart, Tabitha - the middle daughter of George and Judith Stuart

Terhune, Alfred (Terr-HYOON) - the Ardenian cavalry commander at Barley Point

Ubel'la (Oo-BELL-la) - the Udar king

Vines, Mortimer - a powerful Delegate of the Ardenian Parliament from Belgarden

Wade, Alice - a wealthy widow in Dunnansport, and the fiancee of Patrick Baker

Well, Charles - an Ardenian Marine lieutenant from the naval ship Adelaide, attached to the rescue force

53384412R00190

Made in the
USA
Lexington, KY